ODEON PARADISE

ODEON PARADISE

A Night at the Movies with Jesus and George

A Novel

by
John L. M. Palmer

ISBN: 978-1-4669-0178-0 (sc)
ISBN: 978-1-4669-0179-7 (e)

Trafford rev. 03/12/2012

 www.trafford.com

North America & International
toll-free: 1 888 232 4444 (USA & Canada)
phone: 250 383 6864 ♦ fax: 812 355 4082

Acknowledgements

Thanks to Victor McCorry, a master musician and organist/ choirmaster who taught me to play that mighty instrument and encouraged me to write a book on the world of church music. Thanks also to Hugh Meyers, who gave me extensive feedback on the manuscript, Kathryn Board, a fine writer who gave me endless encouragement and a keen eye with the proofreading, and Daniella Molinari, a talented young artist who painted me the perfect cover.

Chapter, the First:

Not the Way to Arrive in Heaven

George, the young organist/choirmaster from St. Christopher's United Church, died Easter Sunday morning before the disbelieving eyes of its horrified congregation, the clergy, the choir, and his beloved Kathy. George, himself, took it no better than they did. Worse, in fact. Not to mention more personally.

The music ended abruptly. His spirit drifted upwards. There was a tunnel . . .

Suspicions began to form in George's mind.

He felt as if he were rising on a powerful current of air inside an enormous organ pipe. A low moan rose up in his throat, growing louder in volume and higher in pitch with a pronounced musical quality which, under other circumstances, the young church musician might have appreciated.

As he approached the proverbial light at the end of the tunnel, George's moan became a ragged surround-sound scream, the light rushed in upon him, and he was blown, cork-like, out the end of a huge organ pipe: one very specialized entrance to Heaven. He reached a respectable height, hovered for a split-second at the apex of his trajectory, descended rapidly, and landed heavily, in a heap, yelling.

St. Peter looked over the counter.

George's raw vocalizations sorted themselves into vowels and consonants, then into syllables, finally coalescing into these, the first coherent words to come out of his mouth: "JESUS CHRIST!!!"

"Taking the Lord's name in vain," St. Peter tutted, "is *not* the way to arrive in Heaven."

Breathing hard, George took in his surroundings: a bearded man in white robes behind a marble counter . . . several others (some with *wings*?) retreating in the face of his unholy outburst . . . what appeared to be *gates*? White, shiny, almost translucent—huge!

"Are those, by any chance, made of . . . p-pearl?"

"They are."

"The Pearly Gates?"

"That's right."

"You mean *the* Pearly Gates? Of *Heaven*? I'm . . . *dead*?"

"That you are."

George's eyes bugged out as his head tilted slowly to one side.

St. Peter nodded deeply. "I see that you're beginning to grasp the situation. Now, about the matter of your taking the Lord's name in vain . . ."

"I did not 'take the Lord's name in vain'," said George, panicking.

"Yes, you did."

"Did not."

"Did, too. I have witnesses." St. Peter indicated a flock of angelic assistants behind the counter.

"Well . . ." George offered lamely, "I may have said the *words*, but I was not actually 'taking the Lord's name in vain'." *Was I?*

"What, then, were you *doing* with it?"

"I . . . uhhhh . . . I was . . . I was asking to *see* Him." *Now* there's *a thought.*

"That's a new one!"

"But I *was*," George insisted. Indeed, the more he considered the idea, the more it appealed to him: *Jesus! Yes, I want to see Jesus!*

"That's what you *really* want?" St. Peter asked shrewdly.

"Jesus!"

"Hmmm." St. Peter stroked his beard thoughtfully. Satisfied that George's answer did not constitute a fresh infraction of the second commandment, he said, "Very well, then. The Lord will see you."

George stared. "He will?"

"He will." St. Peter nodded matter-of-factly. "'Ask and ye shall receive.'"

"Uhhhh . . . when?"

St. Peter arched an eyebrow. "Now."

"Now?" George looked around. "Where is He?"

St. Peter pointed to a spot just behind the puzzled organist. And from the location thus indicated, Jesus Christ, the only begotten Son of God the Father Almighty, Maker of Heaven and Earth, answered, "Right here, George."

Chapter, the Second:

Not Quite What He Expected

"Lord?!"

"Yes, George."

"Is it . . . ?"

"Yes, George. It is."

Jesus? Jesus! It was Jesus!!

The young organist/choirmaster from St. Christopher's United Church followed Jesus out of the reception area into a wide hallway with white plaster walls, green oak molding, and oriental runners that he recognized immediately: St. Christopher's! Then, they went through a door on the right that should have been Rev. Parker's office, but the name engraved on the brass doorplate was "Jesus".

Reaching the chair behind "Parker's" desk, Jesus rested one hand on its high back and extended the other, inviting George to sit.

George sat.

On the left side of Jesus' desk there was a Bible; on the right, a reading lamp, its base a mildly stylized wolf lying down with a lamb. Between them, underneath His own portrait—the one with beard and flowing blond, shoulder-length hair that hangs on the walls in Sunday school classrooms everywhere—sat Jesus.

Jesus!

"George, you're staring."

"I'm sorry. It's just . . . Lord . . . that You're . . . *this* . . . is not quite what I expected."

"Actually, George, I'm almost exactly what you expected, as is 'this'."

"This is *Your* office?"

"It is . . . for *you*. For others it looks a little different: I like people to feel comfortable here. How do you like it?"

"It's . . . it's . . ."

Jesus nodded. "Not quite what you 'expected'."

On the far wall there was a large picture of what looked like . . . George identified some of the nearer faces, first in the choir, then the congregation: St. Christopher's! There were daffodils and lilies everywhere. That made it today! Easter Sunday. His first Easter at St. Christopher's. And the picture had been taken from the chancel. At the *front* of the church. But who had a camera up there? No-one that *he'd* seen. George's gaze snapped over to Jesus.

Jesus smiled. "I took it."

"You?"

"I."

"Today?"

"Water to wine was a miracle, George. Same-day photography is a piece of cake."

"I meant—"

Jesus smiled. "I know what you meant. But seriously, George, what can I do for you?"

George looked down. "Where should I start?" he reflected morosely. "I lost my job, or at least I would have lost it if I'd lived. The only woman I ever loved won't even speak to me, or at least she wouldn't if I were still alive. And yes, to top it all off, I'm dead. And there's nothing I can do about any of it. But you know what the worst of it is? Most of it, I don't even understand."

"Like what, for instance?"

George shrugged. "Like . . . why it had to be that way. Why nothing ever worked. How everything went so wrong. And I tried *so* hard! But people interfered. They wouldn't listen. They didn't understand. They—"

Jesus raised His hand. "Stop right there, George. 'They'?"

George nodded sincerely.

"I see. 'They'." Jesus regarded George thoughtfully. "Then, let's start there, shall we? What we need, I think, is a little fresh perspective." Jesus stood. "And I know *just* how to go about it."

"Lord?"

Jesus motioned for George to follow, leading him back out the door and down a wide hallway towards what should have been the church gymnasium. Once they passed through its double doors, however, George saw that there were no windows, no clocks, no basketball hoops . . . and the floor was covered with rows and rows of comfortably padded seats, gently sloping towards a large . . . *screen?*

By the look of it, George was about to watch a movie.

With Jesus!

"*Lord?*"

Chapter, the Third:

Welcome to the Odeon Paradise

"Welcome to the Odeon Paradise," said Jesus, leading George to his seat, front row center. "Here, have some popcorn."

Too distracted to wonder how it got there, St. Christopher's young organist/choirmaster accepted his brimming bucket of *Paradise Popcorn* from Jesus' hands in a hesitant if not downright awkward fashion, several stray kernels spilling into his lap, and another few landing by his feet.

"It won't bite you," said Jesus.

"No . . . no, I guess it wouldn't."

The house lights dimmed, and the soft strains of organ music wafted through the theater as the film's opening credits began to roll: *Seventh Heaven Productions* was proud to present a Cecil B. DeMille production of *Pipes: the Story of George.*

"Catchy title, eh, George?"

"Catchy," George agreed. "Lord?"

"Yes, George?"

"Cecil B. DeMille?"

Jesus nodded. "Mr. DeMille was between pictures, and there's no-one better at this sort of thing in all of Heaven. Now, this is how it will work: *you* are the narrator . . ."

"I am?"

" . . . and *I* am here to keep you honest."

"You are?"

Jesus nodded deeply. "And when you're not actively narrating, you may eat your popcorn, which, by the way, you've hardly touched."

"But, Lord—"

"Shh, it's starting."

Chapter, the Fourth:

Happier Days

Onscreen, George was walking down the sidewalk with a sense of purpose. Bernie, George's St. Bernard, trotted loosely at his side, tail wagging and jowls swaying, as they passed the large, upper middle class, two and three story, brick and stone houses on the lushly tree-lined, North Toronto street.

"Happier days?" Jesus asked.

George nodded eagerly. "I waited for that position to open up for years. Everyone wanted that church. St. Christopher's had the best pipe organ in the city. And the choir? What an opportunity!"

George and Bernie rounded the corner, turned up the short flagstone path, slowed down under the cover of autumnal red, yellow, and orange maple leaves, and made for the side door of the church.

"I thought I'd died and gone to Heaven—" George froze for a moment, but he and Jesus both let the opportunity for comment pass, aside from the Lord's elevated eyebrow, and George's slowly lowered chin.

* * *

Faces from the congregation and the choir appeared on the screen of the Odeon Paradise as Reverend Parker preached the sermon. "Music has always been important in the life of the

Church, especially at *this* church. St. Cecilia, the patron saint of music—"

"I remember that!" said George. "My first Sunday at St. Christopher's. He managed to work in a reference to St. Cecilia as part of his welcoming me to the church."

Then, a young woman's face filled the screen.

"Tell me about her," said Jesus.

"Kathy," George answered hoarsely. "Rev. Parker's daughter. I . . . loved her."

"No, George. Now you're telling me about you—your feelings towards her. I want you to tell me about *her*."

"I . . . I don't know where to start."

"Then let's start with something simple: what color are her eyes?"

George frowned. He looked at the screen. Kathy's face was no longer there. "I don't know . . . *why* don't I know?"

"Because of the *way* you loved her: through the filter of your own needs, defenses and ideas of how things ought to be. Sadly, that made it difficult for you to catch much more than a glimpse of *her*, and impossible, apparently, to remember the color of her eyes."

For the first time since he died, George began to question himself.

Kathy's face reappeared.

"Her eyes are *blue*."

"Yes, George."

"And her hair is red!"

"My, but you do have an eye for detail," said Jesus, smiling.

"She's . . . very pretty."

"Yes, she is."

*　　*　　*

George was opening his music on an antique brass stand at the front of the church. Plain, stackable chairs and black, metal music stands for the orchestra were arranged before him in the red-carpeted chancel, with more chairs for the choir on wooden risers at the rear. He pored over the score, making small rhythmic gestures, mostly with his right hand, turning pages with his left and humming snatches of melody.

"Looks like I'm getting ready for my first concert with the choir," said George, "taking a last minute look at the score. That's the overture to Handel's *Messiah*. They put it on every year."

"Let's have a listen."

The scene changed again, this time from George's pre-concert score study to the evening performance. The choir sang the Hallelujah Chorus.

"They're good," said Jesus.

"Yes, they are," George agreed. There was a touch of pride in his voice, tinged with sorrow. Dead for only a few short hours, George was already beginning to remember some aspects of his life with a growing sense of nostalgia.

Everyone (performer and audience, even the ushers and ticket takers) was obviously moved as the choir and orchestra settled into their final, massive cadence in the final bars of the mighty chorus. There was a moment of silence, electric in its stillness, as the congregation of St. Christopher's sensed that something besides the instrumentation had changed at their annual performance of the *Messiah*, and then . . . thunderous applause.

Chapter, the Fifth:

More Than 'Hi' and 'Bye'

George walked down the center aisle of the church, looking for someone to talk to. The audience had left, for the most part; a bare remnant of choir members, their friends and families remained, scattered around the church.

Near the foot of the aisle, he slowed down, recognizing the minister's older daughter, Kathy, in all her young, red-haired splendor.

"Time for a little narration, George?"

"Do I have to, Lord?" George was beginning to mist up despite his best efforts at self-control.

"You can pace yourself if you need to."

Ready at a moment's notice to pace himself, George began. "This was the first time that Kathy and I had said anything more than 'Hi' and 'Bye' to each other."

"Hi," said George, nodding.

"Hi," said Kathy, smiling.

"How are you?" he continued.

"Fine," she returned.

"Looks like everyone's gone."

"Pretty much." She glanced around the empty pews as the faint sounds of the few remaining parishioners echoed from the hallway beyond.

"Do you think they liked it?" George asked.

"Yes!" She smiled, blushing slightly. "Looking for a detailed report?"

"There's a little café just out on Yonge Street, isn't there? Why don't we go talk there?"

"I'll get my coat."

* * *

George and Kathy sat in the "little café just out on Yonge Street", cups of herbal tea and slices of cherry-cheese and carrot cake nestled on their tiny, glass-topped table.

"He said what?" George asked, obviously delighted with Kathy's detailed report.

"He said, 'Best *Messiah* we ever had.' That's in about twenty years if you count the time he's worked here, and more if you consider how long they've been putting it on. Why do you ask about Tom?"

"The caretaker usually knows more about what's going on at a church than anyone else. He sees and overhears so much. No-one pays any attention to the man with the mop, and he takes care of the place in more ways than one. Some of these guys get downright maternal about it."

Kathy laughed. "I was just trying to picture Tom as a mother," she explained.

George nodded. "Tom may be a tough old Irishman, but he loves the place. You should have seen his eyes glass over when he was talking to me about the stained glass windows."

They both grimaced at the pun.

"You should have seen him last spring after the tree planting session that the environmental group organized," said Kathy. "There was dirt all over the gym floor. I thought he was going to lose it for sure!"

"Yeah? Well, you should have seen him when . . ."

* * *

George walked Kathy back to the manse where she lived with her family, a few blocks west of the church.

She invited him in. They started talking in the front hallway, moved to the kitchen, and ended up on the plain, high-backed couch in the living room where she squeezed herself unequivocally to one end, leaving George acutely aware of the resulting distance, more or less equivocally, at the other.

"Why was she burrowed into the end of the couch like that?" George asked Jesus. "Why all that distance? Didn't she like me?"

"It wasn't that she didn't like you. She did. In fact, that's *why* she was 'burrowed into the end of the couch like that'. It was more of a trust issue."

"She didn't trust me?"

"You, and herself, and . . . 'things'."

"So she moved away?"

"Farther and farther."

*   *   *

Onscreen, Kathy was walking George to the front door. They spoke lightly and pleasantly. Then, she opened the door and stepped back smartly, pulling it wide, wishing George the most perfunctory and formal of good-byes, almost military in its curt perfection.

Offscreen, George said, "I remember wondering, 'What does she think I'm going do at the front door?'"

"And how did you feel about that?"

"I thought it was cute. Maybe that's when I fell in love with her. But *look* at her, Lord. What did I *do* to her?"

"The unthinkable, George, the utterly unthinkable, from her point of view. You made her fall in love with you."

"I did *what*?"

Then Jesus did something that George could have never anticipated—He sang! "'You made me love you. I didn't wanna do it; I didn't wanna do it.'" Jesus grinned. "Remember that one?"

George's face retreated an inch or two in amazement.

"You didn't think I could sing? I started off the first psalm at the Last Supper. 'The Son of Man' can certainly sing. I'm a pretty fair dancer, too. They don't call me 'The Lord of the Dance' for nothing."

The image of George walking away from Kathy's house began to shrink, becoming one square of many in a checkerboard pattern on the screen.

"*Kathy . . . ?*"

"Don't worry," said Jesus, "she'll be back. Now, we should have a look at some of the other people in your life."

George shrugged.

"Pick a square, George, any square."

George stared at the screen.

"Any square at all."

Chapter, the Sixth:

Thank-you, Reverend Parker

George pointed to the bottom left, selecting a square which then grew out of the mosaic until it filled the screen. Outside Reverend Parker's office, he sat in a green leather chair, where he flipped through his red hymn book, closed it, fidgeted, opened it again, and then went back to fidgeting.

"Good choice," said Jesus, "but what happened to the narration?"

"Pacing myself?"

"*I'll* say."

George sighed and resumed his narration. "I used to do a lot of that."

"What? Sighing? You still do, you know."

"I meant *waiting*." George looked up and saw Jesus smiling. "Sorry . . . uh . . . no offense."

"None taken.

*   *   *

"Good morning, George. Come in," said Parker, using the all the facial expressions and body language that he thought necessary to add a note of enthusiasm and sincerity to the invitation.

"Thank-you, Reverend Parker."

"That's a little on the formal side for colleagues, isn't it?"

"Okay . . . Robert."

"'Bob', I usually go by."

" . . . Bob."

Reverend Bob smiled a little wearily, gently smoothing back the hair at one graying temple, and offered George a chair with the easy assurance of one who had done it hundreds, even thousands of times before.

Jesus shook his head. "You two had that same little exchange every time you went to his office."

"Well . . ." George shrugged defensively, "I just figure that it keeps things feeling a little more . . . I don't know . . ."

"Holy?"

"Yes. And I like that."

"Yes, you do, but what does *he* like?"

"Uhhhh—"

"And whose name *is* it, anyway?"

"Oh."

"Not to worry, George. I don't think that he'd insist on being on a first name basis with you right about now."

"No, I guess he wouldn't."

"Listen."

"George," said Parker, "I have to tell you what I've been hearing all over the church: that was the best *Messiah* that anyone can remember at St. Christopher's. Everyone's thrilled."

George half-shrugged, half-beamed. "Well . . . I couldn't have done it without that choir."

For Parker, the connection was effortless: "Well, as long as you mention them, the music committee is hoping that you can increase the numbers a little."

As it was for George: "They all do. But what's the point of filling the choir pews with warm bodies who possess less than room temperature voices?"

Parker nodded stoically.

"I don't understand it," George continued, "the same people who wouldn't dream of letting someone without the necessary expertise do the books, want me to let every Tom, Dick and tone deaf Harry into the choir."

"I see."

"I suppose they have good intentions."

"They do, and they feel quite strongly about it, some of them, which is one of the things I wanted to talk to you about." Parker waited for the tone of the moment to settle. "There are some concerns regarding the music program, and I can imagine a fault line developing between the music committee and the minister of music down the road a bit—I've seen it before."

"What kind of 'fault line'?" George asked suspiciously.

"Different visions of where the music program should be headed, I suppose, especially after your recent musical success. On the one hand, there are those who see the choir as an all inclusive entity, taking anyone in who wants to join, 'making a joyful noise unto the Lord' as it were."

"Heavy on the noise."

"At its worst, yes. But there are also those who would like to hear the heavenly choir itself installed in the chancel Sunday mornings, whatever the cost, financial or otherwise. Organists at St. Christopher's have usually tried to pitch their tents somewhere between those two camps. The ones who have been successful at finding that balance have prospered. The others, whether they were at one extreme or the other, have experienced difficulties, if that's not too blunt a way of putting it."

"And how severe is this 'fault line'?" asked George, wrinkling his nose at the thought of compromise.

"Let's just say the divisions are beginning to appear."

"Who am I up against?"

"Oh, we're all in the same church family, George, but things can get a little heated, even in the best of families, when the various family members are pulling in different directions."

"Which members of my 'family' should I be watching out for?"

"All of them, in one sense," said Parker, the beginnings of a grin appearing on his face. "But you might keep a special eye on the music committee. And watch out for a few of the more, shall we say, opinionated parishioners, especially two or three in the choir, and, above all, try not to get on the wrong side of your favorite alto."

George hesitated. "You mean . . . Molly?"

Parker nodded grimly. "Molly."

Chapter, the Seventh:

A Careful Choice of Words

"MOLLY! THAT'S SO FLAT, IT'S THE WRONG *NOTE*!!!"

"George," said Jesus, shaking his head, "what did Reverend Parker tell you?"

"I know, I know . . . but it was *so* flat."

George stalked over to the grand piano while Molly fumed. He played the alto section its part, and had them sing it back to him. After fixing up the tuning of one especially difficult interval, he had the entire choir sing the passage: standard operating procedure.

Then . . .

"From bar 17. Extreme staccato. Sing each pitch for the shortest possible time value. Nothing longer than a sixteenth note. Short . . . short . . . short . . ." George illustrated the effect with a rhythmic bounce of his right hand on each of his three clipped syllables.

"So much for steering a middle course," said Jesus.

Choir members stared blankly at George, looked at each other, and tightened their grip on their music. The choir sang a cappella, any form of instrumental accompaniment being, in George's estimation, counterproductive. Notes were quitted as soon as they were visited, the overall effect being the aural equivalent of a small cloud of fireflies, individually winking on and off, on a summer evening.

"Interesting, George. You *are* resourceful."

George chose his words carefully. "It does help uncover pitch insecurities, and it encourages the singers to rely on themselves."

"And if they cannot 'rely on themselves'?"

George shrugged defensively.

The extreme staccato passage grew increasingly uncertain, the rapidly evaporating scintillation of clipped pitches finally wobbling, like a dying top, to a stop.

"That needs more time than we can give it," said George, getting up from his piano and closing the lid—the usual signal that rehearsal was over. "It has to be *perfect* for Sunday. If you don't know it by then? I'd sit out there." George indicated the congregational pews.

"A careful choice of words," said Jesus. "And you had counted on it going badly, hadn't you?"

George nodded a little sheepishly.

"Which very nicely set up your suggestion that they learn their music at home or leave the choir."

"I never *said* that."

"True, you never *said* it, but you didn't have to. The implication—the *intentional* implication, I might add—was clear, and it certainly had the desired effect. It was, quite simply, the most effective threat you never made, and it was something else, too."

"What was that?"

"The first nail in your coffin."

Chapter, the Eighth:

Holy! Holy! Holy!

"Woof?"

"Not now, Bernie. Can't you see I'm busy?"

"Woof??"

"Please?"

"Woo-oof?!"

George sighed heavily. "Oh, alright. Let's go!"

"Woof!!"

"Bernie needed to step outside," George explained.

Jesus nodded. "You're an original, George. In the entire history of the church, there has never been an organist/choirmaster who took his St. Bernard to work. St. Bernard—*the* St. Bernard, that is—got a real kick out of it."

"Come on Bernie!" George stood, braced against the cold air at the door outside his office. "Why do you have to do this on a Sunday morning of all times?"

"Woof!"

"A likely story. Hurry up! This is a *big* Sunday!"

"Woof!!"

*   *   *

Everyone was on time for the short pre-service rehearsal except for those who had taken George's "threat" seriously enough to limit their Sunday morning participation to sitting in the congregation with family and friends.

George sat at the organ, ordering his music, double-checking it against the order of service pamphlet. He glanced around the choir pews, and saw the gaps, nodding with approval as he took a quick census of missing choir members: Ted O'Brien (the Irish tenor who couldn't find his music most of the time, let alone his notes), Bridget North (the soprano with the mile-wide vibrato), her husband Jay . . .

But *Molly* was still there. His eyes met hers, and very briefly they locked, he knowing for a certainty that she would stay in the choir until the bitter end. Molly glared back from under her dark bushy eyebrows, which were as ample as everything else about her.

The choir was quiet and intense, waiting for the anthem.

"From bar thirty-seven, extreme staccato," said George. This time, they knew what they were doing. The lone fluff, minor though it was, found itself instantly buried under George's imperious gaze.

*   *   *

Downstairs, the choir made final adjustments to their gowns and music folders, and formed a double line at the bottom of the stairs at the back of the church.

"Good morning, all," said Parker, greeting the choir as he always did before the service. "Let us pray: We thank You, Lord, for the gift of music, along with all Your other blessings. We dedicate our voices to Your praise, and all our talents to Your service. In Jesus' name, Amen." Another encouraging nod from Parker, and the choir started up the stairs, the soft strains of George's organ prelude growing louder as they ascended.

Processing in pairs up the center aisle, they sang, "Holy! Holy! Holy!" in bold unison against a straightforward organ accompaniment, leading the congregation in the processional hymn. For the second verse, the organ part was more complex. By the third, the double line of choristers split in two at the front of the church and began taking their places on opposite sides of the chancel. In the fourth, they broke into harmony. For the fifth and final verse, the sopranos sang a new descant that George had written especially for the occasion, soaring above the choral unison in triple augmentation: one slow, melismatic 'holy' for the rest of the choir's three.

Ian Armstrong, chairman of the music committee, looked up from his hymnbook, sensing something different in the music but unable to identify it. David Bowles, chairman of the finance committee was nudged by his wife, Ellen, who had sung in the choir years before. A ripple of awareness ran through the congregation that *something* in their Sunday morning service music had changed.

At the hymn's final repetition of "God in three Persons, blessed Trinity," a gentle Breeze arose in the theater.

George looked around for an open window. "What was that?" he asked.

"The Holy Spirit."

"The *Holy Spirit?*"

"Come, George," said Jesus. "You're already sitting with the Son of God. Why is the added presence of His Holy Spirit such a shock? Besides, He was in the church when you played that hymn. We All were."

"You *were?*"

"Yes. All three of Us. The whole Family."

"Why?"

"You were playing Our song!" Jesus answered, brightly.

"Then, what about . . . ?"

"Oh, He's everywhere all the time: basic theology, George—you know that."

George craned his neck at the screen, gave the theater another quick sweep, and sank a little lower in his seat.

*   *   *

Following the sermon, on George's signal, the choir of St. Christopher's United Church rose as one, some of its members with enthusiasm, others with grim determination, all in readiness. After a short organ fanfare, the anthem was underway. "We praise thee, we praise thee, we praise thee, oh God!" the choir sang. The counterpoint both within and between the organ and choral parts built an irresistible tension—"To Thee all cherubim and seraphim continually do cry,"—that finally exploded into the chorus—"'Holy! Holy! Holy!'"—accompanied by a sound such as George had never heard, coming from the rear of the theater. He turned and saw what it came from: a rustling of wings in the back row!

"Who are *they?*"

"I'll give you a clue: your choir is singing about them."

"There are . . . *angels* in the back row?"

"Wouldn't you be interested if someone were singing about you?"

And so, George, Jesus, and an enthusiastic crew of cherubim and seraphim listened to the rest of the anthem. Unable to contain themselves, the angels burst into song with the final repetition of "Holy! Holy! Holy!" adding several parts of further harmony. The anthem ended with a sustained fortissimo chord from organ and choir, both terrestrial and celestial.

A fresh rustling of wings arose as the new group of theater patrons settled in to watch the movie, buckets of popcorn appearing in the hands of those who desired them, which were most.

The choir sat down, and George began his organ improvisation, something that was, as a matter of custom, loosely based on the anthem. He combined melodic excerpts from the triadic "Holy! Holy! Holy!" of the processional hymn with the octave leaps that those same words were set to in the anthem, the number and complexity of its musical parts building as he added color and power with rank upon rank of pipes.

Nearing the end of his improvisation, he directed the choir to its feet with a theatrical roll of his head. The congregation rose, then the heavenly gathering in the theater a moment after that. Two beats of pregnant rest, and the doxology began, thundered forth on full organ and sung by all, both ecclesiastical and theatrical, as God's Holy Spirit made Itself felt throughout the theater:

"Praise God from whom all blessings flow.
Praise Him all creatures here below.
Praise Him above, ye heavenly host.
Praise Father, Son and Holy Ghost. Amen."

Most of the clergy, choir, and congregation of St. Christopher's United Church ("all creatures here below") looked straight ahead, reluctant to dilute the power of the moment with any mere human eye contact, while the angels in the back of the Odeon Paradise ("ye heavenly host") grinned at one another, the breath of the Holy Spirit subsided, and Jesus rested His tender gaze on George, the only one of God's creatures on either side of the screen who was steadfastly staring at the floor.

Chapter, the Ninth:

A Bit of a Breakthrough

"What is it, George?"

"I don't know, I just had the strangest feeling." George pointed to the screen without looking at it. "That was what I had been working so hard for. I was so excited about it. But looking at it all now? It just doesn't mean all that much to me." George shook his head. "What's *wrong* with me?"

"Nothing, not on that account, anyway."

"No?"

"No." Jesus smiled. "I'd call it a bit of a breakthrough, Myself."

"You would?"

"I would."

"Und so vould *I*."

"Huh?"

*   *   *

As the angels at the back of the theater basked in the afterglow of George's music, Jesus made the introductions: "George, this is Dr. Sigmund Freud. Sigmund, this is George."

Freud proffered his open hand, which George accepted as if it were a loaded pistol.

"Nice music, George! I have been listening from back zere for a bit."

"Thanks."

The bearded psychiatrist took a seat beside them, and eyed George's popcorn. "Ahhhh! Nice popcorn," he said, and materialized a jumbo-sized bucket for himself.

George watched Freud noisily satisfying his appetite.

Freud noticed himself being noticed. "It is ze tyranny of ze id, ze source of all ze appetites, you know? I am still vorking my vay zrough zat vone, personally."

"They have shrinks—I mean 'psychiatrists' in heaven?"

"Ja, zey do, und vhy not? It's not as if ve vere lawyers or somezing—old psychiatrists' joke."

"I didn't mean it that way," said George.

"Zen you must have been asking about ze *practise* of psychiatry razer zan ze persons who *practise* it. Zere are psychiatrists for zose who vant zem. Even up here, people have zings to vork zrough. Und, perhaps, you may be vondering also vhat's a nice Jewish boy like me doing in a place like zis?"

"No, no; but, but . . . wait a minute . . . weren't you an atheist or something?"

Freud looked embarrassed. "Ja, ja, I vas, but not anymore! Some of my old zeories vere a little 'out to lunch', if you vill. But I revised zem zoroughly vonce I got ze facts!"

"You'd be amazed if you knew who's up here," said Jesus.

"Ja, und some of ze people who have visiting privileges! Zose would amaze you, indeed!"

George, already as amazed as he cared to be, refrained from asking for names.

A cherub alighted at Jesus' side, and whispered something in His ear. Jesus nodded, and the angel smiled at George before floating back to his place among the feathered contingent at the back of the Odeon Paradise.

"There has been a request to hear a little more of your music," said Jesus.

George returned his gaze to the floor as if his answer lay there waiting to be discovered. "Okay," he said, looking up again, "they can listen to the recessional hymn: that much I can handle."

Jesus nodded, grinning. "They would like to hear the postlude, too."

George sighed. "Okay, the postlude, too, but that's *it*."

* * *

Turning back to Freud as the hymn began, George asked, "So . . . am I nuts? Is that why you're here?"

After a chorus of gentle "shh"s from the back row, Freud shook his head in answer to George's question and whispered, "Nein, nein, more an example of exaggeration zan any sort of psychosis."

"*That's* what's wrong with me? I'm exaggerated'?"

"Ja, or neurotic, or obsessive/compulsive, vhatever."

George smiled self-consciously. "Okay, but you said I had a 'breakthrough'. How is being too depressed to listen to my own music a 'breakthrough'?"

"Because it vas a sign of your letting go of your obsession, so zat your doubts—your healzy und reasonable doubts, I might add—could surface like zat."

"Oh . . ."

Meanwhile, the cherubs and seraphs in the back rows were being joined by a host of Heavenly others: some sprinkled in eddies around the theater; others seating themselves near George and Jesus; still others hovering at various elevations. A trumpet descant to the last verse of George's hymn began soaring above the melody as if on wings, which its inventor both possessed and was using.

"Gabriel," Jesus mentioned matter-of-factly. "He appears to like your playing."

"I like *his*. Who *are* they?" George asked, glancing behind, around, and above himself.

"Assorted angels, members of the Organists' Guild, a smattering of psychiatrists now that Sigmund has joined us, mostly in the back corner. There are others, and there will be more."

"*More?*"

"You're not going to get shy on me now, are you?"

"I never thought I'd be watching my life story unfold in the company of *angels*."

"But everyone's does. Remember 'God sees the sparrow fall'? Well, He's not the only one, but remember also: this is Heaven—you're among friends."

"How many more 'friends' will I be making?" George asked, looking around the theater.

"Let's just say, 'as many as you need.'"

Chapter, the Tenth:

A Variety of Opinions

George lifted his hands and feet from the final chord of the postlude. Members of the Organist's Guild nodded their approval as he cleared the registration, shut off the organ, and headed for his office to pick up Bernie and leave quietly.

"Vouldn't be sneaking out now, vould you, George?"

"Not exactly."

"Yes, George, 'exactly'," said Jesus.

George sighed. "Okay, okay, yes, 'exactly.'" He decided to at least put a positive spin on it. "I sensed that a few people were feeling somewhat . . . passionate about the music, and . . . and I thought it most . . . uh . . . diplomatic to let the passions subside somewhat so that I . . . uhhhh—"

"So that you wouldn't have to listen to them?"

George sighed again and sank back into his seat.

"Woof!" Bernie was also eager to be gone from the church. George gave him a quick scratch behind the ears, filed his music, and changed out of his gown and organ shoes. Then, organist and dog walked and bounded respectively down the half flight of stairs outside his office to street level, and slipped out the side door of the church.

"George!"

"Kathy!"

"What are you doing sneaking out the side door?"

"Who's 'sneaking out'?"

"*You* are," she said, laughing.

"What makes you say that?"

"Well, for one thing, this is the side door; you always leave by the front. All you need now is a trench coat."

"That obvious?"

"Yup."

"Which way are you headed?"

Kathy nodded in the direction of the manse.

*   *   *

"I thought the music was beautiful this morning," said Kathy. "And I've never heard anyone improvise like that before! How do you make it sound so good?"

"Well, sometimes by theory, sometimes by ear, and occasionally by happy accident."

Kathy laughed. "Sounds like magic to me."

"Sometimes that's how it looks to me, too. Sometimes . . . I don't know . . ."

"Sometimes what?" she asked, sensing, with the natural acuity that is so frequently the inheritance of ministers' daughters, that George had been about to say something revealing.

They began to walk a little slower.

"Nothing." George shrugged. "Nothing, really, just how it feels, sometimes."

"How?" She nodded encouragement.

"I don't want to sound stupid."

"You won't."

"Okay. Sometimes, it's almost like I'm not playing, someone else is, or maybe it's more like a deeper part of me is playing, a part that knows things that the rest of me doesn't know, a part that's a better musician, maybe even . . . a better . . . person," he added sotto voce, surprising even himself.

Kathy looked up at him, her features soft, her eyes only vaguely focused.

"I guess you'll think I'm some kind of flake now," said George.

"No . . . not at all."

"So you liked it? The improv, I mean."

"Yes! And I'm not the only one. I overheard some reactions."

"Whose?"

"Jay Madison's, for one. He loved it!" She hesitated. "There were . . . other comments, and not just about your improvising, either. A lot of people were talking about the anthem . . . other things, too."

"What were they saying?"

Kathy stiffened. "I don't know . . . different things," she offered lamely.

"Well, what would the average comment have been?"

"Uhh . . . there didn't seem to *be* an 'average'."

George was beginning to look confused. "Then, what *sorts* of things were they saying, for example?"

"Well, everyone agrees that the music sounds fantastic," she said, trying to give her words a tone of pleasant finality.

"Oh, then wouldn't *that* be the 'average'? I don't understand."

"Oops," said Kathy, grimacing.

"Oops?"

"It's just that there's . . . a 'variety of opinions', to use one of my father's favorite expressions, on . . . other matters."

"Like what?"

There was a long pause, then Kathy answered, "Your methods, I guess, but you didn't hear that from me."

"I didn't?"

"*No*, you didn't. You're too easy to talk to, George." Kathy inhaled deeply, and then let her breath out against the resistance of her loosely pursed lips. "Well, I guess I'll have to tell you the rest. Then, if it comes out that I'm a champion blabbermouth, at least *someone* will be happy with me." Kathy waited for George's reaction.

"It's okay." George smiled tightly. "You don't have to tell me anything. And I'll still be 'happy' with you."

Kathy looked surprised. "Are you *sure?*"

George nodded slowly.

"Then I *really* have to tell you," Kathy decided aloud. "Everyone loves the sound, but—sorry, George—not everyone approves of your methods—*sorry*—especially after last Thursday. Some people think that you're going to try to get rid of the weaker choir members, and then let new ones in by audition only. It's not what some of them want."

"Like who?"

"Like the Norths. I saw them talking to Ian Armstrong—"

"Head of the music committee."

"Right. And Molly—well, you know *Molly*. Dad tried to tell her how beautiful the choir sounded, and she muttered something about 'what's left of it.' Let's see . . . Brian Tyler walked around looking a little tense after the service. And I overheard Ted O'Brien saying something about, 'The ministry of music should be open to everyone.'"

"So there's 'a variety of opinions'. What are the numbers like?"

"I don't know. But I think that *you* will soon. I understand that it's going to come up at the music committee meeting Thursday, and you *definitely* didn't hear that from me, or anyone else for that matter."

"How did *you* know? Your father?"

"No. We never talk about the music. He says it wouldn't be fair for him to have 'an inside source of information'. Let's just say I overheard something. I'm going to get into *so* much trouble if I keep talking to you."

"No, you won't. Your secrets are safe with me. Just tell me this, if you can: what should I expect at the music committee meeting? Problems, I guess?"

"I'm not sure, exactly. Let's just say . . . questions will be asked."

The neighborhood maples gave way to evergreens on the front lawn of the manse.

"Well, here we are," said Kathy. "I'd invite you in, but we have some people staying with us from Dad's last church, and I'll be expected to do some of the entertaining."

"That's okay. Call you sometime?"

"Sure."

*   *   *

"Hello? Kathy?"

"George!"

"Hi."

"Hi."

"Uh . . . there's a special screening of *Fantasia* on Friday . . . . that Disney thing? . . . the animation of all those classical pieces?"

"Yeah? I heard it was good."

"Want to go?"

"Sure."

*   *   *

"I think you set a record there," said Jesus.

"Sometimes I get nervous," George explained.

"Not always when you should."

*   *   *

George sat back and looked at himself on the screen, sitting back looking out the window in his study after getting off the phone. It was like looking at yourself in one of those hinged mirrors that multiplied your image out to infinity if it's angled just so, George thought.

"Questions will be asked," George said quietly to himself, in the only office that he had ever had. "Questions will be asked."

Chapter, the Eleventh:

The Thin Edge of the Wedge

"What gives, George?" Bill Seely looked puzzled, squinting behind his round spectacles. Judging from the way several of the other committee members were leaning forward, Seely wasn't the only one.

"In what sense?"

"In the sense of, 'What happened last Thursday?' for instance."

George shrugged in a near-convincing imitation of innocence. "We had a rehearsal."

"At which Jay and Bridgette North say you kicked them out."

"No-one was 'kicked out'."

"They didn't all show up Sunday morning," Ian Armstrong, head of the music committee, observed evenly.

"At least not in the chancel," Seely added.

"And then a certain church organist who shall remain nameless made himself rather conspicuous by his absence after the service," Reverend Parker said in a tone that made everyone smile. After a carefully timed pause, he deadpanned, "I understand that Molly was disappointed," causing everyone to laugh.

"Avoiding your favorite alto, were you?" Ian Armstrong suggested, trying to sustain the note of levity that Parker had introduced. "You won't be able to do that forever, you know."

"No, I guess not." George replied wistfully as he tried to play along. Parker smiled, but the others were fast resuming their former seriousness of expression.

Bill Seely took up his earlier line of questioning more or less where he left off "Molly aside, what's happening in the choir, George? Why are these people complaining about being kicked out?"

"No-one was 'kicked out'. All I did was ask the choir to learn a few notes at home."

"Isn't that what rehearsals are for?"

"People have always taken music home," Oliver Sommers, who had sung with the choir some years before, countered. "Some of them couldn't manage without it. Others are keen. I don't see anything wrong with George inviting them to do so."

"'Inviting'?" said Seely.

"And what if they *can't* learn it at home?" Jason Matthews, another committee member, asked. "Does that mean they can't come Sunday morning?"

"I never *said* that they couldn't come."

"But you'd prefer it if they didn't?"

"I can't deny *that*."

"If you think about it," said Oliver, "why would they *want* to come?"

"For Christian fellowship?" Matthew's suggested. "Isn't that what the church is all about? Do we exclude someone for not being up to some arbitrary standard. Do we have auditions for the altar guild—"

"No-one's talking about auditions," said George.

"Maybe not now," Matthews continued, "but how do we know that this isn't just the thin edge of the wedge? Now, you're suggesting that people who can't learn the notes at home would be 'more comfortable' in the congregation; maybe next, you'll be insisting on it?"

"I have nothing like that in mind."

"Actually," said Jesus, "that's *exactly* what you had in mind."

"There are many opportunities in the church for Christian fellowship," said Sommers, "and we do actively encourage some parishioners in certain directions."

Parker decided it was time to wade into the discussion. "If you think about it, we do put certain restrictions on some positions in the church. I guess that I'm a case in point."

Several committee members nodded.

"So is George, and so, even, is the choir *now*, if you think about it. Those who are not up to a certain musical standard would not be able to keep up, even if they had *daily* rehearsals. And some of our singers are, in fact, paid."

"Section leads and soloists," George agreed, happy to support that line of reasoning, *wherever* it was going.

"Yes," said Parker, "and the music itself, we must remember, is for the glory of God and the inspiration of His people. And to do that there must be *some* standards."

"Yes," Armstrong echoed, sensing a way through the opposing points of view. "Now, I get the feeling, George, that we're headed into a new era in the ministry of music at St. Christopher's, if Sunday was any indication, which some people would welcome, although I'm not certain of the numbers."

"Some people already have, and we *do* know some numbers," Evan Bawdry, who also sat on the finance committee, offered.

Everyone looked over expectantly.

"We counted the collection last Sunday," Bawdry continued. "We expected it to be a little higher than usual because attendance was also a little higher than usual, but, when we totaled it all up, the figure was over forty-five hundred dollars: $4,567.13, to be exact."

"*What?*" said Armstrong.

"You heard me."

"That's . . . a little on the high side for us, isn't it?" Matthews asked, suddenly willing to be impressed.

"A little? We're still doing some checking, but we think that, aside from Christmas and Easter, it's the largest collection we've ever had."

"And you think it's . . . ?"

"Yes, I do. We've seen before that the choice of offertory anthem can make a difference in the collection plates, but nothing like *this*. Of course, we haven't heard anything quite like *that* before, either."

Eyes settled on George with a new respect.

"It's hard to argue with success, isn't it?" said Armstrong, amid much widening of eyes and nodding of heads. For a few moments, he looked around the table. "Does anyone else have something to add?" A sense of closure was rapidly developing around the table.

There were a few seconds of awkward silence that Evan Bawdry's sense of the moment was left to break. "Is there anything that the committee can do to support the minister of music?"

Chapter, the Twelfth:

Their First Official Date

"And *then* he said, 'Is there anything that the committee can do to support the minister of music?' and I thought, 'Let me make you a list!'" George could barely keep up with his thoughts.

"And did you?" Kathy asked.

George nodded quickly, his eyes growing wide at the thought. "Ohhhh, yes!" and they both started laughing all over again as they walked to the local repertory theater on this their first official date.

"What did you ask for?"

"More," George answered. "More everything—more money for the music program, for starters. Now *that* was easy, very easy. Then I asked them to give me a little more wiggle room on the issue of choir membership. *That* was a little harder."

"What do you mean?" Kathy asked, a little less cheerily, not that George noticed.

"Well, Matthews, for one, wants choir membership wide open: let anyone join, no matter what they sound like. Bawdry, on the other hand, was so thrilled with the collection plate that I think he'd happily let me have an all professional choir if I wanted one."

"Would you?" she asked quietly.

This time, George noticed. "Not if it meant not having *you* in the choir," he offered, suddenly vulnerable.

"That was sweet," Kathy said shyly.

"But I *am* going to hire more section leads. Now, we have four. We really should have eight so that I can do more pieces for double choir—professional singers on both sides of the chancel—*and* get a better sound."

· "That would be great!"

"The organ could use some work, too."

"Why? What's wrong with it?"

"Nothing . . . 'broken', but there *is* room for improvement. A few new ranks of pipes wouldn't hurt: a little more sixteen foot tone, for instance, and maybe another thirty-two foot rank in the pedal. Then there's the—"

"Huh?" Kathy was squinting.

"Sorry. More pipes . . . bigger sound!"

"Why didn't you say so?"

George smiled. "You prefer your answers in English, then, do you?"

*   *   *

"So . . . do you want popcorn or a drink or something with the movie?" George asked Kathy.

"A drink would be nice."

"Popcorn?"

"That's okay," she answered, smiling. "I'll have some of yours."

*   *   *

The house lights dimmed as George and Kathy reached their seats. A silhouetted Leopold Stokowski conducted the Cleveland Orchestra as the voice of Disney Productions introduced the "new art form" that Fantasia represented.

Music and animation depicting the creation of the world followed, which moved Jesus to declare, "The staff should see this: very educational."

"Which?" asked George. "*Pipes* or *Fantasia?*"

"Maybe both," Jesus replied, as St. Peter and a group of similarly robed figures began to make their way into the theater, presumably responding to some form of silent summons. "Peter, you recognize, of course . . . more of the disciples . . . a few others. Sunday's a relatively slow day in 'Arrivals'."

They came in, looked, nodded, and/or smiled at Jesus, and quickly took their seats. Peter glanced at George and sat at Jesus' right hand.

The theater oohed and ahhed as Disney created the world . . .

*   *   *

"Now," said Jesus, "one more scene from *Fantasia*, by popular request, and we should get back to *Pipes*. Why don't you choose one, George?"

"I don't know . . . so many to choose from."

"Free associate," Freud suggested.

"Hmmm . . . The Sorcerer's Apprentice?"

Jesus raised his hand, and Mickey Mouse appeared on the screen, eliciting smiles and cheers from every direction. "A popular choice."

Before long, Mickey was overwhelmed by an army of marching brooms, and near-drowning in the relentless buckets of water they were feverishly throwing around, until the Sorcerer appeared, eyes flashing, to rescue his hapless apprentice.

In an aside to Jesus, Peter whispered, "Makes me think a little of what happened to George."

"Me, too," Jesus replied quietly.

George kept his eyes fixed on the screen as Kathy reached for a handful of his popcorn . . .

Chapter, the Thirteenth:

Hug?

After the short walk from the old Capitol theater, George and Kathy climbed the stairs to George's apartment.

"Woof!"

"Bernie!"

"Woof!!"

When the door was finally opened, Bernie used all the expected canine body language to greet George, and made an even bigger fuss over Kathy with a profusion of wags and sniffs, rubbings and lickings.

"Bernie! You're going to knock her over!"

Bernie sat down, thumping his great tail on the floor, and shifted his weight restlessly from one massive front paw to the other.

"Bernie, go lie down," said George, pointing to the living room.

After a long last lingering look at their new visitor, Bernie lumbered off.

"Can I get you something?" George asked as he took her coat. "I have coffee, orange juice, or chamomile tea. Not much to choose from, I'm afraid."

"Tea sounds good."

As he showed her to the living room, he asked, "Would you like to hear anything?"

"I don't know. What kind of music does an organist collect, I wonder?"

"Mostly church music, some classical . . ."

"Do you have recordings of any of the stuff that we've been doing?"

"Lots."

"What about the anthem from last week? 'Holy, Holy, Holy'?"

"Two versions: King's College, and St. Anthony in the Fields' with the composer conducting. What's your pleasure?"

"I don't really know any of those choirs, except for King's College, I think. They do that carol service every Christmas, don't they?"

"That's right. Have you seen it?"

"I don't think there's anyone in the choir who hasn't."

"Okay, let's start with that one."

George took the CD from its case and nestled it in the player with something approaching a flourish, hit "play", and went to the kitchen, Kathy in tow, to put on the kettle and get better acquainted.

*　　*　　*

At the end of the anthem, precisely with its final chord, the kettle went off, its shrill whistle matching the pitch of the sopranos' last note precisely. George and Kathy looked at each other, eyes wide.

"Bernie lifted his massive head, and looked around vacantly before slowly settling back down into sleep.

"What are the odds of *that* happening?" Kathy asked.

"I don't know. Not good, I wouldn't think."

"Not bad, actually, if I'm around," a female voice chimed in from the row behind George in the theater.

"Who are *you*?"

"You know *me*, George. My name is Cecilia. It's a pleasure to meet you, although I've sat at your elbow many a time."

"*Saint* . . . Cecilia? Patron saint of music?"

"Yes!" she answered brightly.

"*You* did that?"

Saint Cecilia nodded eagerly. "Kettle solo was fun!"

*   *   *

The last chord of the second version of "Holy, Holy, Holy" died away in the echo of St. Anthony in the Fields.

"That was *beautiful*," said Kathy.

"Which was your favorite?"

Kathy smiled shyly, and answered, "Yours."

"Mine? Why? Those two have better choirs."

"It's not the choir . . . it's what you do with it, somehow. I like yours better."

"You do?"

Kathy smiled and nodded.

"Do you like candlelight?" George asked Kathy.

"Sure," she replied, flushing slightly.

George sought out the matches, and made his way over to the mantelpiece, lighting the large ceremonial candle in the middle first.

"You have a huge . . . candle." Kathy flushed a little more deeply, and looked down, as George's gaze fell, full of interest, upon her.

"I got it at the liturgical supply center. I get most of my candles there. This one's designed to last the full liturgical year."

"*What* kind of year?"

"Starting at Easter. I would have thought that you'd heard lots of that sort of stuff, being a minister's daughter."

"Heard, yes; listened, not always; understood . . . ?" Kathy shrugged. "You do sound a bit like Dad sometimes."

"Not *too* much, I hope?"

"No, not *too* much," she answered, smiling.

*   *   *

George put on another CD and sat down beside her, noting that she was sitting closer to the center of the couch than to the end.

"What's that?" she asked.

"Brahms."

"It's beautiful," Kathy gushed.

"It is," George agreed.

Kathy looked around the room. "I like it here," she volunteered.

George did not seem to know what to say, finally suggesting, somewhat clumsily, "Hug?"

"Sure."

They embraced.

Neither George nor Kathy seemed to be in any hurry for the hug to end.

George progressed unsteadily to stroking her hair. She didn't pull away, but something in the way of an expected response, a softening of her posture or some other form of welcoming body language, was missing, it seemed to George, who looked puzzled, uncertain of what to do next.

"Do we have to watch this part?" George asked Jesus.

"Yes."

George sank a little lower in his seat as he watched himself beginning to clumsily kiss the side of Kathy's head.

After a moment's hesitation, Kathy slowly but deliberately disentangled herself from George's embrace. She stared at the cushions for a moment, straightened up, blinked several times, and said, "I just want to be friends."

Chapter, the Fourteenth:

Friends?

Bernie roused himself long enough to look sadly from George to Kathy, and then back again before closing his big, brown, drooping eyes, giving forth the deepest of dog sighs, and going back to sleep.

The theater audience waited for George's response. He squinted painfully, barely able to bring himself to utter the syllable, "Friends?"

Kathy nodded, almost imperceptibly.

George sank back into the couch and muttered, "That's just great."

George sank ever lower in his theater seat and muttered, "This is just great."

There was silence, both in George's living room and in the Odeon Paradise.

Finally, George roused himself from his numb confusion, turned to Kathy, and asked again, "*Friends?*"

Kathy looked steadily at her hands.

"Why?" he asked.

"'Friends' lasts."

"So can—"

"Hardly ever." Kathy shook her head. "You meet someone, something happens, it's great for a while, and then come the problems. Sooner or later, it all falls apart. Then you can't even stay friends."

George thought fast. "I have a friend who stayed friends with every girlfriend he ever had."

"How often does *that* happen?" she asked bitterly.

"Zat obviously comes from *some* place," said Freud.

"Some place very painful," St. Cecilia added.

"What's wrong with 'friends', anyway?" Kathy asked.

"Nothing . . . I *guess* . . . but . . . but . . ." George looked back and forth, around his living room, and then, as if he had seen something he had been looking long and hard for, said, "but it's not what we *feel* . . . is it?"

The theater was filled with sighs and groans.

"It's what *I* feel," Kathy insisted.

"Such denial," said Freud.

"That's what *I* told her," said George, relieved to find some support.

"Und did I say on whose part zis denial vas?"

George and Kathy sat in silence.

"I don't understand," George said finally.

"*What* don't you understand?" Kathy asked wearily.

"It's just that I have this . . . this . . . radar."

"*Radar?*" Kathy asked.

"Something like that. Whenever I've . . . you know . . . wanted to . . . kiss a girl, I've always known if it would be okay or not before I tried."

"But I don't *want* that. I want to be *friends.*"

Defeated, and suffering a severe case of radar failure, George slumped back in the corner of the couch. "I have lots of friends," he muttered, folding his hands in his lap.

The thoughts of the two couchmates echoed over the theater's speakers as the camera panned across their faces . . .

"*(This is just great,)*" thought George.

"*(This is just great,)*" thought Kathy.

Chapter, the Fifteenth:

Crossed Wires and Mixed Signals

"I do not understand," said George.

"What do you not understand?" Jesus asked, signaling the projectionist to stop the film.

George waved his right hand vaguely at the screen. "That . . . that!" George pursed and unpursed his lips several times, the corners of his mouth beginning to twitch.

"'That'?"

"My . . . my *ra*dar!" George sputtered, his voice jumping an up octave on his cherished ability's initial syllable.

"The trouble with your radar," said Jesus, "is that it cannot cope with mixed signals, and life, George, is one great swirling mass of mixed signals."

"But it's not fair," George said quietly, lowering his eyes.

"What . . . precisely . . . is 'not fair'?"

"I don't know . . . or . . . I guess I do."

"Ze mixed signals?" Freud asked gently. "Jesus is right, you know. Life is full of crossed vires und mixed signals."

George shook his head.

"Vhat, zen?"

Achingly slowly, shedding his last shred of dignity, George answered, "I hadn't had . . . anyone . . . in my life . . . for more than two years."

Somewhere in the back of the theater, a seraph whispered, "That is so sad."

And Jesus answered, "Neither had Kathy."

*　　*　　*

"When Kathy said she only wanted to be friends," Jesus explained, "what she actually felt was, 'This is all happening too fast for me, so I want to be friends . . . *first.*'"

"It *was?*"

"It was."

George sat, stunned.

"Essentially, your precious radar was right. Imagine that! You just interpreted the results a little too rigidly."

"You mean that, underneath it all, we both wanted the same thing?"

"Yes, just not in the same way, and certainly not at the same time. Even so, you both acted as you did for the very same reason."

George tried to ask what that was, but could get no closer to doing so than staring, open-mouthed.

"*You* wanted a romantic relationship in a big hurry because you were lonely and feared rejection. *She* wanted to take her time because she, also, was afraid—afraid of something else, however."

"What?!"

"A different kind of being vulnerable," said Jesus, signaling the projectionist. "Listen to this . . ."

"I have a friend who stayed friends with every girlfriend he ever had," the replay began, George, off screen, nodding his approval of his own words onscreen.

"How often does *that* happen?" she asked bitterly.

"See?" Jesus asked, signaling the projectionist again, this time to stop, leaving the two couchmates frozen in a tableau on the screen of the Odeon Paradise.

"*What?* That it hadn't happened for *her*. With some other guy?"

"Yes. And remember when you were over at her place, and she stood so far away from you at the door as you said goodnight?"

"Because she *liked* me?" The exertion of trying to follow Jesus' analysis was beginning to reveal itself in small, sometimes involuntary gestures: at this point, he was massaging his temples.

"Exactly."

"She didn't *look* like she liked me."

"Doesn't matter," Jesus said emphatically, Freud and St. Cecilia nodding deeply. "She liked you, which made her nervous, which, in turn, caused her to keep her distance; and the more she liked you, the more distance she put between you, and not just physically, but emotionally, too."

George took a moment to digest the implications. "So Kathy *wanted* to be friends . . . because she *didn't* want to be friends?"

"Now you've got it!" said Jesus, as various members of the theater audience who were within easy earshot nodded and whispered their agreement, while others took advantage of the break to stretch legs and/or wings.

"So . . . it was all just . . . a lie?"

"Well . . . 'lie' sounds a tad harsh, if you ask Me."

"Besides," said Freud, "sometimes a lie is just ze truz standing on its head. Ve see zat in dreams all ze time. Ze . . . sorry, sometimes I do go on."

"Okay . . . but if we both wanted the same thing, why didn't we work it out?"

"Perhaps ze two of you just need a little more time?"

"But I'm dead!"

"And so is she," Jesus said gently.

"She is?" George's voice dropped to a whisper. "She . . . died . . . *too?*" George looked up, silently pleading, at Jesus, who nodded grimly. George looked gloomily at his feet, his eyes beginning to glisten. Apparently, being dead did not preclude wishing that you could die.

"Will I ever see her again?"

"Yes. When the time is right."

George spoke slowly. "None of this would have happened if it hadn't been for me . . . all because of me. I'm dead . . . *she's* dead. A tragedy . . ." George shook his head slowly " . . . a tragedy of . . . of . . . Shakespearean proportions, wouldn't it be?"

"Oft' times, that which we deem a tragedy is but a comedy stood on its pate."

"Who said *that*?"

Chapter, the Sixteenth:

Rising to the Occasion

"I."

"'I'?"

"Aye!" he said, nodding his head. "I!" he said, tapping his chest. "Or else take this," he continued (pointing to his head), "from this," he concluded (indicating his body). "My name is William Shakespeare, by your leave."

"You, *too?*"

"Thou didst invoke me, didst thou not, good sir?"

George closed his eyes, sighing and rubbing his temples afresh. "I'll never get used to all these famous people."

"But vhen you zink of it, you know, you're becoming kind of famous *yourself*, at least in zese parts."

"And I will soon immortalize thee, sir," said Shakespeare.

"Actually," said Jesus, "I've already done that, William, or Dad did, if you prefer—not to quibble over the credit."

"'Tis even as Thou say'st; I meant no slight: 'twas only of his deeds I planned to write. In sooth, my Lord, Yours is the greater part; I merely sought to fuel my humble art."

"Yes, Will." Jesus smiled. "I understand."

"I thank Thee, Lord. The play's the thing for me."

"I look forward to seeing it," said the Lord. "I will have seen the *movie* . . ."

"And who will write the book?" George groaned.

Shakespeare shrugged. "I know not, but Charles Dickens seems most meet."

"A book . . . a movie . . . Shakespeare is going to write a play. About *me*? Why?"

"You inspired him," said Jesus. "Not everyone can say that."

"Und you should be *glad* zat he's here," said Freud.

"I should?"

"Ja. Some zings are easier to understand in ze context of art zan zey are amid ze frenzy of life, und so, he vill, on occasion, be helpful in giving you a greater understanding of yourself, I am certain, being practiced in his art, as he is."

Shakespeare bowed.

"Und know zis, George: in understanding is healing."

"Then he'll have to ease off a little on the . . . the . . . ?"

"Iambic pentameter? George, I shall."

"William is here to help you," said Jesus.

"Ja, und, if you're finding all of zis confusing . . ."

"I am."

" . . . try *zis* vone on for size: sometimes, ze cure may feel worse zan ze disease, but you can draw some comfort from knowing zat it *is* ze cure."

"That's a cure?" said George, waving one hand at the visual record of his radar failure—or was that success standing on its head?—on the screen. "And this?" he added, waving the other at the theater, which Shakespeare noticed immediately . . .

"George, it would appear that you have gone from tilting at windmills to becoming one."

George allowed his arms to settle at his sides. "This is a cure?" he asked quietly.

"That's up to you," said Jesus.

"But it *hurts*." George reflected long and hard. He also sighed, something that he had been doing more often of late. "Who was it who said, 'If I had to choose between pain and nothing, I'd choose pain every time'?"

"This time," said Shakespeare, "it was you."

"Anozer breakzrough!"

George circled his right index finger in the classic *let's hear it for me* gesture.

"Yes," said Jesus. "Our George is fast developing the habit of rising to the occasion."

George sighed, again. "Okay, okay. So there's the movie, the play, and probably the book. Who's going to do the T-shirt? Picasso? Will *he* be showing up next?"

"No," said Jesus, signaling the projectionist to resume. "Someone else who you have a *lot* more in common with."

Chapter, the Seventeenth:

The Sanest Musician in All of Heaven

Surrounded by a thicket of organ pipes, George scanned the pipe room.

"What's zis, George?"

George looked up at the screen. "The committee had promised me some money. Looks like I'm sizing up the pipe room to see where to spend some of it."

"And how did it look?" a voice asked from behind George.

"Well, it was—who's *that*?" George asked, looking around.

"You know me well, at least through my music. I had the same job as you and your father did—as did mine, more or less, and his father before him—for the better part of my life."

"You're . . ."

"Allow me to make the introductions," said St. Cecilia. "Johann, this is George; George, this is Johann . . . Sebastian Bach."

"*The* Johann Sebastian Bach?"

"Yes, assuming that you're not thinking of my great uncle, also of that name."

"Stupid question, I guess. It's just that it's not every day that a dead organist finds himself sitting with . . . Bach."

Bach shrugged. "I may be 'Bach', but I'm just a dead organist, too, George. And I'm very curious about the development of that organ. Give me the details," he said, leaning forward.

George reported on the capabilities of the instrument as Bach listened intently, asking a short question about one division or another of the organ, or making an observation on the balance of eight and sixteen foot tone, but speaking seldom, and nodding often.

Bach sat back and considered what he had heard, as George, onscreen, continued his perusal of the pipes. "Impressive. Five keyboards. Eighty-seven ranks of pipes. I never had such an instrument."

"It's half the reason I took the job."

Bach grew thoughtful. "I had a job like that, once. Wonderful instrument. Not as big as yours, though. In the end, it was nothing but grief. Now that I look back on it, I was much happier at home with my harpsichord."

"Nice alliteration," said Shakespeare.

"A *harpsichord?*" said George.

"Oh yes!" Bach stopped for a moment, gathering his thoughts as if he were a commission-based salesman facing a tough sell. "Music is still a collection of twelve semitones sounded in different combinations for varying lengths of time. That's it! So simple!"

George's eyes widened, struck by the simplicity of the concept.

Freud's did also, but for another reason altogether. "Semitones? Vhat's a semitone? I have heard ze term before, but I have forgotten, I zink."

"George?" said Bach.

George explained: "A semitone is the smallest difference in pitch that can be notated in western music: A to B flat, then B, C, C sharp, and so on. You can play those notes in different octaves—that is, their frequency divided or multiplied exactly by twos—but an A is still an A; an E is still an E, no matter how many octaves apart they are . . . twelve notes . . . that's it."

"Exactly," said Bach. "The rest is decoration. Some of the best times I've ever had with music were simply writing it, and I don't even use an instrument for that."

"Never?"

"Never. I do it in my head."

"But I've heard some wonderful music that was written sitting at an instrument," George objected.

"Yes, there *are* happy exceptions," Bach admitted, nodding to George "but most such composers are nothing but . . . klavier cavaliers, if you ask me."

George, his German hovering somewhere between rusty and non-existent, looked puzzled.

"Sehr gut!" Freud chuckled. "Keyboard cavalry. I can *see* zem."

"Yes," said Bach, "charging up and down the keys, finding whatever pattern of notes the fingers chance to fall upon, whether it be by habit or by chance."

George started to look nervous; Shakespeare, delighted.

"As I said, 'There are exceptions.' That descant to 'Holy, Holy, Holy', for instance? Wonderful!"

"But you could have come up with something like that in a minute, not poring over it for an hour like I did, more like . . . between the coffee and the cornflakes."

"Corn . . . *flakes?*" Bach shrugged. "But *I* didn't compose it at all. *You* did."

George relaxed a little, and for the first time since he died, began to look pleased with himself.

"Of course," Bach added quietly, "*my* music didn't get me killed."

Chapter, the Eighteenth:

Opportunity

George made his way the few short feet from the pipe room to his office, and sat heavily in his gray, padded, high-backed, swivel chair. As he put first one then the other foot up on his desk, something caught his eye.

"I remember this. That's a copy of *The United Church Observer* I'm reading." George brightened at the memory. "It was like a gift from Heaven."

"It wasn't from anyone up here," said Jesus. "Trust me."

George thumbed through its pages distractedly, then more attentively, until he turned a page, which he scanned, still slowing. When his finger reached a point midway down, he sat upright.

"What did you see?"

"Opportunity. A source of cheap pipes—free, in fact. I called Hillsborough United that same afternoon."

"A church was getting *rid* of its organ?" Bach asked.

"Yes," said George. "It was an inner-city church, most of whose aging congregation had either died or moved away as the neighborhood demographics changed. It had an old pipe organ they didn't know how to dispose of. I told them that I'd take it off their hands."

"Churches closing *down*? That didn't happen often, I hope."

"All the time."

"Sad," said Bach.

"Sad but true," said Jesus.

Bach sighed deeply, saddened to his Lutheran roots. "Well, at least the organ was put to use," was the bravest face he could put on it.

"Yes. They were happy to let me have it in return for giving it a good home, and I suppose it didn't hurt that I was calling from a fellow United church. A week later, I was incorporating some of its pipes and fittings into St. Christopher's' organ."

"Und how vas zat, George?"

"It was fun," George answered stonily. "It got my mind off . . . things. I used to love puttering around in the pipe room."

"Nice turn of phrase," said Shakespeare, making a note of it.

"A new project," said George, "is like something . . . holy—I don't know what other word to use—the creation of something new, something fresh."

"And this time, it was something else, too," said Jesus.

"Lord?"

"The second nail in your coffin."

Chapter, the Nineteenth:

Up to Something

When the choir entered the chancel for their regular Thursday rehearsal, George was waiting at the front with a piece of paper for each of its members.

"You appear to be up to somezing, George."

"A new seating plan."

"Interesting," said Bach, as he watched choir members finding their new places. "They don't appear to be getting back into sections."

"They're getting into pairs, more or less."

"Pairs?"

"Yes. I saw something like it done when I was in university. The conductor of the faculty choir had us all split up. You weren't allowed to sit beside anyone who was singing your part. He did it for a little variety, I suppose, and just once, but the effect was incredible! The sections blended perfectly, and the tuning was beautiful! So I thought I'd try it, not completely 'sprinkled', of course, or there would have been several nervous breakdowns, but at least in pairs."

Molly eyed George suspiciously before snatching her copy of the seating plan from his outstretched hand, glancing at it too briefly to make anything of it, then handing it back to him. "I have been sitting in the same choir pew for thirty-five years," she said, tilting her head back and sighting him along the line of her nose as if she were placing him in the crosshairs of an automatic assault weapon, anticipating an answer that she was determined to reject, whatever it might be.

"So have I," said Mona, who stood beside her, also disdaining the proffered piece of paper.

George smiled, having prepared himself for their rejection. "You still *are*." He stuffed the seating plans back into their hands, and turned to the next choir member before Molly could even fully open her mouth.

"Of course, no-vone *else* is, I'll vager." Freud chuckled.

"Pretty much," George admitted.

"Vait till she sees zat!"

George smiled at the thought.

"And who's that?" Bach asked, indicating a middle-aged man in the second row of choir pews on the north side of the chancel.

"Bill Smiley," George answered.

"And neither of those two," said Bach, pointing to the choristers on either side of Smiley, "is particularly helpful to you, are they?"

"No, they're not. They're actually quite a detriment . . . but how did you guess?"

"Not exactly a guess." Bach smiled. "Look at how they're eyeing that fellow's feet! Now what might be the reason for that?"

"Well . . . there is some thought in the choir that Bill Smiley should change his socks a little more often. Behind his back, some of them refer to him as Bill *Smelly*."

Bach nodded. "I had a feeling it was something like that. Back in Leipzig once, where *I* was organist/choirmaster for many years, I tried something of the sort on *them*, only the fellow I counted on to drive them out of the choir pews and back into the congregation had bad breath, not smelly feet."

"I—"

"Don't even try to deny it, George. I've been there, and I've had my share of friction with choir members. I hate to admit it, but our Gunther got moved around a lot, and he was probably more use to me, in his own unique fashion, than some of my best singers. A rare talent, his."

Shakespeare shifted restlessly in his seat, glanced up at Jesus, apparently trying to restrain himself, and finally said, "Yes, a talent for turning choir pews into *pee yoos*," then settled back, looking relieved.

"A bit of a compulsion," Freud confided to George. "Ve're vorking on it, und he is making considerably progress."

"Alright, William," said Jesus, "that one's allowed." Turning to George, he said, "*You*, on the other hand, are getting sneakier all the time! Even the music committee wouldn't have guessed what you were up to there."

"But that was *then*," George protested weakly.

"And you were smiling about it *now*."

"Did it work?" Bach asked.

"More than once," said George, glancing at Jesus, any hint of a smile necessarily stillborn.

"Vait a minute. *How* exactly did you get avay viz your razer unorzodox use of Herr . . . who vas he?"

"Smiley, Bill Smiley. I don't know," he shrugged. "I just did."

"Nein, George. It had to be more complicated zan zat. First of all, vhy didn't Herr Smiley practice better foot hygiene?"

"He didn't realize that he had a problem."

"But, if it vas *zat* bad, how could he miss it?"

"I never could figure that out. I heard various explanations: childhood illness, congenital nose defect . . . but, whatever it was, he couldn't smell the broad side of a barn door."

"What a *breathtakingly* mixed metaphor," said Shakespeare.

"Oh, Smiley was the undisputed champion of taking people's breath away."

Shakespeare smiled.

"But vhy didn't somevone tell him; somevone complain; or . . . or *somezing*?"

"Political correctness, of which the United Church was a seething hotbed, by the way."

"Political vhat? Correctness?" Freud's eyes shifted rapidly back and forth. "Ah, ja! I remember hearing somezing about zat. A razer recent sort of zing, ja? But how did it apply in Smiley's situation?"

"It's hard to explain, but basically, it would have been considered unspeakably insensitive to draw attention to his disability."

Freud shook his head. "Vhat about his family, zen, assuming zat he had vone? Vhy didn't *zey* tell him?"

"No-one could figure out why Smiley's wife hadn't brought it to his attention, but of course no-one could ask."

"He looks a trifle disoriented."

Smiley was busy surveying the results of the four choral sections subdividing and rearranging themselves into pairs of singers, after the switching places, pews and/or sides of the chancel.

"He's looking for other tenors," said George, "without a great deal of success."

"Vhy is zat?"

"First, because there aren't many tenors—there never are. Second, because I'm trying to keep every tenor I can. I'd lost too many already because of his feet. "There . . . he's just noticed one, Wayne Elston." Smiley had finally looked behind himself. Grinning broadly, he received a tight smile in return.

"Looked like entropy in action there for a minute," said Smiley, his raised eyebrows and little nods indicating his anticipation of some form of acknowledgement of his wit. None, however, was forthcoming.

"Poor Bill," said George. "No-one ever laughed at his jokes."

"That was a jest?" Shakespeare asked.

"*Just . . .*"

Shakespeare grinned.

"... and only to another high school physics teacher. Someone said that he's called 'Smiley' because, after one of his jokes, he's the only one left smiling, at least that's what ... Kathy ... said."

"I see that you've put the Parkers together," said Jesus, "and Kathy is in her usual seat." Indeed, the Parkers were engaged in an animated three-way conversation, and Kathy tried to smile at George, but he was too busy observing his new creation to notice.

George arpeggiated a G minor chord on the piano to get the the choir's attention. "Alright! Rely on yourselves, and tune to your neighbors. Turn to the Brahms."

"You chose this deliberately?" Bach asked.

"Yes. Brahms blends so beautifully this way."

"And the weakest singers get lost and discouraged in the complicated chromatic harmonies that Brahms loved so much to write? Maybe sit in the congregation again?"

"I had to improve the choir."

"Was the Brahms as useful as that fellow with the smelly feet?"

"Not quite."

The choir quickly fell into a state of intense concentration, either relying on themselves as George had suggested, or leaning desperately on a stronger pew partner.

"Next week, something of mine?" Bach asked. "Perhaps one of the more contrapuntally complex cantatas?"

"How did you know?"

"Und viz ze extreme staccato, ja?"

"How did you guess?"

Chapter, the Twentieth:

Busy Hands are Happy Hands

Two men walked up the side aisle of the church towards the organ, where George sat, studying a piece of music.

"Delivery from Hillsborough United," one of them called out.

George looked up. "The pipes!"

"And that's not all," the other man added. "Two wind chests, a blower, swell shutters . . ."

"Bob Harvey," said the first, extending his hand as George rose to greet them.

"Steven Murphy," said the other.

"A pleasure, gentlemen, a genuine pleasure. Let's have a look."

*   *   *

George sat cross-legged in the middle of a jungle of pipes. The wind chest and associated mechanisms had been laid out more or less where he intended them to end up.

"Busy hands are happy hands, eh George?" said Bach.

"I knew *you'd* understand."

"How vere you going to fit zem all in?" Freud asked.

"In the pipe rooms."

"Not *all* of them," said Bach, craning his neck a little, and nodding his head from time to time as he performed a series of mental calculations. "The only place you can use the swell box is mounted on the south wall of the near pipe room, and then you still have at least two extra ranks. What about those?"

"'Those' I mounted on opposite walls of the chancel."

"Out in the open?"

"Yes."

"How did the choir like it?"

George smiled. "Reactions varied. Jay Madison loved it. Brian Tyler liked it, too, I think . . . he kept looking at it, anyway. Not as much as Molly, of course. She *hated* it," George grinned, "but by that time, she hated everything I did."

"*You* saw to that," said Jesus.

George's grin dissolved. "I didn't use them all the time," he said defensively, "and it helped the tuning, especially with the tenors."

"And that's why you got them?" Jesus asked.

"Well . . . not entirely."

Chapter, the Twenty-First:

On His Feet and Pacing

George, robed in red and white, was seated at the organ console, playing the final verse of the final hymn on Sunday morning as the choir recessed from the chancel.

"Ah, Sunday morning!" said Jesus. "My favorite time of My favorite day."

"Days matter up here? In eternity?"

"'The seventh day is very big 'up here'. Dad and I both have very fond memories of it. He 'rested', if you remember your scripture—something He got to do exactly once—and I got to rise from the dead. Not bad! We *have* been told that We're living in the past, but some memories are worth preserving, don't you think?"

George's brow furrowed. "'Living in the past'? Who would say such a thing to God the Father and His only begotten Son?"

"Satan, in this case."

"Satan? You talk to *Satan*?"

"All the time."

"All the time? You *are* open-minded up here."

"I told you that you'd be amazed by who had visiting privileges. In Satan's case, it's mostly to let him see what he's missing."

The hymn ended and the chancel party gathered at the back of the church. Reverend Parker closed his hymnbook, folded his arms, took a deep breath and intoned the benediction. "May the Lord bless you and keep you. May the Lord make His countenance to shine upon you, and give you peace."

The choir sang the choral amen, Brian Tyler leaning forward, as if into a stiff breeze, his right hand describing improbable circles as he conducted, his eyes wide, glued to the hymnbook.

"Amen," Jesus added.

"Amen," the theater echoed.

A short pause, and the organ postlude began.

"Nice timing," said Bach.

"Thanks. I worked on the dotted rhythms: I thought that if I kept them crisp, the piece would move along a little better."

"Not the music, George—although there's nothing wrong with that—the pause."

"The pause?"

Bach nodded. "The pause . . . between the choral amen and the organ postlude."

"Ohhhh . . . right. I like to pay attention to that. At other points in the service, too. I like to let the . . . I don't know . . . the magic . . . hang in the air for a bit."

"It has not gone unnoticed," added Jesus. "In fact, it expiated a number of your sins."

"It did?" George brightened.

"Not *that* one."

George dimmed.

"*That* one is why you're here."

George sat quietly as the last few bars played out.

"Same thing there," Bach noted as George released the final chord, leaving his hands poised in the air, absolutely still at first, then, fingers slowly unflexing, finally allowing his arms to float down to his sides.

"That's even better," said Jesus.

"It is? Why?"

"Because nobody knows that you do that. No-one sees it. It makes no difference to the sound. It is a form of true reverence. Dad loves it."

George stole quick glances around the Odeon Paradise as if the walls were one-way mirrors in a police interrogation room.

"Yes, George. He's watching you now, too, but *He's* not making a big deal out of it, so don't *you*."

"It's not every day that God is *watching* you," said George.

Jesus sighed. "Actually, yes, it is."

George nodded, very slowly indeed.

*   *   *

Onscreen, George was making his way to his office, without enthusiasm.

"Woof!" Bernnie had been waiting for what he obviously deemed to be an inordinate length of time. George removed his robes and collapsed on the couch. Bernie stood beside him, then sat, and finally rested his head on George's thigh.

"Your head's heavy, Bernie. You're going to put my leg to sleep." George shifted, drawing his left knee up, dislodging Bernie, who reluctantly lifted his great head and sulked his way to the corner where he sank down on the floor and gave forth a St. Bernard-sized sigh. George stared at the ceiling and shifted again, this time raising his right knee while lowering his left. The theater watched as George rearranged himself in a variety of positions, the length of time between them growing progressively shorter. Now, George had one leg over the back of the couch and one hand on the carpet. Suddenly, he was on his feet and pacing.

"Where will he end up?" someone asked two rows back.

"The phone," another whispered.

"Ze telephone? You zink?"

"Yes."

"There, he's looking at it."

"Ja, he is, but vill he actually bring himself to use it?"

"No."

"Nein?"

"Well . . . maybe . . . yes, yes he will."

"Ja, I zink so, too."

The theater was more or less evenly divided on the question. An increasing number of persons and angels had an opinion to express.

George, who knew the outcome, began to squirm.

Onscreen, George sat down at his desk and eyed the telephone, looked out the window, and returned his gaze to the telephone, only to get up and resume his pacing.

"Maybe he won't."

"Nein, nein: he is merely postponing ze inevitable. Soon. Any second now."

As if hearing and responding, George returned to his desk, but frustrated Freud's prediction by sitting down on its side, and looking at something on the top. In a moment, he picked up the envelope he was staring at, and removed something from it.

"Vas ist das, George?" Freud whispered intensely.

"Two tickets to the symphony."

"Und zey figure somehow to all zis pacing und so on?"

"They do."

"Vhen did you get zem?"

"They appeared on the organ console that morning. Someone left them there. I never did find out who." Just at that moment, George caught St. Cecilia's eye. She was smiling. "*You?*"

St. Cecilia shrugged.

"It *was* you. I can tell."

"Not directly, George. I just whispered something in someone's ear."

"Huh?"

"A certain someone was given two tickets for the symphony, and had no-one to go with—very short notice. I suggested that she leave them for you."

"She?"

"Yes."

"*Who?*"

"Oh, I really couldn't name any names. Let's just say that you're about to call her."

Meanwhile, in his office, George had already picked up the phone and put it down again several times, but this time, he was dialing.

"Kathy . . . ? Hi . . . yes, it's me . . . uh . . . I have two tickets to the symphony, and I . . . uh . . . do you want to go? . . . Okay . . . . Yeah? . . . oh, soon; in less than an hour . . . . Yeah? You *will?*" he asked, his eyes growing wider "Sure. See you then . . . bye."

George replaced the receiver and sat down in his chair.

"Vhat happened, George?"

"She offered to pick me up." It was a pleasant memory, and pleasant memories were in short supply.

A moment later, and George got up from his desk, saying, "Come on, Bernie. I just have time to get you home."

"Woof!"

Chapter, the Twenty-Second:

Time to Give In

The Toronto Symphony Orchestra was playing Tchaikovsky's love theme from Romeo and Juliet as George and Kathy sat stiffly in the twelfth row of the sterile gray acoustic perfection that was Roy Thompson Hall.

"Und vhat zoughts vere running zrough ze young lovers' minds, I vonder?" Freud turned to Jesus.

"No." George was definite —

"Yes."—as was Jesus, who raised his index finger, signaling the projectionist to add George and Kathy's thoughts to the sound track.

"(I don't know what to say to her,)" thought George, staring straight ahead.

"(He's hardly said a word to me.)" thought Kathy, glancing at George.

"(I can't get comfortable.)"

"(Maybe he's just uncomfortable.)"

"(Maybe this was a mistake . . .)"

"(I hope this wasn't a mistake . . .)"

"(. . . knowing my luck with women.)"

"(. . . knowing my luck with men.)"

And so on . . .

"We're going to listen to my *thoughts?*" George whined to Jesus.

"Only when it is important for you to hear them," Jesus answered.

Kathy and George sat stiffly in the front seat of her car.
"Did you like it?"
"Yes, I did. Did you?"
"Yes."
Silence . . .
"It was good, wasn't it?"
"Yes . . . it was."
More silence . . .
"Good players."
"Yes, very good."
And so on . . .

*   *   *

Back at George's apartment, George and Kathy sat stiffly on the couch.
"*(I still don't know what to say to her. Why is it so hard?)*"
"*(He's still hardly saying a word to me. How hard can it be?)*"
"*(She's probably waiting for me to say that we can just be friends.)*"
"*(He's probably holding out for me to say that I'm willing to be more than friends.)*"
"*(I do like her, and as a friend, too, only not just as a friend . . . but . . . maybe it's time to give in.)*"
"*(I do like him, and like . . . that, too . . . maybe it's time to give in.)*"
"*(Maybe my stupid radar was wrong.)*"
"*(Maybe his stupid radar was right.)*"
George sighed. "*(Well, I guess it's 'friends' or nothing.)*"
Kathy sighed. "*(Well, I guess it's 'more than friends' or nothing.)*"

She took a deep breath, blew a lock of red hair off her forehead, and twisted around to half-face him.

"I've been thinking . . . about . . . things." She paused, feeling the awkwardness of the moment.

"You have?"

"Yes. Like . . . the last time I was here . . . for instance . . . maybe you were right."

"I *was*? About what?"

"You know . . . your stupid . . . *radar*."

George's mouth hung open, and he promptly forgot everything that he had been about to say.

"Okay?" she asked, unable to bring herself to go into greater detail.

"Okay . . ." George looked puzzled, but somehow possessed the presence of mind to slip his left hand around her waist.

Kathy inclined herself towards him, searching his eyes as if for some evidence of the rightness of her decision.

George reached up with his right hand and brushed the hair off her cheek, leaned forward, and kissed her.

Freud sighed wearily. "Oopsie."

"Huh?"

"If only you'd spoken up a moment earlier," said Jesus, "or if she had hesitated a moment longer . . ."

"I do *not* understand."

"No, you don't," said Jesus, "but you'll have to wait—yes, *wait*—for the full answer. For now, all that I will say is this: it would have caused everyone a lot less wear and tear if you had just piped up and agreed to be her friend."

"It should not have been that hard for an organist to '*pipe* up'," said Shakespeare.

A rhythmic banging arose on the theater's surround sound system.

"What's *that*?" George asked.

"A sound that you should be getting quite familiar with by now."

The organist's eyes darted back and forth under his furrowing brow. "What *is* it?" he asked again, alarmed.

"It's a hammer."

"What? *Another* nail in my coffin?"

"Yes. The third. And George?"

"Yes, Lord?"

"If you ask Me, you're beginning to accumulate them at a rate that is becoming alarming."

Chapter, the Twenty-Third:

A Certain Amount of Resistance

"So I was in a bit of a rush," George admitted, "but we both had romantic *feelings*, and so we got into a romantic *relationship*. What's the harm in that? Isn't it just like jumping into the water when it's cold instead of wading in an inch at a time? I mean isn't it better to just—I don't know—get it over with?"

"Let's put it this way," said Jesus. "'You shall know a seed by its tree'."

George squinted. "Isn't it, 'You shall know a tree by its fruit'?"

"Yes, that too, but then how do you think the *tree* got there?"

* * *

George and Kathy were lying together on his living room couch on another occasion, judging by what they were wearing. Her hair was slightly disheveled, the reason for which was obvious.

"You're not going to show *that*, are you?"

"You asked."

"I get so tired of . . . 'sex'," said Kathy. "Whenever I went out with a guy, it was fun until we got back to his place, and then it was just . . . 'sex', even on the first date."

Onscreen, George looked both hopeful and disappointed at the same time. "Are you trying to say that you're a . . . a . . . I don't know . . . 'loose woman' or something?" he asked, the asymmetry of his facial expression reflecting his mixed emotions concerning the possibilities.

"*No,*" said Kathy, italicizing her denial with a sharp blow to George's upper arm.

"Ouch!" George sat up and rubbed his arm.

"Too much pressure," said Freud. "Und on such a little flower!"

"Little *flower*? She *hit* me!"

"Only after you sullied her honor," said Shakespeare.

"I *what*?"

"Zere are zome questions zat a gentleman does not ask a lady."

"Apparently not." George rubbed his arm in remembrance.

"What was *that* for?" George asked Kathy.

Kathy did not answer, preferring to simply fume until she calmed herself enough to blow a single red curl off her forehead. "No," she said again.

George winced an inch or so away from her.

More quietly, she added, "No. They *tried.* They *always tried.*"

"Und so did you, George."

"It was *not* our first date."

Silence . . .

"Okay, I admit that I was in a bit of a rush."

"Which is beginning to sound a bit familiar, isn't it?" said Jesus. "As I said, 'You shall know a seed by its tree'."

"Huh?"

"Think about it, George. Being 'in a rush' got to be quite a habit."

"Wait a minute . . . is this a parable or something?"

"Something like that. Your romantic relationship started off with you being in a rush—that was the seed—and you never stopped rushing it—that is the tree. What followed was the fruit and you know how *that* turned out. He who has ears to hear, let him hear."

*   *   *

"This is *so* embarrassing."

"Yes, it must be."

George spoke quietly. "It wasn't really about the sex. I just didn't want to feel so . . . alone."

"There were better ways," said Jesus.

"I guess there were."

"Especially when you consider what Kathy had been through."

"What had she . . . 'been through'?"

"A bad experience. Enough to put her off men for two long years. Then, when she was barely ready to take the plunge again, she fell for *you*. But you were never happy, always pushing for more. So she pushed back. And then things got complicated."

George hesitated. "Well . . . it was *not* easy."

"True, and, to be fair, she didn't make it any easier for you than you did for her."

"No?"

"It doesn't get you off the hook, of course, but what she was doing was, in a sense, the mirror image of what *you* were doing."

"It was?"

"Let's have a little look at a few examples."

"I don't know if I'm up to it."

"Just a few." Jesus signaled the projectionist, the house lights dimmed, and the film resumed. "He who has eyes to see, let him see." Jesus pointed to the screen, which split into multiple images, each containing George and/or Kathy. "You've done this before."

"Pick a square?"

"Exactly."

"Uhhhhh, there." The square towards the bottom right that George had indicated expanded to fill the screen . . .

"Were you mad at me on Sunday?" George asked Kathy as they walked in from Yonge St..

"No," she answered, tensing.

"It's just that . . . I don't know . . . we get along fine when it's just the two of us, but whenever anyone else is around, like at church, you seem to ignore me."

"I do?"

"Yes."

"I didn't know."

"Actually, she did," Jesus said quietly. "What she did not know was how much she did it, and why she did it. Let's skip ahead a little . . ."

George looked at the second example as it appeared on the screen. "That's the kitchen downstairs at St. Christopher's. Coffee before the service. We get there pretty early."

"All by your lonesome," said Freud, shaking his head, as George, all by his lonesome, filled his coffee cup.

"Not for long," said Jesus.

Kathy slumped in, plopped herself on a stool, where she crossed her arms on the table before her, settled her head on them, and mumbled, "Hi."

Jesus gestured for the thought track.

"*(If I must, I must,)*" thought Kathy.

"Hi," said George. "Late night? *(I wonder where she went.)*"

Kathy shrugged.

"Passive, aggressive, ja? You asked her not to ignore you at church, so she sat down beside you, und ignored you up close razer zan ignoring you at a distance." Freud laughed. "Pretty neat, huh?"

"Yeah, really 'neat'," said George, rolling his eyes, "and only once, as I recall."

"Hardly vorz ze effort, ja?"

"Ja." George sighed.

As the scene in the kitchen shrank back down to its original size on the screen, Jesus looked at George, who pointed at the screen again, causing another scene to replace it . . .

"The choir party," said George, "at the manse."

George and Kathy made eye contact, each with a nervous smile. Kathy quickly turned back to her conversation. George stood uncertainly, and headed for the kitchen.

"Zame zing as before, only perhaps a little more so."

"The more things change, the more they stay the same," said Shakespeare.

"*You* said that?" asked George.

"I did *this* time."

"This is not a copyright convention," said Jesus. "Now, watch. We'll move ahead to your phone call the next evening."

The scene dissolved, and refocused on a split screen consisting of George on the left side, and Kathy on the right, each of them holding a telephone receiver, apparently part way into their conversation.

"Sometimes, I don't even want to come to the phone," Kathy complained. "I think, 'Okay, what have I done wrong *now*?'"

George was silent.

"A certain amount of resistance, eh George?"

"Always."

"Not *always*," said Jesus. "Only when she felt that there was something to resist. Like here . . ."

George and Kathy were sitting together again on George's couch.

"What's wrong with it the way it *is*?" said Kathy. "Why does it have to be more, always more?"

"I don't know. It just seems that relationships either grow, or they die."

"Oi!" said Freud.

"Ouch," said St. Cecilia, several voices around the Odeon Paradise echoing the same syllable.

There was a distinct rustling of wings from the rear of the theater, and even George, who did not know even one word in the tongues of angels, could tell that they were uncomfortable with what he had said.

"'He who has ears to hear'—and I'm saying this to you, George—'let . . . him . . . hear'."

Chapter, the Twenty-Fourth:

All God's Children

"I think that a change of pace would do everyone some good," said Jesus. "Let's go to church. That always cheers a soul in Heaven."

George could see himself, seated at the organ, as the choir, all red and wide pageantry, processed up the center aisle singing *Jesus Loves Me*, followed by the youth choir and then the children's choir, with clergy, robed and crossed, in tow:

"Yes, Jesus loves me,
Yes, Jesus loves me,
Yes, Jesus loves me,
The Bible tells me so."

"One of My favorite hymns," said Jesus.
"For the children," said George, remembering.
"We are *all* God's children, George, even Me."
By the last verse, everyone in the theater was singing with full voice and cheered considerably, just as Jesus had predicted.

*   *   *

"Let the children come forward," said Reverend Parker standing at the front of the chancel, cradling his red hymnbook before him.

"'Suffer the little children to come unto Me'," Jesus whispered, nodding. "I like that man. He *gets* it."

"He used to spend the 'moment with the children' at the beginning of the service before they went to Sunday School," said George, "then he gave it to that new young minister they hired, Wendy Richardson, but he kept finding ways to stay involved, never could completely let go of it."

"Good morning," said Reverend Richardson, after the children settled into the steps and front apron of the red-carpeted chancel, sounding genuinely happy to see them. They warmed immediately to *her* warmth with their own "good morning", as parents and other parishioners looked on.

After a few quiet individual greetings, she continued with, "Can someone tell me something that makes them happy?"

"Presents!" declared one.

"My kitten," said another.

"Dessert!" a third volunteered, utterly absorbed in the spirit of the moment.

"Me, too," said Richardson, grinning.

A more thoughtful young voice emerged shyly. "My Mom."

The young Reverend nodded. "I'm sure that your Mom will be glad to hear that." A brief onscreen appearance of "Mom" confirmed that she was.

The group seemed to have run out of answers, but Reverend Richardson kept smiling . . .

"Going to church?" a very young girl with blonde pigtails answered uncertainly.

"Good answer!" said Robinson, who was grateful for any answer.

But there was another, longer, pause . . . .

"Helping others?" a young, dark-haired girl of about eight finally ventured in a manner which suggested that she may have had a dim memory of hearing something like it before in Sunday School.

"Yes!" said Robinson, visibly relieved. "And what is it about helping others that makes us happy?" she asked, scanning the group, taking an answer . . .

She continued to ask leading questions, summarizing and reshaping the children's answers until she succeeded in directing the discussion to the desired destination, the now immortal theorem of Sunday schools everywhere: If you love Jesus, Others, and Yourself, in that order, you will have: Jesus—Others—Yourself = J.O.Y. = Joy! She had even brought a small portable blackboard into the chancel to make the derivation of the acronym clear, leaving the children with a certain pleasure in the appearance of order to it all, even the few who had not yet learned to read.

"Corny," said Jesus, "very corny, but useful. It sticks!" Jesus was plainly excited. "I would have given that one to the disciples if it had worked in Aramaic."

Meanwhile, at St. Christopher's United, the children, thus prepared for spiritual life in general, and their Sunday school lessons in particular, were thanked and sent downstairs to the strains of another children's hymn, with the children's choir, hymnbooks held at various angles, recessing behind them.

"It's nice to see so many children in a church these days," said Jesus.

"St. Christopher's is one of the lucky ones," George agreed. "There are actually more baptisms than funerals."

"You should have learned to ap*pre*ciate zem a little more zen. Vone day zey vould have been paying your salary."

"But I *did*."

"Not the youth choir," said Jesus.

George groaned. "*Teenagers.*"

"Zey're alright, George. Just full of *hor*mones, zat's all."

"Full of 'hormones'? "Full of—"

"Careful, George: 'Suffer the children . . . '"

"Ohhhh, 'I suffered' . . ." George grimaced " . . . with the 'big' ones, anyway—I suffered, alright."

Jesus nodded. "It was a two-way street as I recall."

Chapter, the Twenty-Fifth:

More Pipes?

"Where do you think *you're* going?" George demanded.

"Uh, sorry, George," said Rob Taylor, one of the more responsible members of the youth choir. His friend David North nodded reluctant agreement, and Ben Smiley shifted nervously from one foot to the other.

"You were sorry the *last* time."

"Yeah. It's just that . . . uh . . . we know how much you hate us being late for rehearsal, and we didn't want to miss anything, so . . ."

"So you cut through the pipe room . . . *again*. How many times have I told you not to *do* that?"

In the theater, George sat a little straighter, and leaned forward an inch or so, mouthing the words of his annoyed onscreen self.

"Looks like you've delivered zat lecture once or twice before," said Jesus.

"Once or twice? Dozens of times! There are hundreds—" George began off screen.

"—of pipes," he continued on screen, "and some of them are—"

"—'rather delicate'," Rob finished. "I know. Sorry, George."

"'I know', 'I know'. 'Sorry', 'sorry'. You always 'know', and you're always 'sorry', but no matter how many times I tell you, someone still cuts through the pipe room to the chancel for youth choir rehearsal."

"What'ya doing?" Rob Taylor asked, staring at the clutter of pipes that surrounded George where he was sitting cross-legged on the floor.

"I'm putting in a new rank of pipes."

"*More* pipes?" Ben Smiley asked.

"Yes."

"Who is zat? He looks familiar somehow."

"Ben Smiley," said George. "His father sings in the adult choir."

"Ze fellow viz ze feet?"

"*And* the sense of humor. I don't know which is worse."

"Zat's because you don't have to sit beside him."

Smiley continued, "My Dad says that, if you put in any more pipes, you're going to have to hire a plumber."

"He certainly has his father's sense of humor."

Rob and Dave rolled their eyes, as did George, as did most of the theater audience, as did almost anyone who had ever heard one of either Smileys' attempts at humor.

"Careful!" George called out as he saw their feet coming perilously close to a pile of pipes.

"There's so many pipes here, George. Someone could trip over them," Rob Taylor suggested helpfully.

"I know! That's why I want you to stay *out* of here!"

The teenage trio quickly made their way through the secret panel as George glared after them.

"Let's follow them a moment," said Jesus. "You should hear this."

Jesus signaled, and the 'camera' followed them into the chancel where David North asked, "Why are you being such a suck-up?"

"My parents," Rob Taylor replied. "They're in the adult choir."

North nodded. "Mine *were*." As they took their seats in the back row of the bass section, he added, "George really hangs off those pipes, doesn't he?"

"Yeah, he does," Taylor agreed, nodding.

"Yeah . . ." North repeated slowly . . . "yeah," a smile slowly forming on his lips.

*   *   *

"Yeah," said George, nodding excitedly. "Yeah, yeah, yeah!"

Jimmy, the organ tuner, had just solved George's most pressing problem for him. "You can do it with about a foot, foot-and-a-half, to spare."

"Why didn't *I* think of that?"

Jimmy shrugged modestly.

"Couldn't see the forest for the trees?" said George.

"The pipes," Jimmy added helpfully.

"Are you sure they'll fit?"

"If you put the lower pipes over there above that wind chest you just got from St. Stephen's, and then knock together a frame to anchor the upper half of the rank lying *sideways*, you'll *just* get them in. Of course, you have to increase the wind pressure substantially."

"I've been doing that everywhere." George was plainly too thrilled with Jimmy's solution to worry about the practical details of delivering a few more pounds per square inch of air pressure, or even many more.

"Jimmy, you're a magician! I could . . . I could *kiss* you!"

"Ahhhh . . ." Freud reached for his pen.

"It's a figure of speech," George told Freud.

"Und *you* picked it."

Jimmy wasn't taking any chances. "No thanks, George. I'm happily married."

"It's a figure of speech," George repeated, on screen.

"I've never seen such a full pipe room," said Jimmy, shaking his head. "You're not thinking of adding any more, are you?"

George shrugged noncommittally, but a grin was creeping onto his face.

Jimmy looked around the pipe room. "But . . . where?"

George's grin was replaced by a look of deep reverence as he slowly shifted his attention to the ceiling, looked back to Jimmy, and solemnly pointed upwards.

"But there's no room. There's only a foot or two between some of the tallest pipes and the ceiling. You can't fit any more in."

George smiled again, wider.

"You wouldn't!"

"I would."

"You vouldn't!"

"I did."

"You're going to extend the pipe room into the *attic?*" Jimmy asked.

"Well, it's just a thought at this point, but it's a very attractive thought."

Jimmy closed his eyes, shook his head, and reopened his eyes, raising his gaze doubtfully to the ceiling. "How?"

"I haven't worked out all the details yet, but I'm getting ideas."

"Does the music committee know what you're thinking of doing?"

"What they don't know can't hurt them."

"Do *you* know what you're doing?"

George shrugged a third time. "Going for broke?"

Jimmy looked at George, over to the pipes, and back to George. "Call me superstitious, but I think I'd feel less concerned if you'd stop shrugging."

Chapter, the Twenty-Sixth:

Smooth Symmetrical Gestures

George leaned back in his chair with his feet up on the desk in his office and an organ pipe balanced between his two upraised hands, running his eye over it from several different angles as he turned it this way and that, like a diamond cutter studying a stone of great value.

"It's a beautiful thing," said Bach.

"Indeed," said George. "A miracle . . ." glancing at Jesus, he corrected himself, " . . . almost."

"A miracle?" Freud asked. "How is zat?"

George looked surprised to hear someone questioning what he considered one of the most obvious truths in the world, at least in his old world.

"Well . . . look at that one," George finally answered.

There was considerable interest in Heaven in miracles, so the entire theater joined the two Georges, one on screen and the other off, in their perusal of the pipe.

"A piece of wood," George explained, "not so special, but cut it, shape it, bore it, glue it, split the air stream . . . just so . . . combine it with others in a rank, then add rank on rank of different sizes, materials, and patterns of construction, and it has the power to move the human heart, even to tears. Isn't *that* a miracle . . . almost?"

"Ja, but zat last bit you could manage viz ze original block of vood."

"How so?" George demanded.

"Bop!" Freud replied, pantomiming a swift blow to the head. "Zen zey vould be in tears for sure! If zey vere still conscious."

On screen, George took the short pipe in one hand, looking for all the world as if he were contemplating using it for the purpose that Freud had suggested.

The choir was arriving for Thursday rehearsal, and George could hear the familiar sounds of conversation and music folders being plunked into choir pews. He heaved himself up with one hand, shouldered the pipe, caveman club style, with the other, and headed for the "secret" panel to the chancel.

*   *   *

Some of the choir members were already in their seats; most of the others started heading that way when they saw him arrive. Paul Bartholomew was just entering the chancel as George reached the piano, pipe in hand.

"New method for dealing with wrong notes?"

George looked puzzled.

Paul inched closer and almost whispered, "You're going to let Molly have it over the head with that, *aren't* you?"

"Don't give me any ideas."

George looked around the chancel, trying to decide on a suitable place to put the pipe, and chose the top of the organ console.

Molly, uncharacteristically late, lumbered up the aisle, into the chancel, and then to her choir pew. Mark Elston saw her at the last moment, and wisely removed himself from his position at the near end of the row rather than have Molly drag her prodigious girth past him in such a restricted space. Settling into her time-honored position, Molly was greeted warmly by Mona, who, uncertain of her notes at the best of times, was grateful for any help she could get and clung to Molly as if she were the last life preserver on the Titanic.

Feeling thus appreciated—something which she clearly considered her due—Molly wore a pleasant smile as she surveyed the chancel. George was similarly assessing his view of the choir pews, contemplating further decentralization of the sections. Then . . .

. . . their eyes met.

George was startled and temporarily disarmed by the friendly face that seemed to be greeting him. Through normal social habit, he began to reciprocate until he fully realized just who the mouth and eyebrows belonged to. The result was an utterly inscrutable series of facial contradictions.

Meanwhile, the left side of Molly's face dropped like a rock, thanks to the organist/alto eye-lock (which was rapidly approaching World Wrestling Federation proportions) while the right drooped into a quivering grin, sustained only by Mona's continued effusions on that side. The overall effect suggested a chameleon on a Scottish tartan who was getting a nervous breakdown from trying to effect a suitable camouflage against the wild profusion of Highland hues beneath its skittering feet.

In the end, each participant decided that the other was making faces at him/her, and made a mental note to exact appropriate revenge at a suitable opportunity.

George's presented itself almost immediately:

"Wayne and Bill, switch places!"

Molly's eyes grew wide, and her mouth gaped as she saw the infamous feet of Bill Smiley headed her way.

George drank in Molly's reaction. A second smile, more satisfying and heartfelt than the first, formed at the corners of his mouth, which she also saw and most definitely received in the spirit in which it was given.

"How long had you been thinking about doing that?" Bach asked.

"As soon as I realized that it was an option."

"So vhy did you vait so long?"

"I was afraid of her reaction. Then it finally dawned on me that she couldn't say a thing about it, especially in public, seeing as Smiley was nasally challenged."

George announced the first piece for rehearsal. To further express his joy, he improvised melodramatically at the piano on the main theme of the anthem while choir members fished out their music.

In the theater, George basked in the warmth of the pleasant memory of, however temporarily, having had the upper hand with Molly.

"You wouldn't be smiling," said Jesus, "if you knew what she was thinking, George."

"No?"

Jesus signaled the projectionist, and, for the first time, George actually looked forward to hearing the thought track, anticipating the sweetly satisfying act of savoring the cerebral sputterings of Molly's impotent rage.

"Wayne and Bill switch places," George said for the second time.

"*(Wayne? . . . Wayne and . . . Bill?! . . . Switch PLACES??!!)*" Molly erupted inwardly, her eyes darting back and forth, and her great chest heaving spasmodically.

"*(Gotcha now, Molly.)*"

"*(George!)*"

"*(That'll fix you.)*"

"*(George, I'm going to FIX you!)*"

"Hooh! Strong stuff!"

"Truly."

"Not *that* strong, surely," said George, seeing no reason to surrender his enjoyment of Molly's predicament, even after the thought track.

"You wouldn't say that if you knew Molly the way *I* know Molly," said Jesus, Who softly began singing, "If you knew Molly like I know Molly: Oh . . . ! Oh . . . ! Oh . . . !"

"Huh?"

"Do you know what career she wanted to pursue . . . really, *really* wanted to pursue . . . before she got married?"

"No."

"Veterinarian," said Jesus, clearly enunciating all six syllables.

All around the theater, knees came together, all of them male, including those of several disciples, many a dead psychiatrist, and most emphatically, one young church organist/choirmaster from St. Christopher's United Church.

*   *   *

The choir members fished through music folders and book racks on the backs of the choir pews for their music.

George, at the piano, ended his improvisation with an Apollonian cadence in C major, sounded the notes for the a cappella anthem, stood, and began conducting the piece with smooth, symmetrical gestures, left hand mirroring the right.

"We did it differently in my day," said Bach.

"It's the modern approach," said George. "It's considered better for the singers: it encourages better support, posture, and other aspects of good vocal technique—'monkey see, monkey do' sort of thing."

"A little too 'modern' for me," said Bach, "although I can see how it would encourage proper carriage in the singers."

"Ze conductor, also," said Freud, "in more vays zan vone."

"Huh?"

"Zat vas ze closest you ever came to possessing a balanced psyche: vhen you vere conducting."

"Spiritually as well," Jesus agreed, "and not solely when you were conducting with 'symmetrical gestures'. Whenever you lost yourself in the music, you actually found yourself."

"When I disappeared?"

"Let me tell you a story."

One raised finger stilled the action onscreen. Jesus rose and faced the theater audience.

"Zey love it vhen He does zis," Freud whispered to George.

"There was a certain competition for church choirs," Jesus began, "and three organist/choirmasters were leading their choirs into the final round of judging.

"The first had gone to bed the night before, and prayed, saying, 'Lord, please don't let me make a mess of this. I have worked long and hard, my reputation is on the line, and I couldn't stand the embarrassment and disappointment if I did poorly.' The second prayed, saying, 'Lord, please don't let the choir make a mess of this. They have worked long and hard, and they would be embarrassed and disappointed if they did poorly.' The third prayed, saying, 'Lord, be with us, and help us, so that we might better serve Thee and glorify Thee in song.'

"And it came to pass that the first, who had prayed only for himself, won third prize; the second, who had prayed for his choir members, won second prize; and the third, who sought, on behalf of himself and his choir, to give the glory unto God, won first prize. He who has ears to hear, let him hear."

"Lord, tell us the meaning of this parable," asked a robed and bearded figure whom George supposed to be one of Jesus' disciples.

"Thank-you for asking. The first organist put himself above all, and lost his heart's desire. The second thought of others, and won at least something, both for them and himself. The third, who sought solely to serve God, won a great honor for everyone, including himself.

"Truly, truly, I say to you: He who would be first shall be last, and he who was last shall be first. He who would save his life shall lose it, and he who would lose his life for My sake shall save it. And *he*," Jesus concluded, looking at George, "who would lose himself in his music, will happily conduct a choir that sounds very, very good, with or without using smooth symmetrical gestures."

Jesus smiled.

The theater audience, with the sole exception of the author of those same smooth symmetrical gestures, also smiled.

"Lord, I'm not certain that I understand . . . completely," said George.

"Let me put it to you this way then: did you hear the one about the three organists?"

"That part I understood."

"You're just not quite sure how it applies to you personally?"

"I don't know . . . maybe I do."

"Take a stab at it."

"Well, I can relate to part of it."

"Which part?"

"The part about losing yourself. I do that every time I make music."

Jesus nodded deeply. "What I am suggesting is that you should do that very same thing when you make . . . 'life'."

" . . . ohhhhh . . ."

Jesus nodded, smiled, and turned to face the full theater audience. "This parable also shows us the truth of what Reverend Wendy Richardson was telling the children. 'If you think first of Jesus, then of Others, and then, finally, Yourself, you will have J.O.Y. Joy!' Just ask the organist/choirmaster who won first prize."

"It is easy to see zat *George's* choir looks not so joyous."

"Not their best night," George agreed.

"And why might that be?" Jesus asked.

George shrugged.

Jesus waited.

"Off night?" George suggested.

"Yes, but 'off' *why?*"

George looked up dumbly.

Jesus pointed to the screen. "Watch and see."

George silenced the choir with an imperious wave of his right hand. "That was a little too chesty, altos.

"Watch the tuning, tenors.

"Basses! Stop bumbling about in the basement!

"Get out of the mud!

"There were some smelly notes in that last phrase, tenors.

"A few birds loose in that last chord, sopranos.

"More breath for that phrase, ladies.

"More support, tenors.

"More focus . . .

"More . . .

" . . . more . . .

" . . . MORE!"

"I get the idea, Lord."

"Not so fast, George. There is, as you say, 'more'."

"Bill, that's so flat it's the wrong *note!*"

"Careful, George," said Bach. "You don't want to lose Smiley!"

"No breath, there, sopranos!

"I said 'No breath'!

"No breath, Diana!

"No breath . . .

"No . . .

" . . . no . . .

" . . . NO!"

"That was a little selective, wasn't it, Lord?" said George, looking and sounding a little hurt.

"Yes, it was, but only a little, and there was a lot to select from."

"But I only wanted the best from them."

"True, but for whose benefit?"

George shrugged.

"Think of the parable."

George looked distinctly "caught in the headlights".

"For Me?" Jesus continued. "Others, perhaps? Yourself? And in what order? Did it bring you or anyone else any JOY?"

George was silent.

Jesus leaned toward George, and said quietly, gently, and earnestly, "He who has ears to hear . . . let . . . him . . . hear."

Chapter, the Twenty-Seventh:

Friends?

George closed the piano lid with a bang, startling several people in both the choir and the theater. He smiled sheepishly to show that it had been unintentional, but many looked unconvinced.

"I think I was starting to get a little tense."

"It vould seem so."

Choir members filed out of the chancel, some of them nodding or saying a few words as they passed the piano. The Parkers were among the last to leave, and George had been taking his time collecting his things so that he would still be there as they passed. Of the three passing Parkers, Kathy was the farthest from George. He tried to catch her eye, but she didn't seem to see him.

"Kathy?"

Kathy hesitated a moment, turned without breaking step, smiled mechanically and said, "Hi, George," as she was leaving the chancel.

"Kathy . . . ?"

This time she stopped, whispered something to her sister, nodded towards the back of the church, and waited for the people between her and George to pass.

"Hi."

"Hi."

"Can I walk you home?"

"Well . . . my mother and Joanne will be waiting for me."
Kathy again nodded towards the back.

"Oh."

"She has the car."

"It's a beautiful night out . . ." George said hopefully.

Kathy hesitated. "I don't know . . ."

"I'll be right back," said George, scooping up his music and heading for his office.

When he returned, she was coming back up the aisle, presumably from sending her mother and sister on their way.

"She looks a little uncomfortable if you ask me," said Jesus.

"Yes, she does. I don't remember noticing it at the time."

"It was not the only time."

"Let's go this way." George indicated the not so "secret" panel, through which they went to the half flight of stairs that led down to the street level door.

"Your escape hatch," said Kathy.

"I find that I'm using it more and more."

Kathy studied the side of his face as if instructions for how to handle the situation were printed on his cheek. "Molly didn't look very pleased with you tonight," she said finally.

"So what else is new?" George shivered ever so slightly.

"Are you cold?"

"No, just a little tired."

"Why?"

"I don't know. Too busy, I guess."

"I guess! You look tired, George. What have you been up to?"

"This and that." George smiled. "I've been working on the organ a lot, and at some odd hours."

"Oh . . . is it a secret or something?"

"Not *exactly*. The committee knows that I wanted to make some . . . improvements."

"Do they know how many?"

"No."

"How many *are* you making?"

"Let's just say that you'll notice a difference at Easter. I'm writing some new music, and the organ renovations should be complete by then."

"You must *really* want Easter to be special."

"Yes," said George, looking suddenly serious. "I have this feeling that I need to play 'catch up', and this may do it."

"Dad says you look tired," said Kathy.

"I thought your father didn't discuss choir matters with the family choir members."

"He doesn't," said Kathy. "He wasn't referring to choir matters."

"Oh."

Kathy paused. "Why do you think you need to play 'catch up'?"

"Things feel different than when I started." George focused on the distance. "I wanted to really improve the music program. I saw how much potential it had. I knew that there would be *some* resistance, churches and choirs being what they are. Maybe it's just that 'the honeymoon is over'."

Kathy flushed slightly. "Can't last forever."

George paused. "Sometimes, I wish I had a better idea of where I stood."

"With who?" Kathy stiffened.

"With . . . the choir . . . and . . . certain others?" At this, they both looked away.

"Oh . . . I don't think that Molly's all that thrilled with you."

"No kidding."

They both smiled tightly.

Kathy filled the silence. "There are a few others."

"A few?"

"Well, maybe a few more than a few." Kathy looked away again, then back. "Sorry."

"No. 'Forewarned is forearmed.' What will they do about it? Any idea?"

"I don't know how to *say* this."

"Sounds serious."

"It is. There's talk. I can't give you too many details. It could be a lot of trouble, not just for me but for Dad, too, his job, even."

"Confidences?"

"Sort of. A minister's daughter hears things, you know?" Kathy took a deep breath. "Some of them are talking about staying on till the end of June . . . and then not coming back in September."

"How many?"

"A few."

"A *few*?"

Kathy nodded. "And a few others would like to see . . . someone else fail to return." Kathy looked *really* worried.

"Not to name names, I suppose," said George, who came to a full stop.

"No!" said Kathy, her worry graduating to alarm. "Not to name names." Her eyes were pleading.

George swallowed slowly, breathed in deliberately, and nodded.

They resumed walking.

"She's hoping zat you von't press for details."

"Yeah, I knew that."

"Zat's a good fellow."

There was silence . . .

"Spoken like a true gentleman," said Cecilia.

"But I didn't say anything."

"Exactly."

"Thanks," said Kathy, visibly relieved.

"Apparently she thinks so, too," said Cecilia.

"For what?" George asked Kathy.

"For not asking too many questions."

*   *   *

George, both on the sidewalk and in his theater seat, was so busy obsessing over what Kathy had told him that he took in very little of what she went on to say:

" . . . friends?"

" . . . sorry . . . what?" said George, surfacing from his thoughts.

"Nothing," Kathy replied.

"You should have paid more attention, George," said Cecilia. "That was important."

"Why? What did I miss?"

"What Kathy said was, 'I wish we could be friends. Couldn't we just be friends?'"

"You mean she—"

"Listen."

"So, I haven't seen you in a while," George was saying.

"I guess rehearsal doesn't count?"

George smiled briefly. "Yes and no?"

Kathy smiled briefly.

"There's a concert Friday night: the choir down at Metropolitan United."

"I can't."

"Are you busy Saturday?"

Kathy hesitated. "I don't know about *this* weekend."

"Should I be asking about *next* weekend?"

Kathy smiled awkwardly. "I'd *like* to . . ."

" . . . but?"

Kathy took a deep breath. "Not that I *never* want to see you," she said, sounding halfway between justifying her decision and backpedaling from it. "It's just that . . . George?"

"Yeah?"

"Are you okay?"

"Yeah, I guess It's just that things have been kind of piling up lately."

"How bad?"

George stopped, and looked down at the sidewalk. "I'm not sure yet. I . . . I could kinda use a friend."

Kathy's eyes widened. "That concert sounds good."

"Zat didn't take long!"

"That's what she wanted all along," said Jesus. "That's what you missed when she asked if you could be friends a minute ago. Now she thinks that maybe you'll be her friend, finally. Poor girl."

"'Poor girl'?" George asked. "Why are you calling her *that*?"

"Because she is going to be so disappointed."

Meanwhile, George looked over at Kathy, confused. "I thought you . . ."

"Oh . . . yeah. Let's do something Saturday, then."

*　　*　　*

"So sad," said Jesus, as Kathy walked up the path to her house and George continued along the sidewalk.

"Lord?"

"You parted, seemingly in agreement yet with completely different understandings of what you had agreed on."

"*That's* what happened?"

Jesus signaled for the thought track.

"*(That was easy!)*" she thought, flopping down on her bed. "*(He agreed! Why, I wonder? Does he mean it? He must. That was so easy.)*"

"Too easy, as it turns out," Jesus said darkly.

"*(Of course, I hope that doesn't mean he thinks that I **just** want to be friends.)*"

"Not a danger," Cecilia added.

"*(He couldn't, could he?)*"

"Nein."

"*(Not with the way **he's** been carrying on. The pressure! I thought I was gonna have to dump him! Now I wish that I could see him **both** nights.)*"

"Thus encouraged, Kathy slept the sleep of the well satisfied and much relieved," said Jesus. "Now, *your* turn."

George instinctively lowered his head.

"*(Friends?)*" thought George, heading homeward. "*(I told her I wanted a 'friend'. That's not the same thing, is it?)*"

"Only if you speak the same language," Jesus said grimly.

"Going . . ." said Cecilia.

"Huh?"

"*(I hope she didn't think I meant that I **just** wanted to be friends.)*"

" . . . going . . ."

"*(Certainly not with the way **I've** been carrying on: it's not like I haven't been clear. This must mean that she's finally willing to get more involved!)*"

"Thus encouraged," said Jesus, "you headed home amid much fantasizing and all manner of wishful thinking."

" . . . gone."

Chapter, the Twenty-Eighth:

The Stuff of Legend

"And where do you think you're going with *those?*"

Molly stood in the doorway of the flower room, squarely framed by and almost entirely filling it, blocking George's path as he stood just outside the doorway with an armload of pipes.

"It's temporary, Molly."

"I've heard *that* before."

"Seriously! Just until I finish with the wind chest."

"What about *your* office?"

George shrugged sheepishly, the pipes beginning to weigh heavily in his arms. "Full."

"The pipe room?"

George rolled his eyes wordlessly to convey the impossibility of the suggestion.

"You cannot store your pipe . . . your *pipes* . . . in *my* room!"

Freud grinned.

Molly was just warming up. "The last person who tried something like that . . . in case you haven't heard!"

"I've heard." George, pipes teetering, backed up.

"Narrator?" said Jesus.

"Everyone had heard. It was the stuff of legend at St. Christopher's. Tony Patterson (their organist about twenty years ago) had the misfortune to lock horns with Molly, and he paid a terrible price for it."

"Vhat vas zat?"

"Patterson tried keeping his bicycle there—it was closer to the side door than his office—and Molly, on behalf of her fellow flower guilders, took umbrage, and one thing lead to another . . . Suffice it to say, in the end, there were flowers and bicycle parts everywhere, and he was gone by the end of June."

Molly advanced, but without entirely quitting the entrance to *her* flower room.

George accelerated his retreat, his armload of pipes looking less than stable, scurried up the hall, the pipes rolling around in his arms, and disappeared as quickly as he safely could down the stairs.

"Now, there you go again, George!" Tom, who had been caretaker at St. Christopher's about half as long as Molly had been in the choir, shook his head as George descended the stairs, his armload of pipes balanced precariously. "Have a care there."

"It's all right, Tom. I've got them."

"If you say so."

George lurched halfway down the stairs, and steadied himself against the railing before continuing.

"George, I can't watch."

"Then don't . . . or *help* me."

Tom shook his head. "Those pipes are going to be the death of you if you don't watch it a little."

"Here, then," said George, reaching the bottom of the stairs. "Take a few? I'm in a hurry: meeting with Rev. Parker in a few minutes."

Tom nodded stolidly, took a few off the top, and followed George into the choir library where they placed them on the work table.

"If they keep coming in like this, you'll have to start putting them in the pews."

"The thought has occurred to me."

"All these pipes! You keep adding and adding, and more of them are stacked up all over the place waiting to be added God knows where, and here you are with still more of them. Why do you bother? The organ's a beast as it is."

"For the sound, Tom, the sound."

"The sound? It doesn't sound any different to *me*."

George blinked, shook his head, and grimly declared, "I haven't finished yet."

"Oh, we're all finished before we know it. Have a care, George. Have a care."

*   *   *

"Here today, gone tomorrow," said Rev. Parker, essentially expressing the same sentiment as Tom. "We are but as blades of grass."

George hesitated, finally saying, "I was hoping to stay around at least until next Sunday."

"Oh, I think you're good till then."

"Seriously," George asked Rev. Parker, "how serious is it?"

"Serious enough . . . but hang in there."

"And be hung?" asked George.

"Well . . . passions sometimes run high in the music committee, but I don't think they've ever ordered an execution."

"Things were piling up," said George.

"As fast as zose pipes?" Freud asked.

George hesitated, and bit his lower lip before answering, "That I could have handled."

Chapter, the Twenty-Ninth:

A Night In

"Bernie, down!"

The great St. Bernard lumbered off the couch and onto the rug in the center of the room, then retreated to the corner as George steered the vacuum cleaner nearer.

Next, George hurriedly threw papers into piles, removed glasses and plates from here and there, and struggled to straighten out the music on the piano, until the sheer number of musical scores and sheets of manuscript, together with a glance at his watch, convinced him to abandon the effort.

"Looks like a romantic dinner," said Freud.

"Not exactly."

George was busy putting candles out on the dining room table.

"Actually, yes," said Jesus, "'exactly'."

"But it was Kathy's *idea*."

"After you hinted that, following a full day of throwing pipes around in the pipe room, you would prefer a night in."

George smiled weakly.

Meanwhile, George got out the wine glasses, subdued the lighting, and fluffed up the pillows on the couch.

Any man in the theater who had ever been a bachelor understood.

*   *   *

"Hi, George."

"Poor girl," said St. Cecilia.

"Truly."

"Ja."

"Forsooth."

George opened his mouth, and then closed it again, just as quickly.

"Kathy!"

"Poor guy," was the muffled comment from somewhere in back of the theater.

George perked up a little.

"Him again?" St. Peter asked.

Jesus nodded matter-of-factly. "You should know the voice by now."

Peter nodded.

George perked down again.

Kathy walked into the kitchen with George in tow, and pulled a collection of plastic food savers out of her bag. "Quiche," she announced, pouring the contents of a plastic bottle into a ready-made pie shell.

"Great! Get you a glass of wine?"

Kathy looked surprised. "Tea . . . for now?"

"Okay." George readied the cups, and put on the kettle as Kathy continued her preparations.

"How's work going in the pipe room?" she asked.

"Pretty good, but I seem to have more 'pipe' than 'room'."

"Dad says he's getting reports of stray pipes from all over the church. Bill Smiley says they're multiplying."

"He *would*."

"What are you going to do?"

"I don't know. I guess I'll have to think of something."

"Will you have to get rid of some of them?"

"No!"

Kathy looked up.

"Sorry." He smiled sheepishly. "I guess I'm a little wound up."

*   *   *

"We're not going to watch *all* of it, are we, Lord?"

"Would that bother you?"

"Well . . ." George sighed. "Some of it's a little . . . uh . . . personal."

Jesus nodded. "I will instruct the angels to cover their eyes with their wings at the appropriate moments. I wouldn't want them to be embarrassed."

George put his hand to his forehead. "It wasn't them that I was worried about."

"Very well, then, George. You may cover your eyes also."

George sighed. "You won't let me get away with anything, will You?"

Jesus leaned forward and lowered His voice. "Sooner or later, everyone is held to account . . . and this," He indicated with a modest sweep of His hand, "for you, is 'sooner or later'. So, no, I won't let you get away with anything. You didn't really think you could fool *Me*, did you?" Jesus sat back in His chair. "Narrator?"

"*All* of it?"

"*All* of it . . . one way or another."

George looked up. "I have options?"

"Yes, in this *one* regard: any events of this evening with Kathy Parker that you narrate to My satisfaction, we will leave off the screen."

George nodded thoughtfully, and took a deep breath. "We had dinner . . . annnnd she went home?" George raised his eyebrows hopefully.

Jesus watched George intently.

"Well . . . what does 'to Your satisfaction' consist of?" George asked.

"Remember why you're here. This movie is a part of it. There is much for you to learn from it, and ultimately, your very hopes of Heaven may rest upon that sole foundation. Perhaps that will give you some idea of the expected standard?"

"Yes, Lord."

"But of course, if you can show Me that you have the understanding that renders a scene or some portion thereof unnecessary, then there is no need for us to watch it, *is* there?"

"Ohhhh . . ."

"And no-one need suffer any embarrassment."

"Okay . . ." George took a deep breath. "Kathy came for dinner . . ."

Jesus looked at George expectantly, left eyebrow elevated.

" . . . she brought a lovely quiche . . . knowing that it was my favorite. She . . . put a lot of . . . *work* . . . into it." George felt many eyes upon him. "But was I *grate*ful?" His voice broke like a pubescent thirteen year old's, and he tried to compensate by clearing his throat with a massive bass rumble, which was difficult for a natural tenor.

"Not good enough, George. Let's walk through this. It's important. Why did she come?"

"Because I asked her nicely?"

"Perhaps we should just roll the whole scene?"

"She came because . . . she *missed* me."

"Yes, but more."

"Because she . . ."

Freud leaned over and whispered something in George's ear. George stopped, thought about it, and looked at Freud, who nodded encouragement. Turning back to Jesus, he said, "She came under false pretences."

"Zat's not vhat I said!"

George leaned towards Freud again, who whispered furiously into George's ear, causing him to wince visibly.

"*My* false pretences."

"Zat's better!"

"I led her . . . *mis*led her . . . without meaning to, of course . . . at least, not at first . . . I, uhhhhh—"

"Get on with it, George."

"She thought that I wanted to be friends."

"And whatever could have given her *that* idea?"

"I guess . . . I must have . . . told her?"

"You're getting warmer."

"I wasn't *lying* to her. I really needed a friend . . . but that wasn't . . . all that I . . . felt."

"Nor was it all that *she* felt. And this is all beginning to sound a little familiar, isn't it? Next, we'll be hearing about your 'radar'. But you asked her to be your friend—we can run the replay if you have any doubts on that score—and then you did not *treat* her like a friend. You didn't even *want* a friend so much as you wanted the *comfort* of a friend. There's a huge difference."

"Yes, Lord."

"And—here's where you really have to pay attention—once she gave you that comfort, you sought *other* forms of comfort, if you know what I mean—and I know that you do—when her guard was down."

"You took advantage of her," St. Cecilia said sadly.

"I didn't mean to."

"Zat's debatable."

"Let's not debate," Jesus said calmly. "Now . . . George has been forthcoming enough, with a little help, to get out of watching the dinner meal itself."

"That's not the part that I was thinking of, Lord."

"I'll bet, but it's up to the narrator, George."

"Yes, Lord." George looked at the screen. "Now, we're clearing the table."

"Then?"

"Then, we sat on the couch . . . there we go—you're not going to run the *whole* scene, *are* You, Lord?"

"As I said, 'It's up to the narrator': that's *you*, George."

George swallowed hard. "We started off just talking about this and that, I think. Then we talked about church, the choir, and so on."

"Let's pick up a little of that. You don't mind *that*, now, do you?"

"I guess not."

"Good." Jesus signaled the projectionist.

*   *   *

"I'm counting on Easter to save me," George said to Kathy. "That's what I said to your father, too. You know what he said?"

"No, what?"

"He said, 'So is the congregation, if you think about it.'"

"That sounds like Dad."

"What I meant, of course, was I thought that, if the music was inspiring enough, certain other matters might be forgotten."

"Do you think that will work?" Kathy asked quietly.

"It had better."

They sat wordlessly . . .

George looked up. "Do *you* think it will?"

Kathy pursed her lips.

His eye was caught by the slight movement.

"I don't know," she answered.

George looked at her steadily.

Kathy breathed in slowly, and then blew the hair off her forehead. "I don't know how you get these things out of me. I've been . . . hearing things. I don't know how much it will help you, but . . . I don't know where to start."

"Start anywhere."

"Well, it's worse than I was telling you before."

"How much worse?"

"Those people I told you were thinking of not coming back after the summer? It's about . . . a third . . . or so . . . of the choir."

"'Or *so*'?"

"Uh . . . more . . . actually."

"*More*? How *many* more?"

"Oh, George! I don't know. Now, I wish I hadn't said *anything.*"

George whispered, pleading, "How *many* more?"

"Almost half," she answered miserably.

"I didn't know that it was that bad. What about the others you were talking about? The ones who want to see *me* leave?"

"There's fewer of those, so far at least, but then, there's a few former choir members . . ."

"What about them?" George stiffened.

"You know . . . I guess you know . . . that there's a rule against choir members joining the music committee . . . as a safeguard, Dad says . . . you know? Conflict of interest? Well, there's no rule against *former* members joining."

George's eyes widened.

"And there are a *number* of former choir members."

"The Norths?"

"Yes."

"O'Brien?"

Kathy nodded. "Others, too. And there's another new committee member; one who wasn't in the choir, at least not during *your* time here."

"Who's that?"

"Don Braden."

George's eyes narrowed in non-comprehension. He looked back at Kathy, the connection swimming to the surface of his thoughts just as Kathy said it aloud.

"Molly's husband."

"Molly's *husband?*"

"Yes. Dad wonders about that, too. Mr. Braden hardly ever comes to church, so why he'd ever want to sit on a committee . . ."

"He doesn't," George said flatly. "*She* does, but she can't, not directly at least, so he's doing it *for* her."

"That's what Dad says."

"Right. And the others, and all this at once? *Something's* up."

"Dad says that too."

"I thought he didn't discuss choir matters with family members?"

"Usually, he doesn't, but he says that he's bending the rules a little . . . temporarily . . . because the situation is getting so serious. Besides, he's not my only source of information."

"No?"

"A minister's daughter hears many things, and when it comes to *your* name . . . I seem to have developed a bad case of what my mother calls 'Mummy ears'."

"She loves you, George," said Cecilia. "Poor girl."

"Ja, even viz your stubborn insistence on getting romantically involved viz her, she *still* loves you."

"Hug?" George asked Kathy.

"Zere you go."

"Sure."

"Poor girl."

"Stop *saying* that."

And they hugged a long and lingering hug.

"Can we leave out this part?"

"That's up to you."

"If I talk?"

"Talk."

"What can I say? I felt . . . fragile . . . and I needed a hug."

"And how do you think *she* felt?"

George was kissing the side of Kathy's head, caressing her curls with one hand and guiding her closer to him with the other. She allowed herself to be guided, first with a start, and then a little more willingly.

"Friends?" said Jesus.

"It seemed all right with *her*," George protested.

"*Seemed*," said Cecilia, "because you had overcome her resistance, her desire not to be overwhelmed, by engaging her maternal instincts. That was *sneaky*."

"I didn't mean to."

"You didn't mean *not* to."

"Also," said Jesus, picking up the thread, "you were benefiting, whether you meant to or not, from the guilt that she felt at being the one to tell you how desperate your situation was at the church—but she was not comfortable. *That* you should have known."

"Ja, George: she vas heavily conflicted."

"Yes," said Cecilia, "and remember that when she decided to come over to see you, she was expecting something quite different."

"Otherwise," said Jesus, "she would not have come."

"She wouldn't?"

Jesus looked grim. "No, George, she wouldn't."

Cecilia continued. "She'd had enough pressure. You barely got her to come over as it was. Don't you remember?"

"Well . . . she sounded really busy."

"Until you said the magic word."

"The magic word? What magic word?" George thought about it. "'Please'?"

Cecilia shook her head. "'Friends'."

Meanwhile, George had Kathy in a lip lock.

*   *   *

"But why was she so nervous about getting involved with me, anyway?"

"Haven't you been paying attention?" Jesus asked, raising his hand to freeze the scene, the lip lock filling the screen in all its stillness.

"I know. 'Bad experience,' You said, but . . . how bad could it have been?"

Jesus, Cecilia and Freud looked at each other.

"Will You tell him, or shall I?" Cecilia asked.

"We'll both tell him."

"Lord, viz Your kind permission, ve'll all zree of us tell him."

*　*　*

Cecilia began. "Kathy's first real boyfriend sang in the church choir with her when her father was minister at St. Luke's in Windsor, Ontario. She went out with him for five years."

"Five *years?*"

"Yes. And at first, it was fun; then it was a lot of fun. Later . . . ?" Cecilia shrugged. "He was a little on the wild side,"—she chose her words carefully—"but not *too* wild, not at first, anyway: just about right for a minister's teenaged daughter who was eager to come of age."

George thought about the implications of what Cecilia was saying, and then the inevitable question arose, typical for the fragile male ego, "And did . . . she . . . ?"

"Yes, George, she did . . . with *him.*"

George blushed.

"Serves you right for being so nosey. Now, for the first two years or so, the relationship was wonderful for both of them, but then he got a little wilder, then a little more . . . and then the doctors diagnosed him as a paranoid schizophrenic."

"Serious stuff, zat."

"Yes, and the jealous type, too," Cecilia said.

"Truly," said Jesus, "and, no matter how close they became, he wanted to become closer still. Finally, he became suffocating, alarming both Kathy and her parents in the process."

"So how did this all end?"

"Not too keen on old boyfriends?" said Cecilia. "She escaped—she had to—with him in hot pursuit, of course: he did not take rejection well."

"He's the . . ."

" . . . 'bad experience'. After a few years of avoiding the male sex in general, punctuated by the occasional exception—mostly jerks, as luck would have it—she finally met someone she could 'put up with', to use her expression. Not the best choice perhaps, she thought, but someone, at least, who she could relate to: her second real boyfriend—or at least he could have been if he'd taken a slightly different approach."

"And what was *he* like?"

"Passionate . . ."

". . . intense . . ."

". . . neu*rotic.*"

"Who was 'he'?" George asked suspiciously.

Cecilia and Freud looked at George, then to each other, then back at George, answering in one voice, "You!"

"Me?"

"Do you see now why she wanted to take it slow?" Jesus asked.

From the look in his eyes, it was apparent that he did.

* * *

George could hardly watch.

There was a faint rustling of feathers from the back of the theater as the winged members of God's court shielded their eyes in order to preserve their angelic sense of modesty.

George kissed Kathy, the expression of his passion increasing as rapidly as her crumbling resistance would allow.

George looked imploringly at Jesus, who shrugged and returned His attention to the screen: tough love, it might have been called, on His part.

Ere long, organist/choirmaster and minister's daughter were prone on the couch, becoming increasingly intertwined.

"No peeking between your feathers," said Jesus, over His shoulder, which was followed immediately by a quick rustling from the rear. "George?"

George stared at the screen. He saw his right hand inch away from its former, modest position in the small of Kathy's back, brushing, as if by accident, the upper margin of her hip; tracing a line up her side before lifting off her subtly stiffening form, and describing an arc further upwards and forwards through the air, millimeters, then centimeters, and then inches above her reclining form; then closer, in the descending arc with which every young male is so achingly familiar, declining through those same units of measurement, above the intoxicating curves that lay below.

Jesus' hand crept upward, and the speed of the film began to decrease . . .

"Narrator?"

George huddled forward, crossing his arms protectively in front of himself, mesmerized by the progress of his onscreen hand.

The film's speed decreased further . . .

"George?"

George, rapt, losing the tug of war between silence and self-horror, did not respond.

The film ground into extreme slow motion . . .

"George!"

"Okay! Okay!! I *used* her! There, I *admit* it! *Happy*?!"

George's admission was accompanied by a now-frozen frame which prominently featured his right hand poised pregnantly just above Kathy's left breast.

"And GeT THaT O*FF* THe Scr*EE*n!!!"

* * *

The film broke, and after a few stray frames danced dizzily across the screen, a grainy whiteness prevailed at the front of the theater, causing many members of the audience to blink at the unaccustomed brightness.

A profound silence descended over the theater, punctuated only by the distant rhythmic thwipping of the severed film strip in the projection booth at the rear, which eventually slowed and stopped.

There was the soft sound of many rustling feathers, as wings were lowered.

George's breathing became tight, slow and shallow. He bowed his head, and his shoulders began to quiver, as his best defenses swiftly dissolved in tears.

*   *   *

"This has not been a good day," George snuffled miserably.

"That depends on how you look at it," said Jesus.

"Well, let's see: I died, I'm reliving all of the horrible things that ever happened to me, and as if all that weren't enough, I'm beginning to feel really *bad* about myself!"

"Zen, zere's hope for you."

"Truly, which might make it a very good day indeed."

"That sounds suspiciously like, 'Here, drink this: it's good for you.' Well, maybe it is, but it never tastes any good."

"Oh, I don't know," said Jesus. "Sometimes it does . . ."

Chapter, the Thirtieth:

What'll It Be?

When George looked up again, he was no longer front row center in the Odeon Paradise, but seated on a stool, a nice stool: tall, solid, and generously padded. The air was cool. The lighting was soft and indirect. The ambience soothed.

Jesus, dressed in casual slacks and a white shirt, sleeves rolled up, His hair pulled back in a ponytail, was wiping down the hardwood bar that stood between them.

"Welcome to the Cross and Crown, George. What'll it be?"

George's left foot slid off the bottom rung of the stool. "What happened to the movie?" he asked huskily, not that he wanted to see any more of it.

"Intermission, let's call it. You looked like you could use a little glass of something." Jesus took a wine glass down from the rack above the counter. "Something that 'tastes good'."

"Lord?"

"Yes, George?"

"Why did I *do* that?"

'You mean with Kathy?'

George could not bring himself to answer.

"Oh, let's not get too complicated about it. How about 'hormones and loneliness'?"

George nodded weakly.

"Maybe a change of topic . . . ?" Jesus suggested helpfully.

George nodded several times in swift succession, as if trying to set a new standard in sincerity.

Jesus filled George's glass. "Here you go, then, George: the house brand, Chateau Cana. It'll settle your nerves."

"You drink? In Heaven?"

"Sometimes." Jesus smiled apologetically in advance. "When the Spirit moves us."

George looked skeptical.

"Remember your scripture, George? 'I will not drink of the fruit of the vine again until I drink it with you in Heaven'? Well, this is Heaven, one little corner of it, anyway."

George reached for his glass.

"It's a very good year," said Jesus. "They served it at a certain wedding in Cana. I liked it so much that I ordered some for the Last Supper, and now . . . here."

"Alcohol? In Heaven? In a bar? Wait till Mona sees *this*. She's not the type to let a man drink in peace, even at the choir's Christmas party. Lord?"

'Yes, George?" Jesus, being an excellent bartender, put down his cloth and leaned over the bar, indicating his willingness to listen.

"I know I'm not perfect . . . but why is it that there are so many people in the church who are always telling me what to do? Like . . . Mona." George took another sip, a bigger sip this time. "Why are there so many people like her? What makes *her* so perfect? And why in a church of all places?"

"Many reasons, and some of them would amaze you. Mona, for instance, really wants to be a better person, but she doesn't know how to go about it, so, she joined the local church."

"Which makes her feel good and holy?" George suggested unenthusiastically, twisting his now half-empty glass by the stem.

"Exactly! And then she suggests to anyone else who will listen, and some who won't—like you, for instance—how they, too, can be better people. Then, she goes to bed most nights feeling that she's done her bit to help make the world a better place, whether people have the good sense to appreciate her best efforts or not.

Every once in a while, though, she gets around to praying very hard for *herself* to change—yes, George—and she *means* it."

"She does?"

"She does! Trust me. I've heard her. It would melt your heart."

George cradled his chin, and frowned. "She's not the only one who's dispensing free advice."

"They each have their own little story, as do *you*. Consider *that* if you will."

"I know." George sighed weakly. "Lord?"

"Yes, George?"

"Why did I have to . . . die . . . like that?"

"Cause and effect," Jesus answered gently. "And there's no escaping it, really. The angels themselves respect it above almost everything. Even Dad tiptoes around it most of the time."

"What's so wonderful about 'cause and effect', anyway?"

"Cause and effect," said Jesus, lifting his left hand, as if he were holding the concept in his open palm; "free will," He concluded, similarly raising His right, balancing His hands like scales seeking equilibrium. "It's difficult to have one without the other. We don't like to fiddle with the equation if we can help it."

"Maybe someone should," George muttered sourly.

Jesus shrugged. "Einstein tried tinkering with it for a few decades after he rewrote the Theory of Relativity and cracked the Unified Field Theory, then he gave it all up for the violin. 'God does not play dice with the universe' was his final word on the subject—Dad liked that."

"But, how did it apply to *me*?"

"That, among other things, is what we're here to see," said Jesus, glancing at his watch, "and, it's just about time that we got back to it."

"*Already?*"

"I see that you've drained your glass."

George still held it, empty though it was, in his hand.

"We can't have you falling asleep during the last reel." Jesus put away the bottle, whose progress was followed by George's tender gaze. "Feeling a little steadier?"

George pursed his lips and nodded slowly.

"That's the spirit!"

The theater chimes began to sound in the background. Intermission was over.

Chapter, the Thirty-First:

Lord, Hear Our Prayer

George had barely put his glass down on the counter when he found himself back in the theater. A large soft drink sat on the apron of the stage before their front row center seats. George had preferred the wine, much preferred the wine. He was sure that he could have easily managed another glass of Chateau Cana, and he had really liked it! Jesus had turned *water* into wine. Maybe if he asked Jesus nicely, He would do the same thing with this. George looked to Jesus, full of hope.

But Jesus knew George's question even before he asked it. "There are no drunks in the Kingdom of Heaven, George. Strength!"

"I'm going to need it."

"Now, about the broken film," said Jesus, pointing to the screen.

"Did *I* do that?"

"You did. In Heaven, thoughts are as tangible as actions, and you appear to be rapidly acquiring the knack."

"Sorry about that." George looked around, and noticed that some of his nearer neighbors were quietly moving a discreet seat or two further away. "Sorry about that," he said again, this time to them, receiving scattered, cautious nods in return.

"And now," said Jesus, "let's see what happens next."

*   *   *

Kathy sang with the rest of the choir, sneaking the occasional peek over a neighbor's shoulder at George, and then sat down with the others at the end of the hymn, stealing another glance before riveting her gaze to her hands when he looked up.

And Kathy was not the only sneaker of peeks that morning. He was also stealing glances at her while he closed his hymn book, turned off the organ, and waited for the sermon to begin.

"Two unhappy people," said Jesus, very quietly.

Reverend Dawson, minister emeritus with special responsibilities for the older members of the church, led the congregation in the prayers of intercession:

"Father, we pray for the aged, for those who face illness and death and the loss of beloved spouses after a lifetime shared together. Lord, hear our prayer."

"And in Your love, answer," the congregation responded, either reading from the service bulletin or repeating it by rote.

"We pray for those of all ages who are facing difficulties in their lives, who are uncertain and insecure, who do not know which way to turn, and would turn to You for comfort, strength, and guidance. Lord, hear our prayer."

"And in Your love answer."

George sighed. "I called him Reverend Neverend. He went on and on."

"He's a good man," said Jesus. "He went 'on and on' because he had a lot to go 'on and on' about. He really cared. The congregation didn't mind; the older ones loved him for it: they really needed prayer, many of them—it isn't easy being old."

"Is it any harder than being dead?"

"You'd be surprised."

"We pray for those who are in conflict, especially those who have relationships that are in difficulty, that they may know Your will for them, and resolve their differences with love and understanding. Lord hear our prayer."

"You two certainly heard," said Jesus.

George and Kathy looked at each other from under the anonymity of near-closed eyelids.

"And in your love, answer."

"He tried," Jesus added, "but someone was not listening very hard, not to name names."

'Reverend Neverend' ended: "All this we ask in Jesus name. Amen."

*   *   *

Announcements were made concerning the weekly life of the church, the name and number of the recessional hymn was given, and clergy and choir recessed to the back of the church, singing, "Now Thank We All Our God".

Reverend Parker intoned the benediction. The choir sang the "Amen", Brian Tyler conducting. George's postlude sounded forth gloriously from the organ as the congregation rose, fortified by the word of God for the rest of the week and ready to go about the rest of its Sunday business.

"Hmmm," said Bach. An improvised postlude based on the tune of the final hymn. Very good, George. But wasn't it a little 'upbeat' for the occasion?"

"I was kind of in a hurry," George responded, a little embarrassed.

"Kathy?" St. Cecilia asked.

"Yes. We had pretty much gotten into the habit of going out for lunch after church. First we dropped off Bernie, and then we carried on to a restaurant."

"So vhy vere you in such a hurry?"

"Well, she didn't seem very happy with me when I walked her home after, well . . . you know. And we hadn't gone the past few Sundays."

George hurried down the aisle to the back of the church, still robed. Turning down the back stairs, he was just in time to meet Kathy halfway up the top flight.

"She also appears to be in somevhat of a hurry."

"Poor girl," said Cecilia, "she looks so startled."

"Und who is zat who she seems to be viz, I vonder?"

"That's what *I* wondered, too."

"Hi, Kathy."

"Hi."

George stopped on the stairs, at a loss for words. People were beginning to accumulate behind both of them.

Kathy took strategic action. "Rob, this is George, the organist."

Rob nodded. George eyed Rob suspiciously. Churchgoers thickened in a knot around them.

"See you Thursday," said Kathy. She looked at Rob to signal their departure, and moved on, leaving George with nothing to do but continue downstairs, where he had absolutely nothing to do.

*   *   *

George, now at home, a half-eaten sandwich on the coffee table in front of him, was on the telephone . . .

"Who was *that*?" he demanded.

"What do you mean, 'Who was *that*'?"

"Rob."

"Someone I know."

"That much I figured."

"He's just . . . 'someone I know'."

"Were you going somewhere?"

"Just for lunch."

"But *we* usually go for lunch."

"I had plans."

"But we haven't gone in *weeks*."

"Then you can't exactly say that we '*usually*' go."

"Well, I *wanted* to ask you, but you were in too much of a hurry."

"We were in the middle of a bit of a traffic jam, in case you hadn't noticed."

"Well . . . I guess you didn't really want to go . . . anyway."
George's indignation was rapidly melting into a puddle of
resignation.

"I was *busy.*"

George was silent.

"Besides, I didn't exactly appreciate the other night," she
continued. "And there's no rule," she added, her voice rising with
accumulated frustration, "there's no rule that says I have to spend
all my time with you!"

More silence.

"I . . . don't know," George said numbly.

"You don't know *what*, George?"

George swallowed hard. "I don't know . . . that . . . either."

"Not easy dealing with her anger, was it?" said Cecilia.

"No."

Finally, George spoke. "I hoped that . . . things would be
different."

Kathy said nothing.

"I wanted to give you something nice . . ."

"Good thought," said Cecilia, "decent, unselfish impulse,
finally."

" . . . if I can't do that . . . then . . ."

The theater audience leaned forward in anticipation . . .

" . . . maybe . . . I shouldn't give you . . . anything . . . at
all."

"Fine!" said Kathy, even though her facial expression clearly
indicated that it was anything but fine.

Silence.

"Well . . . bye, then . . . I guess . . ."

There was a sharp collective intake of breath in the
theater . . .

" . . . bye . . ."

. . . followed by a slow exhalation, accompanied by much
blinking of eyes and shaking of heads.

It had all been a little sudden, especially by Heavenly standards.

* * *

George felt the pressure of many eyes upon him. "I didn't want to break up."

St. Cecilia spoke first. "You did a pretty convincing imitation."

"But it's not what I wanted."

"It's not what she wanted, either."

"She did a pretty convincing imitation."

"Zen perhaps," said Freud, "ve need to examine zis on a deeper level."

"I agree," said Jesus.

"Huh?"

The projectionist was signaled.

George sighed. *The thought track,* he thought.

Once again, Kathy fidgeted in her choir pew, glancing periodically at George. George fidgeted at the organ console, glancing periodically at her.

Reverend Dawson began the prayers of intercession. "Father we pray for . . ."

"*(I need to see Kathy for lunch,)*" thought George, "*(smooth things over . . . or something.)*"

"*(The service is almost over,)*" thought Kathy. "*(**Then** what do I do? What do I do about George? And what do I do about Rob . . . ? Why do they **both** have to be here?)*"

"I *knew* she was up to something."

Jesus shook his head.

"*(Maybe I can get Rob out of here before George gets a chance to ask me . . .)*"

"See, see?"

Jesus sighed mightily.

"(I wish Dad wouldn't ask me to entertain for him. What do I care about some second cousin that I haven't seen for years and years?)"

"Rob?" George asked, the sickening realization flooding in on him.

"(George won't like this.)"

"Ja, almost as much as he doesn't like *zis.*"

"We pray for those who are in conflict, especially those who have relationships that are in difficulty . . ."

"(That's us.)"

"(That's us.)"

"(Going to have to move fast. We haven't had lunch in a couple of weeks now. George'll be looking for me.)"

"(Going to have to move fast . . . haven't gone for lunch in a couple of weeks . . . get downstairs . . . catch her before she leaves . . . she'll have a head start.)"

"All this we ask in Jesus name. Amen."

"Amen," said the congregation.

"Amen," the theater audience echoed, many of whom, Jesus included, were looking pointedly at George.

*   *   *

"Now I see why the postlude was a little rushed," said Bach as it approached the final cadence.

"I was kind of in a hurry," George responded, catching himself. "Isn't that what I said the first time around?"

"Yes."

Again, George looked a little embarrassed.

Onscreen, George hurried down the aisle to the back of the church, still robed.

Bach smiled. "Couldn't even wait to change your clothes."

Turning down the back stairs, George was just in time to meet Kathy halfway up the top flight.

"Hi, Kathy."

"Hi."

"(*Who's **he**?*)" thought George.

"Feel a little silly, now?" asked Jesus.

"As opposed to when?" George sank a little lower into his seat.

"Rob, this is George: the organist."

Rob nodded.

George eyed Rob suspiciously, silently. Churchgoers thickened in a knot around them.

"*(Gotta get outta here!)*" thought Kathy. "See you Thursday."

"Now, the phone call," said Jesus.

"Not the *phone* call!" George whined.

"The *phone* call," Jesus affirmed.

"Who was *that*?" George demanded.

"What do you mean 'who was *that*'? *(What **is** this?)*"

"Rob."

"Someone I know."

"That much I figured."

"He's just . . . *(I should tell him—no! not with **that** tone . . .)* someone I know'."

"Were you . . . going somewhere?"

"Just for lunch."

"But *we* usually go for lunch."

"I had plans."

"But we haven't gone for *weeks*."

"*(Getting cornered—we'll see about that!)* Then you can't exactly say that we 'usually' go."

"Well, I wanted to ask you, but you were in too much of a hurry."

"We were in the middle of a bit of a traffic jam, in case you didn't notice."

"Well . . . I guess you didn't really want to go . . . anyway."

Freud rolled his eyes. "Lame, George. So lame."

In the theater, George grunted.

"I was *busy* . . . *(Pressure, always pressure.)*"

On the screen, George was silent.

"Besides, I didn't exactly appreciate the other night. And there's no rule that says I have to spend *all* my time with you!"

More silence.

"I don't know," George said numbly. *"(What do I do **now**?)"*

*"(What's he going to do **now**?)"*

"(This is . . . horrible . . . all this fighting . . .)" George's thoughts sounded like those of a man edging closer and closer to tears.

"(Why isn't he saying anything?) You don't know *what,* George?"

George swallowed hard. "I don't know . . . that . . . either . . . *(What happened?)* . . . I had hoped that things would be different."

Kathy said nothing. *"(He was only my cousin. I got stuck with him. Maybe I should tell George—no, no, no! I'm tired of being pushed around! I can't let him keep **doing** this to me!)"*

*"(I can't keep **doing** this to her!)"*

"Thinking of *her,* finally," said Jesus.

"I hoped that . . . things would be different. I wanted to give you something nice . . . if I can't do that . . ."

Again the theater audience leaned forward in anticipation, even though they knew what was coming . . .

" . . . then . . . maybe . . . I shouldn't give you . . . anything . . . at all. *(I just can't keep doing this to her . . .)"* George's voice trailed off.

*"(What?! I'm getting **dumped**?)"*

The air in the theater became still . . . very still . . .

"Fine!" said Kathy. *"(How can you **do** this to me?)"*

Silence

"Well . . . bye, then . . . I guess . . ."

For the second time in the theater audience, there was a sharp collective intake of breath . . .

"(Bye?!) . . . bye . . ."

. . . followed by a slow exhalation accompanied by much blinking of eyes and shaking of heads.

*   *   *

"That was a very unselfish thing of you to do," said Cecilia.

"Truly," said Jesus. "Rather than continuing to engage in emotional combat with Kathy, you gave up your own desire for a close romantic relationship with her, rather than causing her further distress."

"Ja, zat vas a tremendously generous impulse."

George looked up in hope.

"Zere vas only vone problem, of course."

"What was that?"

"She didn't understand a vord of vhat you vere saying."

Chapter, the Thirty-Second:

Isn't It Ironic?

George numbly watched the phone on his side of the screen as Kathy did likewise on hers.

After a few moments, Kathy started shaking her head, and then, lowering it, began to cry.

"Poor girl," said Cecilia.

George got up slowly, headed for the refrigerator, and after some hesitation, reached for the wine bottle . . . left over from Kathy's visit.

"Poor guy," came the quiet, half-rasping voice from the back of the theater, that was met by hindward glances from many in the audience.

"Him," St. Peter said sourly. "Again."

"Yes," said Jesus. "We've talked about this, Peter."

St. Peter nodded, and returned his attention to the screen.

"I *must* write a play about this," said Shakespeare. "The irony alone is breathtaking."

"The what?" George asked distractedly.

"The irony."

"Oh, like in the song," George nodded, satisfied with his understanding, his mind not fully engaged in the conversation.

"The song? There's a song? About irony?"

"Yes. 'Isn't it Ironic?'"

"'Isn't *what* ironic? That there's a song about irony? What's ironic about that?"

George shook his head. "No, no. There is a song *entitled* 'Isn't it Ironic?'" George sang unenthusiastically, "'It's a death row pardon two minutes too late . . . ' That one. Sorry, I don't know it very well; it's not exactly church music."

Shakespeare thought for a moment. "Hmmm . . . 'a death row pardon two minutes too late' . . . . To me, that's not ironic, just bad timing."

"Okay . . . uh . . . 'It's a black fly in your Chardonnay'?"

Cecilia wrinkled her nose. "That's just gross."

"Okay, okay . . . 'It's like rai-ee-ai-ain on your wedding day'?"

"You're getting warmer," said Shakespeare, "although, in some cases, that's closer to pathetic fallacy—was in mine. Do you remember the definition?"

"It's been a long time since high school."

"Irony exists when the inner meaning is opposite to the outer expression."

"Oh."

"Such as when you and Kathy thought, 'That's just great,' meaning, 'That's just awful.'"

"Ohhhh."

"Also, in your actions: doing one thing and meaning another, or doing something that guarantees the opposite of what you are trying to accomplish with it."

"I did *that*?"

"All the time."

"Was there anything I was doing that *wasn't* ironic?"

"Not so much," said Freud.

"Often, your left hand did not know what your right hand was doing," said Jesus, "and not in the manner that scripture intended, either."

"Most of the things you did were, in one manner or another, tremendously ironic," said Shakespeare.

"Like which ones?"

"Here," said Jesus, producing a pack of playing cards. "Pick a card, George, any card."

George looked deeply skeptical.

"Any card at all."

Chapter, the Thirty-Third:

Not Quite the Same Committee That It Was

George selected a card—the king of gavels—which Jesus smoothly removed from George's hand, and with a gentle flick of His wrist, sent it arcing towards the front of the theater, expanding in flight as it turned, to fill the screen with a picture of Ian Armstrong, chairman of the music committee at St. Christopher's United Church, who held a mahogany gavel in his right hand.

George looked at Jesus.

"Special effects, á la Heaven," said Jesus.

"I call this meeting to order," said Armstrong, bringing the gavel down then deftly setting it aside. "First order of business is committee membership. I would like to welcome a number of new faces. Let the minutes show the additions of Ted O'Brien, Jay and Bridgette North, Sam Waterford, Ellen Fotheringham, and finally, Don Braden."

"Everyone knew what was happening," said George. "They were going get rid of me if they could, and tie my hands if they couldn't. With that many votes between them, they had a real shot at changing the balance of the committee."

"Had you been thinking of joining for long?" one committee member asked, looking up and down the line of new arrivals, not knowing where to direct his gaze. Consequently, none of them answered.

Oliver Sommers' voice was the first to rise out of the silence. "Perhaps, given their newness to the committee and the relative shortness of the remainder of the church year, we might consider conferring 'observer' status on our newest members for the immediate present, just until they feel a little more . . . 'up to speed'."

There is no precedent for that," said Armstrong with a palpable tinge of regret.

"There is no precedent for *this*," said Sommers.

The newest members of the music committee shifted uneasily.

"It would seem that we are getting into an area where we need to give careful attention to such considerations," said Rev. Parker.

"Agreed," said Armstrong. "And in the absence of any useful precedent . . ."

"We may lack 'precedent'," said Jason Matthews, "but we do have a church constitution."

"Which Matthews had conveniently read up on . . ." said George.

"'Any member of the church may sit on any committee unless there is a bona fide reason, cited in the individual constitution of said committee, for the exclusion of such members'," Matthews intoned.

" . . . thoroughly," George added.

"And . . . do we—"

"No."

"What about the exclusion of choir members?" Bawdry asked.

"'No choir member may sit on the music committee'," Sommers stated, quoting from the music committee's constitution.

"None of us *are* choir members," said Jay North, one of the "new members" of the music committee.

"Recent change of status," said Armstrong.

"Very recent," Sommers added.

Armstrong nodded reluctantly. "Alright . . . there isn't much for us to consider tonight. There is the matter of the preliminary budget for the Fall, of course, but perhaps we should defer that matter until the entire committee has had a chance to consider these figures," he said, passing the page that contained them to members on his left and right. "I'm not sure that we even have enough copies—we were not expecting this turnout—but we can remedy that during the week. All those in favor of deferral?"

A rough show of hands revealed a division of opinion in the committee, with the new members in solid opposition, which threatened to derail Armstrong's strategy before he had even finished handing out all the reports.

"Can I see a show of hands again? In favor?" He counted, a slight nod of his head recording each. "Opposed?" He hesitated, absorbing the implications of the vote. "Nine 'ayes', and nine 'nays'."

There was silence around the committee table as the regular members looked at each other.

"Alright," said Armstrong, "as provided for in the music committee's constitution, the chairman will vote in the event of a tie. Let the minutes show nine 'nays' and ten 'ayes'. The matter is deferred to our next meeting. Other business?" he asked formulaically, reaching hopefully for the gavel.

"Yes."

"Yes?"

"Yes," said Don Braden. "There is the matter of membership in the choir."

"But that is normally the responsibility of the choirmaster," said Evan Bawdry.

"Yes," said Armstrong. "The committee has always left questions of that nature to the choirmaster."

"Still, it would not be improper to discuss the subject," said Bill Seely.

"Now?" said Armstrong. "So late in the season and with Easter not too far off, you want to get into *that*?"

"Easter is our biggest service," said Sommers.

"And our biggest collection," Bawdry added.

"Which is taken up during the offertory anthem," George contributed dryly from the far end of the committee table.

"Finally had to say somezing, eh George?"

"I could see what they were up to."

"And the 'strategy' most likely to net votes," Jesus added.

"I had to do *something*."

"There is also the matter of Christian fellowship," said Jay North, judging it time to edge into the discussion.

"This is all beginning to sound a little familiar," said Armstrong. "So far we've avoided tying the choirmaster's hands in that regard."

"No-one's talking about tying the choirmaster's hands—"

"Not directly," said George, "but I have a feeling that it would end up that way eventually, and when I was hired, it was my understanding that I could set certain minimum standards, at least with new members. I took that to be part of my contract—my *verbal* contract, at least."

Reverend Parker finally judged it necessarily to enter the discussion, albeit cautiously. "It sounds as though there is some desire for a change, but 'timing', as they say, 'is everything'. Do we really want to pursue the matter at this time?"

Sensing the "time" to be ripe for closure, Armstrong asked for a show of hands, and, after much nodding and another tie breaking vote on his part, directed that the minutes reflect it. "I hope that isn't going to be our new voting pattern. I had rather gotten used to the relative anonymity of the chair," he said with a half-smile, but the air in the committee room remained leaden. "Move to adjourn?"

"So moved," said Bawdry, with grim determination.

"Seconded? By Sommers," said Armstrong, nodding acknowledgement for the record. "In favor?" Nodding wearily, he added, "This is beginning to be a familiar sight."

"I believe that this is what Yogi Berra used to call 'deja vu all over again," said Parker, only semi-successful in defusing the seriousness of the moment.

"Okay," said Armstrong. "Let the minutes show . . ."

"Okay, how was *that* ironic?"

"Simple, George: you zought zat you had gotten rid of zem, but zey ended up even more 'zere' zan before."

"Huh?"

Shakespeare explained. "The methods that you used to get rid of a few inconvenient choir members drove them on to the music committee where they were even more inconvenient to you."

"Ja, ja," Freud agreed, pleased. "Zat's vhat I said."

"Oh."

George sat at his desk in his office, balancing one of the smaller pipes in his hands, tapping it for resonance, blowing a short blast into its end to check the tone, locating its center of gravity for no good reason whatsoever, even sighting down its length, one eye squinting hard, at his extended foot, when Oliver Sommers appeared at the door.

"Careful you don't shoot yourself in the foot."

"Maybe I already have?"

"Well, it's not quite the same committee that it was, but you're okay for the moment, as long as Armstrong plays tie breaker for you, which I'm sure he will, at least until the end of the year. Then . . . ?"

" . . . who knows?"

"Who knows."

"And that assumes that the numbers stay as they are," George continued, "which is . . ."

" . . . quite an assumption."

"Making this a good time to pull a rabbit out of the hat?"

Sommers nodded grimly.

"For that, I will need one rabbit, and one hat." George looked around the room.

"Two rabbits would be even better." Sommers smiled gently.

"Will it take that many?"

Sommers shrugged.

"Okay, I'll try for three."

"Don't get *too* carried away."

"What choice do I have?"

"Good question . . . but I *really* wouldn't get too carried away with . . . those," Sommers answered, eyeing the pipe in George's hands. "They're beginning to cause quite a stir in some quarters."

"Which quarters are those?"

"Certain voting members of the committee. Just for now?"

"'Just for now' might be all I have."

A few minutes later, Sommers' presence was followed with Evan Bawdry's. George was inspecting and playing with the metal cylinder as before.

"Saw the light on."

"Got some things to do before I go."

Bawdry shifted his weight as if to leave.

"Not too busy to entertain, though."

Bawdry settled back into his original posture, and remained stiffly in the doorframe, seeming not to know whether to come all the way in or leave after all. In the end, he stayed where he was.

"How bad is it?" George asked.

"We need to buy some time."

"What good will that do?"

"Give you a chance to do something with it?"

"Like what?"

"I don't know . . . win over some hearts and minds?"

"How?"

"Make the offertory anthem on Easter unforgettable?"

"For the collection plate?"

"Like Trinity Sunday."

"Easter will be spectacular."

"And," said Bawdry, looking around at the jungle of pipes in George's office, "these . . ."

"What about them?" George asked, drawing the pipe in his hands a little closer to his chest.

"Careful."

"Don't tell me: they're beginning to cause quite a stir in some quarters, perhaps among certain voting members of the committee?"

"I see I'm not the first one to stop by."

Alone again, on inspiration or out of boredom, George fished a second pipe out of one of the piles, and found that he could play the first four notes of Beethoven's Fifth Symphony, using the two of them together.

"Heard you playing," said Armstrong, entering. "Where's the rest of the instrument?"

George waved the smaller of the two pipes around to indicate that the "instrument" was everywhere.

"You're my third visitor."

Armstrong nodded.

"The pipes, right?"

Armstrong smiled. "They're not the central issue, although they *have* attracted a certain amount of attention."

"Among certain voting members of the committee?"

"Exactly. And we need to hang on to every vote that we can."

"Of course. And 'the central issue'?"

Armstrong exhaled slowly in preparation for his explanation. "As you may have noticed, we have a few new members sitting on the music committee, mostly ex-members of the choir, and I can only break a tie."

George nodded his understanding.

"The central issue?" Armstrong continued. "We don't want anyone else showing up next week."

"Do you think anyone else will?"

"No, I think they've gathered up all the support they can, at least for *this* season. Unless . . ."

"Unless what?"

"Unless you somehow create more ex-members."

"I see."

"Maybe you should take it easy with the 'extreme staccato' thing."

"Maybe I should."

"Good." Armstrong turned to leave. "Oh, and George . . . ?"

"I know, I know. The pipes."

Chapter, the Thirty-Fourth:

Of Pipes and Plaster

"Pick another card," said Jesus, bringing forth the deck of playing cards from a fold in His robe and fanning it out for George, who ran his finger over it and pulled one from the middle.

Jesus took the card and turned it over.

"Ah, ze five of pipes," Freud declared with ill-disguised enthusiasm.

George looked sideways at Freud as the five of pipes traced the same gentle arc that the king of gavels had taken to the screen.

George looked at Jesus.

"I thought you might like to see it again," said Jesus, smiling.

On screen, George sat in one of the pipe rooms, surrounded by a bewildering array of pipes.

"Now, vhat did zey tell you?"

"I know: 'the pipes'. But I couldn't stop *then*."

"Vhy not?"

"Because I had already *gotten* most of them—"

"Most of zem? You mean you accumulated even more?"

"Well, a few more . . . actually, a lot more . . ."

Freud suppressed a laugh.

" . . . but I needed to impress people somehow if I was going to keep my job."

"And there sits grinning irony, if e'er it hath been seen, 'thron'd in its own excess," said Shakespeare, recording his words with quill on paper.

"Huh?"

"You were using those pipes to try to save yourself," Shakespeare explained, "but eventually, they become the very instrument, so to speak, of your destruction."

And there sat George, onscreen, surrounded by loose pipes, scribbling calculations on a small pad before putting it down beside him, picking one pipe up, and cradling it like a newborn.

"Digging your own grave with a pipe," said Bach. "Not what they were originally intended for."

"But vhy do you appear to be so listless up zere, George?"

"It looks like I couldn't figure out where to put them all."

"I think you mean you couldn't figure out where to put *any* of them at that point," said Bach, having busied himself with his own mental calculations.

"True. The pipe rooms were overflowing; the chancel couldn't take any more; I had decided against—"

"Vhat's *zis*, zen?"

The camera angle swung up from George, traversing the walls of pipes, and zoomed in for a close-up of the ceiling twenty feet above his head to reveal a tiny, y-shaped fissure, from which fell a small piece of plaster, coated on one side with cream-colored paint, that floated down in slow motion, to land abruptly, in real time, with a soft "thidt" in the center of George's sheet of calculations.

George who had been considering the pipe in his hand, stopped, turned his head sideways with a look of intense concentration, then budding awareness. Eyes widening, he turned his gaze slowly, slowly upward, alighting, finally and steadily on the ceiling.

"Und?"

"Und," said George evenly, "I decided where I was going to put the pipes."

"You had already discussed the possibility with Jimmy, your tuner, had you not?" Bach asked.

"I had, but then I decided against it, that maybe he was right, maybe it was too much. Now, I was desperate. So many pipes piling up, so much trouble with the committee, the choir ready to walk. I needed a miracle. And that little piece of plaster fell from the ceiling and landed right in the middle of my calculations."

George watched himself looking around the pipe room. "I was trying to figure out how to get them up there. See those grilles set in the ceiling? They're for ventilation. They're large enough for a certain amount of sound to get through, and it's the same in the other pipe room on the far side of the chancel, but I didn't know how to get the pipes, the wind chests, and everything else up there.

"Next, I checked out the ceiling of the chancel itself. Look there . . ." the camera panned upwards co-operatively as George exited the pipe room " . . . there are no grilles, but see those circular vents? They're something at least. And there are ceiling vents running all the way down the church." The camera again obliged. "They were something to work with if I could just figure out how to get up there."

George scanned the church, raising an eyebrow here, squinting there. Finally, he saw what he was looking for: a door in the rear balcony. He set off towards it with a purpose.

"That was it: the door to the bell tower. I just *knew* it."

George slowed down, and approached the door, almost with reverence, and found it locked.

"That was not a surprise. What did amaze me was that I could unlock it with my office key," which he proceeded to do.

George went up the half-flight of steps that preceded the next winding set of stairs to the landing where the person who rang the bells stood on Sunday mornings, and paused again, scanning. Then he saw it: the small white door that faced towards the chancel.

"It wasn't even locked."

George opened the door, which swung open to reveal nothing but blackness.

Just then, the sound of chopsticks being played badly on a piano wafted up to the steeple, and into the theater.

"Youth choir!"

Chapter, the Thirty-Fifth:

Could It Be Any Worse Than This?

"Those two girls," said George, shaking his head, watching himself tramp up the center aisle of the church as the 'two girls' closed the piano lid and scurried for their seats.

Once in the chancel, George glared at them. They smiled back, almost coquettishly, at least until he busied himself at the organ, then they wrinkled their noses at each other.

"Teenagers!"

George looked ready for rehearsal to begin. The youth choir, however, did not.

"Look at those empty seats! I wouldn't even mind it if they'd just stay away, but no, they're late."

Freud shrugged. "Kids."

"Easy enough for you to be sympathetic: you don't have a choir full of them. Most of them don't even want to be there; they only come because of their parents. They're late. They talk through rehearsal. I even found them in the pipe room sometimes, making out!"

"Hormones, George, hormones. Vhat can zey do about it? Zat's how zey vere made."

"Original equipment," Jesus agreed, "straight off the assembly line."

"Do you forget so soon, George? It hasn't been all zat long since you vere a teenager."

"I didn't let it rule my life."

"Could have fooled me," said Cecilia. "*I* saw you two."

"That was different."

"Not *zat* much different."

"I was dedicated. I devoted myself to my music."

"Ja, you sublimated much of your li*bid*o into your practice . . . during ze daytime at least, but zen!"

"What do you mean?" George asked suspiciously.

"Vell . . . zen—"

"On second thought, spare me." George looked around and saw that many in the audience, including Jesus, were looking at him with knowing smiles. "Oh, alright, alright. I'll concede you . . . *that*, but . . . *everyone* did . . . *that*."

"Exactly!" Freud crowed. "Vhich is vhy you should exercise a little more under*stand*ing in *zeir* case."

"Okay, okay, but I was still a little more dedicated than . . . them."

"*Ve* vill concede *you* . . . *zat*."

"Okay, then."

"Okay."

"Well, okay."

*　　*　　*

Meanwhile, David North, Rob Taylor and Ben Smiley entered through the "secret" panel from the pipe room. They glanced furtively around the chancel, and headed for their seats in the back row.

"Sorry, George," said Taylor when George caught his eye with the now familiar glower.

George nodded resignedly, and resumed sorting his music. A few last teenagers straggled in, and George stood.

"Alright! Stand up. Now . . . breathing . . ."

George's teenagers rose with various degrees of reluctance, and endured George's breathing exercises with the occasional whispered, "This again?" or "I already know how to breathe."

George soon lost whatever enthusiasm he had for it, and moved on to tone production.

"I don't think they got much out of that," said Bach.

"They didn't put much into it."

"Vhy vould zey? Look at ze attitude you vere modeling for zem."

"I *used* to put more into it."

"I'll bet zey did also."

"Maybe a little, but it all seemed kind of pointless after a while, so . . ."

"So you vizdrew your enzusiasm, zen zey also vizdrew zeirs, und down it all vent from zere. But vhich came first, I ask you: ze *chicken* or ze *egg?*"

George's eyes narrowed.

"The chicken," said Jesus. "I was there, on the third day of creation. 'Let there be chickens,' Dad said."

"*That's* what He said? Not in *my* Bible."

"That's only a summary."

*   *   *

George looked on as the rehearsal progressed in a series of overlapping scenes. "I thought that at least when I died I'd be through with youth choir rehearsals."

"Not that stupid thing again," said one chorister, to the general agreement of his neighbors as they riffled through the music in their folders. "Who does he think he is?" said another teen, the facial expressions of those who sat around him suggesting that a number of colorful possibilities were forming in their minds.

"Try this," said Jesus, signaling for the thought track, George not even bothering to protest. A jumble of words and expressions swirled out of the theater speakers:

"*(Why do we have to . . .)*"

"*(. . . sure thing, buddy . . .)*"

"*(. . . no way.)*"

"*(What a wiener . . .)*"
"*(. . . loser . . .)*"
"*(. . . are you ever gay!)*"
"This is hell," George muttered.
"Closer, actually, to purgatory," said Jesus, signaling for the thought track to end.
"Maybe we should be watching this at the 'Cinema Purgatoria' then."
Jesus shook His head. "You wouldn't like it there."
"Could it be any worse than this?"
"Absolutely."
"How?"
"No popcorn."

*   *   *

"Jesu, Joy of Man's Desiring," George announced. While the Youth Choir fished out the music, he began the opening organ solo.

At the high point of the first phrase of the lilting triplet melody, the pure pipe tone was colored with an odd dullness and sputtering accompanied by a flapping noise. George stopped abruptly, and sounded the offending note again, with the same result. He signaled Anne Jeffries, one of his organ students, to come over to the console, where he indicated the key in question, and headed for the pipe room. Even with a withering glance from George in transit, a few of the basses in the back row barely managed to contain their laughter, only to erupt afresh as he disappeared behind his not so "secret" panel, certainly no "secret" to them.

Once in the pipe room, George stared steadily at the suspect rank of pipes, his gaze moving slowly towards the place where he felt the offending note had originated. Anne sounded the key in question at regular intervals, and an odd motion caught George's eye. Just as he reached that region of the rank, he was aware of a subsidence of sorts, and began to focus on an object at the top of one of the pipes. Anne sounded the pipe again in shorter durations, causing the whiteness atop the pipe to rise and fall repeatedly.

"Vas ist das?" Freud asked. "A . . . a balloon of some sort?"

"It is," George replied.

"Vhy ze odd shape? Ze elongation? Ze—"

"It's a condom."

"Vas? A kon-*dumb*?! You mean a . . . ?"

"Yes," George sighed wearily.

"Zen . . . vhat's it doing *zere*? Vhat does it mean?"

"It means that the E-flat was giving me the finger."

Anne sustained a particularly long tone, and the condom stood for one final salute before losing its hold on the pipe, and corkscrewing its way flatulently through the air to land at George's feet.

The Organists' Guild was more or less equally divided between deep shock and wild amusement. The Psychiatrists' Guild tended significantly towards the latter, especially the Freudians.

Other reactions in the theater varied widely, but in general, the air quivered with the irony of the situation, which was not lost on Shakespeare: "Now there," he cried, "is the greatest irony yet. You put more care into that organ than some people do with their own children, and look how it shows its gratitude . . . thumbing its . . . *nose* . . . at you!" Shakespeare said, grinning.

"Razer like a teenager," Freud added, visibly pleased with his own insight.

Smiles were raised around the theater.

Even Jesus looked amused.

"I knew who it was, too," George said darkly. "Look there, in the back row."

George reappeared at the "secret" panel, and glared at the rear of the bass section. Rob Taylor, David North, and Ben Smiley were red-faced—North was bent near-double—in their efforts to contain themselves.

He faced the youth choir, glared again at the back row, appeared ready to speak and then to change his mind, a cycle that he went through a number of times, looking something like a fish out of water gasping for air.

"Why the silence?" asked Bach.

"I couldn't think of what to say. Anything that occurred to me was either too mild for the guilty, or too strong for the innocent, and there were a fair number of innocent young things who would have gone straight home to tell their parents that I was ranting and raving about condoms—not something I thought I needed, not on top of everything else."

After one last glare at the back row, which had, by then, effected something approaching a collective straight face, George gave up the effort and returned, defeated, to the organ, and stoically resumed.

David North leaned over to Rob Taylor, and whispered, "He really hangs off those pipes, doesn't he?"

*   *   *

As the last few members of the youth choir left the chancel, George gathered up his music. He cast his eyes to the rear balcony, seeking out the door which led to the blackness that he had been prevented from penetrating by their arrival.

The scene changed and George was looking into that same blackness. After much brailleing of the walls just inside the door, he finally found a light switch and flipped it on, gasping when he saw what it revealed.

He threaded his way down the central catwalk. At regular intervals, it branched off to the sides, doubtless for service access to various parts of the structure, wiring, and so on. When George reached the chancel, he turned to the right and did a visual sweep of the area above one of the pipe rooms.

"How did it look to you?" Bach asked.

"It was even better than I had hoped. There was a solid framing over the ceilings of the pipe rooms but lots of space between the joists, and the best part was that the lath and plaster ceiling that they had everywhere else—very messy stuff to deal with—had been replaced over the pipe rooms with simple drywall sheets—probably after some kind of renovation, maybe repairing some water damage or something—so I could gain access to all that space simply by undoing a few screws, and more of the sound would get through."

"But vouldn't zat leave a big hole?"

"Yes. And that troubled me for a time, but then I remembered something: grille cloth. It's virtually opaque unless it's illuminated from the other side, which of course it never would be, not when anyone was around anyway, and it's perfectly transparent to sound: they used it on the front of both pipe rooms."

"Wouldn't someone at the church notice you working?" Bach asked.

"Mostly I worked at night. First I sealed off the pipe rooms, put up a 'wet paint' sign, and even painted a little. Tom muttered something about that not being my job, so I went on about the danger of damaging the pipes and so on, and he walked away, still muttering of course, but relieved that he didn't have to be involved, I think. Then, I took down the drywall sheets and some of the two by fours, and covered the openings with grille cloth, each section on a removable frame for easy access. Simple! And no-one would notice the difference. Even if they did, they would only see the grille cloth, and I could say something inscrutable about acoustics. I'd worked it all out. Anyway, it was not exactly a high traffic area, except for those wretched teenagers, but what were *they* going to do?"

A soft snort was heard from the back of the Odeon Paradise: *someone* knew *something*.

St. Peter stiffened, but did not otherwise react.

"But someone vould find out about it sooner or later, surely, und you were told to lay off ze pipes. Even if zey didn't see it, zey'd hear it, or vhat vould be ze point of it all?"

"True, but *when* were they going to hear it? That was all that mattered."

"How so?"

"I was going to hold off till Easter, and then, if all went according to plan, they would be so impressed with what they heard that I would be able to stay there forever: I was going to give them an Easter they would never forget."

"You succeeded in that," said St. Peter. "You surely succeeded in that."

* * *

"Should I pick another card?" George asked unenthusiastically.

Jesus shook His head. "I think you get the idea. Besides," He said pointing to the fold in His robe where He had been keeping them, "if we tried to keep track of all the irony in your life, there wouldn't be enough cards in the deck."

Chapter, the Thirty-Sixth:

A Bigger Deal than Usual

"Now, about Easter, George. Have you made any plans?" Rev. Parker asked.

"Oh yes!"

"That's good."

"If only he knew . . ." said Bach.

" . . . he vould increase his insurance substantially."

"A little in the way of inspirational music might go a long way, if you know what I mean," said Parker.

George nodded, encouraged. "I thought so, too."

"What do you have in mind?" Parker asked.

"The usual, so I'm told: the Hallelujah and Amen choruses from The Messiah. I haven't decided whether to settle for brass quartet and tympani with the organ, or to go for a larger ensemble. Other than that, I haven't completely decided. I'm going to do some writing, and I'm bringing in a few extra singers."

"That's good. I look forward to it."

"Ze poor man."

"I wonder if you could give me the hymns a little earlier than usual, too, for descants and perhaps a special prelude or postlude: lots of composing to do."

"Sure thing."

"I want to give the organ an opportunity to shine."

"Yes, the organ," said Parker thoughtfully. "Is it my imagination, George, or does it sound a little . . ." Parker contorted his face in the effort to find an appropriate term " . . . different . . . maybe a little . . . fuller . . . louder?"

"Maybe a little."

"There are a few new pipes in the chancel, are there not?"

"Yes, I put in a new rank last week."

"Yes. I thought something was different. Any, uh, further plans in that regard?"

"No," said George, shaking his head, "no . . . no more ranks in the chancel: I think that's about it for there."

"Equivocator," Shakespeare noted.

"Vas?"

"Using the truth to mislead."

"Ja, ja."

"I've never been called *that* before," said George.

"Not for vant of trying, vone presumes."

Parker appeared to be fishing for the right question to ask. "What about . . . elsewhere?"

"Ze good Reverend suspects somezing."

"Well . . . uh . . . organ maintenance is an ongoing sort of thing, and that can always involve certain . . . improvements, but nothing exactly . . . 'today', you know?"

"That's about a dozen leagues short of the truth," said St. Peter.

"Well, I wasn't—"

"Telling the truth," said Jesus.

"I'm not sure what's happening with all those pipes, then," said Parker, "but they are not going unnoticed. And you know how people are about change."

George nodded.

"Especially now."

"Now?"

"Well, it hasn't exactly been smooth sailing, has it?"

"No, I suppose not."

Parker stared long out the window.

"Thinking of retirement," said Jesus.

"Ze poor man."

"And we both know how the numbers are stacking up in the music committee," Parker continued.

"Yes," George agreed.

Parker stopped, again appearing to be searching for words. "George, I'm not going to belabor this . . ."

"Meaning that he knows you won't listen to him anyway," said Jesus.

" . . . but you're going to have to be mindful of a few things for the next little while."

George nodded.

"First of all, we can't have the balance swing any further in committee, obviously." Parker waited for some sign of recognition from George. "One more vote . . . ." Parker let the thought linger in the air. "We don't want any more ex-choir members, especially Molly. Keep her in the choir at all cost."

George, both of him, sat in silence.

"And I want you to take care of yourself. Whether it be the . . . the rigors of the situation, or the . . . the *whatever* it may be, you're starting to show it, if you don't mind me saying so."

"Well, I was up a little late last night rearranging a few things."

"Like ze church attic, for instance."

"For the fifth night in a row," Jesus added, "and *still* you weren't finished."

"Well, whatever it is, you might consider cutting down on it a little if you can: a person needs to take care of himself." Here he allowed himself to smile. "Especially now," Parker said for the second time.

"Now? Why? Am I pregnant?"

"No, no, nothing like that. Easter's only a few weeks away, and it's going to be a bigger deal than usual this year. It's always a big deal, of course, and not just theologically, but now, what with the Moderator coming."

"The *Moderator* coming?"

Parker nodded solemnly, giving George a moment to digest the news.

"Vhat's a Moderator?"

"A Moderator is the head of the United Church of Canada," said George. "They elect one every two years. Sort of like a United 'pope'."

"Pope? Impressive."

"Not exactly the same thing." Peter sniffed.

"True," said Jesus, "but the analogy is not without merit. Peter, of course was the first pope, if you will . . ."

Peter nodded, dignified.

" . . . and remains, of course, 'the rock'."

"No offence," George said.

"None taken," Peter replied gravely.

"And the church wants to give the Moderator an Easter to remember," Parker continued.

"Oh, I think I can guarantee the Moderator *that*."

"You can say zat again!"

"More irony," said Shakespeare. "I think that I'll stop mentioning it now."

"Good," George said.

"Good," Parker said.

"Ze poor man."

*   *   *

George left Parker's office with a renewed sense of purpose, rounded the head of the stairs, and headed deliberately for his office where he eagerly fished out a mechanical pencil to continue sketching his plans for the new array of pipes in the attic, as he waited for evening to come and people to go home.

Chapter, the Thirty-Seventh:

So Many Pipes; So Little Time

George took a long look at the pile of pipes in his office, sighed, and reached for the smallest one.

"You do look a trifle spent," said Bach.

"I was, and it only got worse, but what could I do?"

"Take a day off?" Freud suggested.

"Not with everything that had to be done, especially with the organ. I had more pipes coming, and now I had to do it all at night. I even had to arrange the *deliveries* at night—that wasn't easy—once to my home, even, and then carry them, *carry* them, to the church."

"So many pipes, so little time," said Shakespeare.

"Exactly! Sometimes I didn't get out of there till the sun was coming up. A couple of times, I ran into Reverend Dawson in the morning and had to pretend that I'd come in early. Then I was stuck there all day, and I had more to do that night in order to stay on schedule! Sometimes, I hardly slept."

"Ja, und you vere getting no emotional support."

"Right!"

"*You* saw to zat."

"Well . . . "

"Und your opponents vere lining up against you."

"Taking numbers!"

"Und you saw to zat also, all of vhich eqvaled a horrible downvard spiral, in vhich your ability to deal viz zese zings vas severely diminished, vhich in turn produced more situations zat furzer taxed your strengz, vhich zemselves produced . . . und so on . . . vell, you get ze idea." Freud sounded fatigued by the mere recitation. "It's a most familiar pattern to any psychiatrist."

"What pattern is that?"

"Ze nervous breakdown."

"Nervous *breakdown*? *That's* what it was?"

"Or, perhaps, I should call it ze latter stages of mental und emotional exhaustion zat is so typical of musicus obsessus."

"Musicus obsessus? What's *that*?"

"Musicus obsessus . . ." Freud clear his throat " . . . is an obsession vhich is particular to musicians. It vas I who named ze syndrome!"

George frowned. "What's wrong with music?"

"Nozing. It's ze *obsession* zat you should get over."

George nodded thoughtfully. "So what's the treatment?"

Freud shrugged and smiled. "Viz a little bit of luck? An evening at ze Odeon Paradise."

Jesus nodded. "Heaven is a place where things get worked out."

*　　*　　*

George struggled up the stairs to the rear balcony with an armload of smaller pipes, and lurched along the catwalk towards the rapidly sprouting grove of pipes at the front.

"You must have nine or ten ranks in place," said Bach.

"Eleven, at that point . . . and counting. Eventually, I had thirty-seven ranks of pipes up there, not just above the pipe rooms and the rest of the chancel, either, but at further distances from the front, also."

Bach considered all this. "But how did they speak? Wouldn't the sound be too quiet and dull by the time it got to the ears of the congregation?"

"I had that all figured out! First, I opened the ceiling in the pipe rooms, as I was saying earlier, and covered the openings with acoustically transparent grille cloth so that the sound could come through there."

"Softly, still," said Bach, "especially the ones further from the front, in direct proportion to the distance, surely, diminishing both in volume and timbre."

"Not *too* softly, though. The ones directly above the pipe rooms were fine, and I noticed that there were vents all the way down the center of the church to the rear balcony for ventilation, which I used to strategically place some of the further ranks of pipes—clustered around them in thickets—so that the sound had another outlet."

"But what of the tone? You would lose so many of the higher partials with all the reflection and absorption in the attic prior to the sound's transmission through those, shall we say, less than generous openings."

"That one was stubborn, but I kept on anyway: I was sure that the answer would come to me."

"And it did?"

"It did."

"And it was . . . ?"

George smiled. "Tin foil."

"Tin foil? What is . . . 'tin foil'?!"

"Actually, a thin layer of I don't know what . . . maybe aluminum?"

Bach looked deeply skeptical.

"There," said George, pointing at the screen where he was busily at work in the attic, attaching reams of tin foil to the ceiling and walls with a staple gun where the ranks of pipes were located.

"I think I see what you're up to," said Bach, his face contorted with the effort of deciphering George's strategy. "The tin foil . . . it has the acoustic properties of metal?"

"Exactly," said George, smiling.

"So the sound of the pipes is reflected off the tin foil covered surfaces, being perhaps even brightened somewhat in the process before it finds the apertures in the ceiling for transmission to the church below?"

"Exactly."

"Brilliant!"

"Thanks."

"But not necessarily ze best zing to get involved viz at zat point."

"Not as it turned out. But it kept me busy."

"Zat vas important to you?"

George nodded sadly.

"But not ze *most* important zing to you, ja?"

George shook his head slowly and sadly, as his onscreen persona paused from his labors, and joined him in mouthing the single word, "Kathy."

Chapter, the Thirty-Eighth:

Where's the Tin Foil?

Molly banged her way through one drawer after another in the church kitchen. By the time she got to the last few, her frustration was echoing through the rest of the church basement.

Mona walked in with the last tray of finger foods from the church's monthly, post-service tea. "What's wrong?" she asked, slowing and stopping.

Molly's bushy eyebrows caterpillared themselves into a horizontal question mark . . .

"Where's the tin foil?"

Chapter, the Thirty-Ninth:

Similarly Oblivious

George sat in his office, looking out the window, squinting at the low angle of the sun filtered through the maples on the west side of the street.

"You look tired," said Cecilia.

George nodded. "It must have been one of the days that Dawson caught me, so I couldn't go home: all night with the pipes, all day in the church."

On screen, he put his feet up on his desk and settled back in the high-backed swivel chair, his eyes closing . . .

"Woof!!"

"Bernie!" George tumbled from his chair, all flailing limbs and twisting torso, to land in a disorganized heap on the floor.

There was a quicksilver giggle from further back in the theater, stifled by its author but nonetheless clearly audible and even more obviously out of place.

"Him again!" said St. Peter, rolling his eyes and sighing, giving the impression of one who was thinking intemperate thoughts while praying for patience.

"Try not to pay any heed," said Jesus. "You know that only encourages him."

"True."

"Who's 'him'?" George asked.

"One of your biggest fans," Jesus answered. "Let that suffice for the present."

"Woof!"

"How many times do I have to tell you not to do that, Bernie!"

"Woof!!"

"Somebody wouldn't be hungry, would they?" George asked, as he picked himself up off the floor.

"Woof! Woof!!"

"Okay, okay."

"I stocked the office for snacks and emergency meals," George explained. "Bernie figured that out in a hurry."

"Bernie may have a limited vocabulary," said Jesus, "but he certainly knows how to use it."

George went to the cupboard, accompanied by much tail wagging and a little drooling from Bernie, to get out some dry dog food, then he dug a little deeper to find something for himself, which turned out to be a peanut butter sandwich and some apple juice.

When they had satisfied their appetites, George stretched out on his office couch, surrendering to a feeling of spreading warmth, with Bernie close by on the floor, similarly oblivious.

Chapter, the Fortieth:

Oops

"They're waiting for you."

"Huh?"

Brian Tyler, de facto assistant conductor at St. Christopher's United, stood over him. "The *choir*, George . . . they're *waiting* for you."

"I just had the strangest dream."

"Come *on*."

"You go ahead. I'll be right out."

Tyler hesitated only long enough to convince himself that George was really awake.

"Vhat vas ze dream, George? Do you remember?"

"I'm an organist, not a shrink. I don't keep track."

"But it must have been important. Maybe, ve could look at it?" Freud, eyebrows arched, looked hopefully to Jesus, the collective eyebrows of the Psychiatrists' Guild of New Jerusalem similarly raised, as if the request had been seconded and passed by acclamation.

"And how would George feel about that?" Jesus asked.

"Not thrilled," said George.

"Not this time, then," said Jesus. "It *is* George's dream, after all."

"*Dreams* . . ." George shuddered.

"'And in that sleep . . . what dreams may come,' eh George?" From Shakespeare, that could possibly be construed as sympathy, but that was not the manner in which George construed it.

"'That sleep of *death*', wasn't it?" George returned darkly.

"It was."

"Yeah, I remember, 'And in that sleep of death, what dreams may come must give us pause.'"

"Woof!"

"Not 'paws', Bernie, '*pause*'." George enjoyed the occasional pun, and he had been deriving blessed little enjoyment from anything for longer than he cared to consider.

"Bernie can't hear you from on screen," said Jesus. "That was just a coincidence."

Meanwhile, Bernie nudged his master, who was now struggling heroically into an upright position.

* * *

George emerged, blinking, from his office, entered the chancel and shuffled his way to the piano, where he opened his music slowly and deliberately. Not quite awake, he omitted his customary greeting to the choir, along with any mention of the piece that he was intending to start the rehearsal with. When he began playing, members of the choir looked at each other, uncertain what was expected of them, even as he glanced up at them, and otherwise comported himself in a manner which told them, from experience, that he expected a good, solid choral entry.

In a matter of moments, the more musically accomplished members of the choir recognized the opening instrumental measures of *The Magnificat*, and pulled it quickly from their music folders; those who were less accomplished and/or perceptive followed their example, and were only a step or so behind; the least able nudged and gestured their need for assistance to anyone nearby. After a good deal of frantic rustling of paper, the choir was ready to sing when their entrance arrived in the ninth bar.

George, unaware of their disadvantage, was profoundly unhappy with the result, and stopped abruptly.

"We practiced this last week. There's no reason for the choral entry to be so ragged. And the page turning! It sounds like the junior choir marching through piles of dry leaves. The congregation would be able to hear that in the back row!"

There were many raised eyebrows in the choir: some puzzled, others annoyed.

"Oops," said Jesus.

"I know, I know." George lowered his head.

"Und look at *zat*."

Molly, who had just managed, barely, to survive her encounter with extreme staccato, was a thundercloud looming large and dark on the far side of the chancel. Mona Cooper, Molly's pew partner for decades, who mortally disdained drinking in all its forms, looked as if she could sorely use one now.

"They all hated me," George said darkly.

"Not all of them," said Jesus.

"Tell me one who didn't."

"I'll do better than that," said Jesus, raising his finger in a gesture that George had come to dread. "I'll show you *two*."

"*No-oo*," George moaned, burrowing face first into his cupped hands, "not the *thought* track!"

"Don't worry, George. It's not you that we're going to be listening to this time."

"*(Damn you, George!)*" Molly flashed.

"That, I could have predicted."

"Hasty, as usual, George."

Molly continued. "*(Why do you have to do things like this when I've been trying so damn hard to forgive you! Lorrrd, give me strength!)*"

"*That's* what she was thinking?"

"It was. Now, listen to *this*."

"*(Oh, George,)*" Kathy thought in something that sounded very much like a sigh. "*(You look so tired. Did I do this to you?)*"

The thought track stopped, but the Kathy's face remained on screen.

"I didn't know . . . I didn't know that she felt like that."

"No, you didn't.

"If I had . . . ." George looked up, miserably and wordlessly, a hitherto essentially unknown combination for him, which did not go unnoticed.

"Anozer breakzrough, George."

"Not *another* one!"

"Yes," Jesus agreed. "It's an entirely new step for you to suffer in silence."

George started to open his mouth, then closed it again, firmly, to the accompanying smiles of everyone around him.

* * *

George was treated to a telescoped, then a kaleidoscoped presentation of himself rehearsing a number of pieces with the choir.

"We don't have to watch *all* of this, do we?"

"No," said Jesus, "we'll be selective. Let's try . . . this." Jesus signaled the projectionist, and the scene changed:

Many of the choir members were getting up and leaving their pews . . .

"Ze rehearsal vas over?"

"No," said George. "It was break time. See? No-one's in a hurry."

"Und no-one seems to be talking to you, eizer."

"I had become somewhat unpopular. Even Brian Tyler, my sometime assistant . . . there . . . seemed to be avoiding me."

Tyler was leaving by the opposite side of the chancel, grim-faced.

"And look at Janet Stewart, over there. Even her."

Janet passed him by with a cheery but uncharacteristically brief greeting. "She used to mother me shamelessly. Now look what I got: two words—'Hi George'—literally, two words; that's all I got."

"You don't look all zat approachable, eizer."

"Truly," said Jesus. "And you deliberately avoided the one person who actually wanted to talk to you."

George chose his moment to get up from the piano and head down the chancel steps when there was no-one else to run into. He got about a third of the way down the aisle when, in the relative darkness away from the chancel, he saw Kathy, a short distance ahead, separate from her mother and sister, and begin walking slowly towards the back, as was he.

"Zat's interesting."

"It is," said Cecilia.

"It appears zat George vill overtake her. He is valking a little faster zan she is."

"Which she was aware of," said Cecilia.

"She was?" George asked.

"She was."

"How do you know that?"

"I'm a woman, and I'm a saint, and I'm not stupid."

The situation was watched with interest and anticipation from all quarters.

"They'll meet."

"Yes."

"Wait . . ."

"What's he *doing?*"

" . . . he's slowing down!"

A groan arose from the audience.

"George! What were you doing?" said one voice from a few rows back, too shocked to observe the formality of an introduction.

"I couldn't handle any more rejection."

"Und so you guaranteed it!"

"I did?"

By now, even Jesus was sighing. "Cecilia, will you explain it to him, please?"

"She was *trying* to run into you."

"She was?"

"Yes."

"And there lies the saddest irony of all," said Shakespeare, "that you, fearing her rejection, rejected *her*."

"Not only sad, but extremely neurotic, if you don't mind me saying so . . . und even if you do."

"I blew it?"

"Again," said Jesus. "And that was your last chance."

*   *   *

George stood bent over the wash basin with his hands over his face, water dripping liberally from his fingers. Lifting his head from his hands, was caught off guard by his reflection, and stared at it.

"Ah, ze obligatory 'mirror scene'. A defining zeatrical moment of some sort; some deep realization, perhaps? An epiphany even?"

"I saw that I looked awful."

"Zat's it?"

"That's it. One bone-tired, rubbed raw, deeply disappointed little organist."

"That's a lot," said Jesus. "Fatigue of the heart, mind, and body can be a deeper well of sorrows and afflictions to the human soul than sin itself."

"Worked for me," George sighed.

"As we shall see."

*   *   *

George looked haggard, sitting at the piano and shuffling his music as the last few choir members came back from the break. Few said hello. Kathy entered on the opposite side of the chancel. She and George avoided each other's gaze.

"You look miserable," said Cecilia.

"An all-nighter will do that."

"Just what you needed the day of a rehearsal," said Bach.

"At least it wasn't youth choir."

"By the time you were finished, as I recall, you might well have wished that it had been," said Jesus.

"The worst choir rehearsal of my life."

George announced the next piece for rehearsal with all the self-possession he could muster. "Kee-here . . . kuh-kee-ree . . . kee-ree-ay? Kyrie!" He looked up from the piano a little sheepishly, a weak smile on his lips, as if someone might laugh with him, but the best that he could get from anyone there was a puzzled look, the other reactions ranging from annoyance to avoidance.

"Not an auspicious beginning," said Bach.

"It got worse."

"At least you told them the piece this time," said Bach, "after a fashion, anyway."

After a single run-through, George moved perfunctorily to the next piece.

"That's it?" asked Bach. "No comments? No directions?"

George shook his head.

The next piece was handled essentially the same as the first. Occasional, half-questioning glances from the choir swept George's way.

"George, vas ist das? Ze cat got your tongue?"

"Something like that."

On screen, at the piano, George grimaced, sighed, and, with an effort, announced a third piece.

"Und now, you're starting to look a little annoyed."

"They were putting so little effort into the music. It was getting to me."

"You certainly veren't *asking* zem for much. Vhy is it, zen, 'getting' to you zat zey aren't *giving* it so much?"

"I was reluctant to ask for more after what Parker said: no more ex-choir members."

"But the music?" Bach asked him.

"That's what finally got to me."

In one particularly demanding passage, the choir, particularly the altos and sopranos, were running out of breath in the long, romantic phrases, some of them gulping for air and dying like gasping fish out of water at phrase endings.

"You left that *alone*?" Bach finally asked.

George nodded. "I couldn't afford any more ex-members, especially Molly."

"So you actually paid some attention to what Parker said?"

"I tried."

"Looks like it was quite an effort."

Indeed, as the rehearsal wore on, the strain showed more and more on George. His responses were more terse and strained, although not directly unpleasant, but some choir members began to look uncomfortable.

George appeared ready to let yet another one of the offending breathless phrases go. Then, with an effort, he checked, struggled with, and finally asserted himself. "More breath, ladies! More breath!"

Immediately, there was a modest improvement, but judging from his expression, not enough to suit George.

"Not rising to the occasion, are they?" said Bach.

"That's what *I* thought."

"But, you were too slack with them for most of the rehearsal, and then, all of a sudden, you went back to making your customary demands."

"Grinding the gears a bit, I know," George agreed.

"And look at Molly there," said Bach. "She also looks like she's getting a little steamed."

George stopped halfway through the phrase this time. Sounding increasingly annoyed, he said, "Breath! Breath! It's all in the breath!" restraining himself, with considerable effort from still further, and less moderate, comments.

Finally, only two syllables into the phrase, he stopped, and after a long silence, during which it could be seen that his frustrations were beginning to master him, expressed his disapproval in steadily rising waves:

"Bigger breaths. Bigger breaths!! Ladies, for the LasT TiMe, YoU . . . NEED . . . *BIGGER **BREASTS*!!!*"

If ever George had wanted silence in rehearsal, this appeared to be a bullet-proof method for achieving it. Mouths and various other anatomical features were frozen in expressions usually found only on ceremonial masks from primitive societies.

After a seeming eternity, flash-frozen in ice, Molly's was the first voice to rise out of the stunned silence, muttering to her fellow alto Mona Cooper in tones that slowly mounted to the threshold of George's hearing, " . . . talking about our breasts!"

Molly stared defiantly at George, not realizing that he had heard her.

George struggled between competing senses of guilt and defense, Molly's glower finally tipping the scales towards the latter.

"I was not commenting on *your* breasts," he commented from between clenched teeth. And anyone would have agreed that Molly's breasts were in no need of augmentation.

"I NEVER!!!" Molly declared, becoming a whirling dervish of music, purse, and coat, exploding from her pew into the chancel, flashing down the centre aisle, and out of the church, a slamming door echoing behind her.

Chapter, the Forty-First:

Answering the Call

Desperate, George looked at his watch, reckoned that there were only about twenty minutes left in the rehearsal, and declared it concluded. After a formal, "Thank-you, everyone. See you Sunday morning," he deserted his music, still open on the piano, and fled with what little dignity he could still command, the choir pews left roiling behind him.

"Well, well," said Jesus.

"Ach du lieber!"

"Holy shit," George whispered.

"I heard that," said Jesus.

"Sorry." George grimaced. "Well . . ." he sighed resignedly " . . . at least it was holy."

Jesus smiled, but not so that George could notice.

The pews on either side of the main aisle of St. Christopher's United Church flashed past as George accelerated out of the church and burst into the outer hallway, retracing Molly's wild path of a few moments previous, not that anyone witnessing his speedy egress would have imagined, even for a moment, that he was pursuing her.

"George!" Tom called out affably as George rounded the corner without acknowledging him.

"Vhat vere you zinking, George?"

"I had to get away. I didn't know where I was going. I just knew that I had to get there, and I knew that there was a 'there' to get to. Don't ask me how I knew. I just knew."

"You were being called," said Jesus.

"I was?"

"You were. I know: I was doing the calling."

George rounded another corner, and avoided two members of the flower committee who scowled at him and seemed to be on the verge of speaking but lacked adequate opportunity to do so.

"Them, I had to avoid. They weren't very happy about pipes finding their way into the flower room, and I was not in the mood to deal with them."

"I know," said Jesus. "I put it in their heads to go there."

"Why?"

"So that you would avoid both them and the corridor they were coming out of."

"So what happened to free will?"

"I have a little more discretion in that department than some—think of it as my 'double O' license to fiddle around with cause and effect—but here I only suggested to the ladies of the flower committee that the flowers for Sunday might be in need of a little water. No-one forced them to go anywhere: cause and effect were left more or less intact."

"But how did that help me get to . . . 'there'?"

"Watch."

George doubled back, using the stairs to the basement at the end of the hall.

"I wanted to get back to my office."

"That was the last place I wanted you to go," said Jesus.

"But—"

"Watch."

At the bottom of the stairs, George turned left, went through some double doors into the basement gymnasium, got a few feet, and noticed that it was stuffed to the bleachers with mostly middle-aged and older men who filled the air with a cloud of tobacco smoke as they watched one of their number at the microphone on the other side of the room intone the formula which they all knew, not only by heart, but by autonomic reflex, by soul and by sinew: "Hi. My name's Fred Williams, and I'm an alcoholic . . ."

Eyes began to turn George's way, but it was too late for him to retreat without looking even more foolish than he already felt. It was also too far to cross the entire length of the gym to the stairs that led to his office without drawing more attention to himself than he cared to, so he made his way, with an apologetic smile, to another door that was only about fifteen feet away.

"You put it *their* heads, too?"

"I'm good, but I'm not *that* good, not unless I really roll up my sleeves, and begin to seriously play fast and loose with time and space in general. I was aware of them when I touched the minds of those two ladies of the flower guild. That was sufficient."

George sped back upstairs, this time dodging a few significant members of the music and finance committees, now out of a need for avoidance in general rather than from any real need to do so.

"I was starting to feel like one of those metal ball bearings in a pinball machine."

"Good analogy," said Shakespeare.

"It's all in the wrist," said Jesus, smiling.

A final rounding of corners, and the sound of voices, out of direct sight but coming from both before and behind, was all the encouragement George needed to push his way through the large oak doors into the chapel.

"Well done, Lord," said Peter.

"Thank-you, Peter."

"Vhat now?" Freud asked.

Said Shakespeare, eyes wide, quill poised hungrily over his writing pad, "The turning point!"

Chapter, the Forty-Second:

In the Chapel

The carved oak doors closed heavily behind him as he stood in the darkened chapel of St. Christopher's United Church. Footsteps and voices approached and receded in the corridor outside. George, finally, was alone.

Jesus signaled for the thought track.

George sighed.

"I thought it might be easier on you than supplying the narration," said Jesus, "especially seeing as you don't have a lot to say in this scene, at least not out loud."

George nodded.

At first, there was silence, then a few thoughts, then a torrent.

"*(Alone . . . alone . . .)*"

George looked around in the darkness, and walked up the aisle, slowing as he approached the altar.

"*(Can't . . . can't . . . do this anymore,)*" he thought, taking a seat in the third pew and closing his eyes.

"*(What a choir! Altos who can't keep their mouths shut, a tenor whose feet are lethal weapons, a soprano with a mile-wide vibrato that I have to listen to in committee now!)*" George shook his head ruefully. "*(It used to be that when someone left the choir they were gone . . . they didn't show up the next week on the music committee . . . don't they know the rules . . . aren't there any?)*

"*(And that youth choir . . . teenagers! I can't deal with them; they hate me! And the tuner, always giving me his wise advice, as if something could go wrong, as if I didn't know what I was doing, as if . . . aS iF . . . AS IF!!)*

*"(And the people who give me the pipes, and the 'flower ladies', always with their stupid questions, and their stupid objections, and their stupid . . . **stupid** . . .)*

"(And the music committee! The very idea! Music 'committee'? That's an oxymoron, isn't it? How can they even say it with a straight face? 'Committee'? It's obscene! But evvvvvvery church has one. They can't resist their little meetings, their, their . . . meddling. As if they were any use, as if they actually knew anything about music . . . as if . . . As iF . . . AS IF!!)

*"(And I'm supposed to work with them? and the choir? and the, the . . . how **can** I? They can't stand me now! I can't stand me now!!)"*

George was paralyzed by the thought.

"You're almost there," said Jesus.

George got up from his pew, and made his way unsteadily to the altar, falling first to his knees, then fully prostrate.

*"(Lord, I can't handle this. I have too many problems with too many people . . . too many people: choirs . . . committees . . . Kathy . . . Kathy . . . I have problems with . . . with **everyone** . . . I can't handle all . . . these . . . problems . . . I can't . . . I . . . **I** . . .)"*

"That's it," said Jesus.

"(. . . 'I'? . . . Oh . . . My . . . God!!)"

"Yes!"

*"(**I'M THE PROBLEM!!!**)"*

"That's It!"

Shakespeare nodded gravely. "Epiphany," he whispered, his quill scratching its way across his pad.

Freud smiled. "Bingo!" he cried.

"(My God! . . . the one common factor to all of these problems is . . . me?)" George looked up. *"(. . . **me?**)"*

George, both on screen and off, began to weep: on screen, with the fresh wound of bitter and hard realization; off screen, with the dull ache of remembrance.

Respectfully, the theater audience sat silently, most of them with their heads bowed . . .

"*(Wait a minute.)*"

Heads rose.

"*(Wait . . . a . . . minute!)*"

"Good, George. Sehr gut! Ze vheels are turning now!"

"*(If I'm the* **problem** *. . .)*"

"That's it," said Jesus.

"(. . . then maybe . . . maybe . . . I can be . . . the solution, too . . . *if I* **did** *this . . . maybe I can* **undo** *this.)*"

"Yes!"

"Epiphany number two," Shakespeare whispered, scratching the words on his writing pad. "Twins!" He grinned.

"Ja! Bravo, George!"

George sat in the chapel pew, his back a little straighter now. Wiping the tears from his cheeks, he sank deep into his thoughts . . .

Jesus nodded, satisfied.

"*(Alright,)*" George thought, slowly, deliberately. "*(One at a time . . . one at a time.)*"

Chapter, the Forty-Third:

One at a Time

George sat at his desk, staring out the window, staring at the phone, and staring out the window again. Then he picked up the receiver and replaced it several times before dialing the number and stopping, dialing and stopping, until he finally succeeded in hitting the last digit, and waited for someone to pick up.

"Hi . . . Kathy?"

At Jesus' signal, the screen split, revealing Kathy on the right.

"Hi, George."

"Hi . . ."

"You said that already."

"Yeah, I know . . . I guess I'm, uh . . ."

"Look, I'm really busy."

"Thought track," said Jesus.

George was beyond caring.

"Okay, uh . . . I just called to tell you that I was not very . . . happy—"

"*(So what else is new?)*" thought Kathy.

"—with . . . how I've been handling things . . . and I really want to do better . . . and I guess I just wondered how *you'd* like things to be instead of, uh . . . me trying to get my own way all the time . . . you know?"

Kathy was silent. "*(What?!)*"

"You have her attention," said Cecilia, "but she's been burned too many times to buy it just like that."

George shifted uncomfortably in the silence. "*(What do I say now?)* So . . . what would you like?"

"Too sudden," said Cecilia.

"*(Nothing!)*" Kathy thought. "*(I'd be nuts!)* Nothing!" Kathy answered aloud.

"*Nothing?*" That was the *last* answer that George had expected to hear.

"Nothing!"

"Nothing . . . ?" George repeated slowly, softly, sadly; disappointed and disbelieving.

"Nothing," Kathy reaffirmed, a little more quietly. "*(What's happening?!)* I . . . my feelings have changed."

"They *have?*"

"Yes. *(They have not!)* I . . . met someone. *(Why am I lying?)*"

"You did?!" George was on the edge of tears.

"Yes—*(No!)*"

"Ze time has definitely come for your radar, George."

"I lost it."

"Bad timing," said Bach.

"Oh . . ." George was too crushed to express himself with any other part of speech.

"She's not used to you giving up so quickly," said Jesus.

" . . . good-bye?"

"*No*, George," said Cecilia.

"Vhat a time for you to get over being so manipulative! Und so completely!"

"The wrong thing for the right reasons," Shakespeare said wearily. "More irony than I can stand."

"Bye," said Kathy. "*(Huh?)*"

The two telephone receivers were replaced on their respective cradles.

Kathy first stared at the phone, then off into the distance. "*(What the **hell**, George?!)*"

"Now you've *completely* confused her," said Cecilia.

George looked out the window, then lowered his head, and laid it on his folded arms atop his desk.

"A fat lot of good my little 'epiphany' did me," George said miserably, watching his own despair unfolding silently on the screen.

"You had to give it time," said Jesus. "You had to . . . *wait*."

"Poor George. You zought, perhaps, zat after your moment of realization, your situation vould improve immediately."

"Silly me," said George. "Things got worse, and I was disappointed. And that was only the beginning."

"Actually, it was the ending, pretty much," said Jesus. "In the chapel, you said, 'one at a time'. That was how you decided to tackle your troubles, remember? Then, instead of 'one at a time', it became 'one time'."

"Dreadful revision, George," said Shakespeare.

"Yes," said Jesus. "You tried your new 'I was the problem so I can be the solution' strategy—which was a pretty good one—exactly once."

"That was enough for me," said George. "After that, I gave up on everything except the music."

In an irony that did not escape Shakespeare's quill, St. Cecilia said, "Some things are more important than music, George."

"Not then, not to me they weren't."

"Let's have a look," said Jesus, grim-faced.

Chapter, the Forty-Fourth:

Musicus Obsessus

The entire forward portion of the attic above the chancel resembled a futuristic New York City skyline, pipes everywhere with a tin foil sky above. More modest clumps of pipes radiated down both sides of the main catwalk, directly over the centre aisle of the church, clustered around the ceiling vents.

"I had more pipes, actually a lot more pipes, and no way to use them."

"How so?" Bach asked.

"I had more pipes, more wind chests, motors, you name it, but I had finally used up all the available space. The pipe room was full, the chancel was too visible, and there were no more platforms in the attic that were strong enough to take the weight."

"I'm surprised zat you let a little zing like zat stop you."

"I wouldn't have if I could have worked openly on it. There were solutions, but I would have needed a crew to do the necessary reinforcing."

"So vhat zen?"

"That," said George, pointing at the screen where he sat down amidst his pipes, staring blankly into space.

"Even your beloved pipes vere bringing you no sense of purpose."

"None," said George, also staring blankly ahead. "'What's the point?' That's what I was probably thinking. My girlfriend had no use for me. My job hung by a thread. Nobody liked me, that's for sure. And now? Now, I'm dead on top of it all. What *is* the point, anyway? Well, I guess *that's* the point, isn't it? Without the love of someone or something there *is* no point. That's why I felt," he said, pointing at the screen, "and feel . . . so . . . utterly . . . pointless."

"Well done, George," said Shakespeare. "Another epiphany."

"That's nice," said George, unenthusiastically, "but it won't give me Kathy back, or my life . . . my *life*."

"It *will* give you back your soul," said Jesus.

George was not consoled, so Jesus took a different tack. "I suppose a friendly face would go a little further right now than any theological concept. Let's see what I can do for you in that department." Rubbing His hands together, Jesus said, "George, if you could have your choice of anyone, absolutely anyone, to see at this moment, who would it be?"

The theater became intensely quiet in anticipation of George's answer.

"Kathy," he said miserably.

"As you will, but right now, that would be a little premature. Who would be your second choice?"

On the verge of shrugging his dismissal of the question, George brightened a little as he said, "Bernie."

"Ask, and it shall be given!"

Chapter, the Forty-Fifth:

Woof!

"Woof!"

"Bernie!"

"Woof!!"

Bernie romped his way in, wagging and woofing and spread-eagling on his forelegs before face-clothing George with his immense, dripping tongue. George threw his arms around Bernie's neck, and rested his teary cheek thankfully on the great dog's furry flank.

"There are times when a boy simply needs his dog," said Jesus.

"Thank-you, Lord," George said quietly.

Bernie's great tail thumped on the red-carpeted floor of the Odeon Paradise.

"You're . . . dead, too, Bernie?"

" . . . woof . . ."

"No need to look so sad," said Jesus, "either of you. Bernie is more abundantly alive here and now than he ever has been, and so are you, George."

Bernie wagged his tail.

If George, on the other hand, had a tail, it certainly would not have been wagging. "Could have fooled me . . . about me, at least—"

"Woof!"

Bernie was up on his paws again, looking first at the screen (where George was still wearily contemplating his creation in the church attic), then at his master beside him in the theater, and then back at the screen . . .

"Your friend up there is stirring," Jesus told Bernie, indicating George onscreen.

"Friend?" said George. "I wasn't much of a friend to Kathy, that's for sure. What kind of friend I was to anyone, even to myself?"

"Not always the best, but you're improving, George, you're definitely improving."

Chapter, the Forty-Sixth:

Any Port in a Storm

Surrounded by pipes, George strained his ears at some distant sound in the building. "No-one here but us mice," he said to himself.

In the theater, George explained. "They did it to me again." He sighed and corrected himself. "*I* did it to me again. I'd just pulled another all-nighter, and Reverend Dawson was in early, as usual. I had to dodge him on the way out, if I could, or be stuck there for hours, and he was already suspicious of something."

Meanwhile, in the attic, George listened intently, threaded his way down the catwalk to the door in the rear balcony, locked it silently, and crept down the stairs to the rear of the church where he halted abruptly, almost militarily. Satisfying himself that the coast was clear, he straightened up and headed for the half set of stairs that led to the outside door before they joined the main staircase to the basement.

"Good morning, George!"

George jumped.

"Sorry about that. Didn't mean to startle you. In early again?"

"I thought I'd try out a few things on the organ before everyone arrived."

"Forgot about *me*, I see."

"Never."

"I imagine that you're working on something special for Easter."

"Yes."

"Good." Reverend Dawson had appeared ready to be on his way, but he hesitated, pivoting on his left heel. "And how are things going?"

"Oh . . . they're . . . 'going'."

"Well, I guess that's better than the alternative," said Dawson, uncertain as to what degree he should be encouraging or inquiring.

"I hope so."

"So do I, George, so do I." Reverend Dawson turned again to go.

"Uh, Reverend?"

"Yes, George."

"The prayer of intercession . . . do you ever take . . . requests?"

"All the time. Got one?"

"At least."

"Okay," he smiled. "Give 'em to me one at a time."

"Yeah . . . one at a time," said George, mostly to himself.

Jesus looked over at George, eyebrows arched.

"I don't know," George said to Dawson. "I *do* know, but I'm not sure how to put it."

"You mean, for public consumption?"

"Something like that."

"Leave that to me. What's on your mind?"

"Reconciliation . . . of the . . . estranged? Something like that?"

Dawson nodded gravely. "I'll see what I can do."

"Thanks."

"Don't work too hard," said Dawson, turning.

"Asking—vhat vas ze name?—'Reverend Neverend' for as*sist*ance?"

George looked embarrassed as he nodded.

"Any port in a storm?"

"Something like that."

Chapter, the Forty-Seventh:

Never Saw This Before

"Vhere to now, George?"

"To the organ, seeing that Reverend Nev—uh . . . *Dawson* thought that was why I was there."

"You don't look very happy about it," said Bach.

George turned back, moving a little more slowly than when he had been when he thought he was leaving, a minute before.

"I wasn't, not after a night with the pipes. Throwing them around for hours, and then I had to *play* them."

"A trifle fatigued for your obsession?"

"Well, yeah, but that wasn't it."

"Vhat zen?"

"Boy, did I stink."

"You mean—"

"I mean that my playing was awful."

"Can we have a listen," Bach asked, grinning.

"No!"

"Just kidding, George."

"Good." George sighed heavily. "I was *so* out of practice."

Jesus signaled for the thought track.

"*(No rest for the weary . . . and little help for this prelude.)*"
George sat on the organ bench, staring blankly at his music.
"*(I wish I hadn't run into Dawson: I could use a little sleep before Parker.)*"

"Vhat does zat mean, George?"

"I must have had a meeting with Rev. Parker that day. Yes, now I remember. I had to drag myself—no sleep—to our regular weekly meeting."

"We'll skip ahead," said Jesus.

George buried his head in his hands. "No playing, though, right? This is *so* embarrassing."

"It's alright, George: no playing."

"Promise?" George asked, peeking out between tentatively fanning fingers.

"Promise . . . at least until Easter or so."

"That I can live with."

*   *   *

George shut down the organ, presumably after a lengthy practice session, judging by the profusion of books on the music stand, and the slowness with which he dismounted the organ bench.

In the theater, George breathed a sigh of relief.

"Sometimes," said Jesus, "I believe you care more about what Herr Bach thinks than what I do."

"No, Lord—"

Jesus waved him off, smiling. "At least in some areas. Now, let us see what develops."

A gaggle of voices was heard coming from the back of the church.

Jesus gestured discreetly for the thought track.

"*(God help me, it's the flower guild, and I still have some pipes in their room.)*"

"Und Molly told you not to do zat."

"No choice."

George began gathering up his music, dropped a few sheets, picked them up, fumbled with them, then gave up the effort entirely, beating a near-breathless retreat through the "secret" panel to his office as the flower guild rounded the corner into the church.

"*(There . . . safe . . . for the time being . . . Let's see . . .)*" he thought, surveying his desk, and picking up seemingly random pieces of paper, "*(that one, that one . . . and . . . that one.)*"

The door had half closed behind him when he reappeared. "*(Can't forget that . . .)*" He scooped up his hymnbook, which bristled with little scraps of protruding yellow, and left again. Just outside his door, he went through his materials one last time, double-checking slowly and thoroughly to compensate for his lack of sleep. George's ears pricked up at the sound of the ever-nearing flower guild, then he bolted down the hall, past the flower room and down the stairs.

"*(Yea, though I walk through the valley of the shadow of death . . .)*"

"Being a little melodramatic there, weren't you?"

"Not really: Molly's voice . . . I heard it." George hit the bottom of the stairs, and burst blindly ahead, throwing open a door, and stopped dead in his tracks, facing, at some short distance, a brick wall.

"*(What's this, then?)*"

*   *   *

George advanced slowly into the room. Halfway in, he stopped suddenly, and looked around. "*(How did I get here? Hmmm . . . bottom of the stairs, turn left, then a quick right . . . Never saw **this** before.)*"

"Was somebody up here guiding me?" George asked, looking around for a likely candidate, only to be greeted by a vigorous shaking of heads.

"Nein, George. No-vone here. Zink about it, given vhat it led to."

"Nor I," said Cecilia. "I would have steered you away, if I could have."

"Certainly not I," said Jesus, "But I do know who did."

A muted giggle from the rear.

"*Him* again," said St. Peter. "And again and again."

"*Who?*" George asked.

"One of your greatest admirers," said Jesus, "whom, I might add, you will be hearing more from, but first things first." Jesus nodded at the screen.

"*(I must be under the pipe room . . . yes, but it's not as long . . . or as wide. Why is it here? Storage? Not much room, especially with that . . . column . . . in the center . . . ohhhhh . . . that* **column** *in the* **center**. *That support column extends up into the rear of the chancel, right beside the pipe room . . . Yes! I* **know** *it.)*

"*(But wait . . . why build a room around it? How odd! Hmmm . . . then there must be one on the other side, too, for the other column. Wait a minute . . . I see . . . the walls are for support,* **too** *. . . good thing, with that grand piano in the chancel . . .)*

"*(Wow! If I were really nuts, I could* **use** *these . . . or could I? Not enough height to put in any reasonably sized pipes, though. Let's see . . .)*" he looked around, "*(. . . concrete block walls . . . poured concrete floors . . . considerable cracking: must be thin . . . easy to . . . easy to . . . dig . . . through. Hmmmm . . .)*"

George looked around the room a third time, long and hard, leading to this, his final pronouncement:

"*(If I were really, really nuts, I could somehow lay claim to these rooms, lock them, dig out the floor . . . part of the floor, anyway . . . down eight or ten feet for the sake of the longer pipes—Wow! The resonance!—open up an access for the sound at the back of each of the pipe rooms, and cover it with a little more grille cloth like I did to the attic! It would work! It would . . . if I didn't get caught . . . and if I were really, really nuts!)*"

George scanned the room one last time, snorted in amusement, and closed the door behind him. Still grasping the handle, he drifted into a look of quiet intensity, then shook it off with an effort, followed by a wry smile and a shake of his head.

"*(. . . really, really nuts . . .)*"

Chapter, the Forty-Eighth:

Desperate Situations . . .

"Sorry to keep you waiting, George."

George unfolded himself stiffly from the green leather chair outside Rev. Parker's office and managed an apologetic smile for taking his time about it.

"Showing a little more patience in the green leather chair than on previous occasions," Jesus noted.

"What was my hurry?"

"Come in," said Rev. Parker, his tone hovering between friendly and firm. "Have a seat."

George refolded himself into the new chair.

"Working hard?"

"I guess you could say that."

"I could, I'm sure. You look like you've been up all night, if you don't mind me saying so . . . and . . ." he added, his voice veering to the serious.

" . . . even if I do?" George smiled grimly.

Parker let out his breath slowly. "I have to level with you, George, and for whatever it's worth, I feel deeply conflicted about it. My managerial and pastoral hats are both twirling about my head. I scarcely know which one to put on."

"How bad is it now?"

"I see that you've been thinking it over," said Parker.

"Pretty hard to avoid the subject."

"True. I'm hearing about it everywhere: from the finance committee to the flower guild to the—"

"I narrowly avoided them a little while ago."

"Not a bad idea. And a number of people are concerned about all those pipes. They're everywhere! You're going to have to do something about that—what, I don't know."

"I know a place. No-one else is using it."

"There *is* such a place at St. Christopher's?"

"There is."

"It's yours. *Do* it . . . as soon as you can, if you would. One thing less to worry about would be nice. The situation has deteriorated somewhat since the last time we spoke, unfortunately."

"How are the numbers in the music committee holding up?"

"The same, so far, but I was sorry to hear that you succeeded in creating another ex-choir member. I'm not big on 'I told you so's, but . . .'"

"I know. You did tell me. So did Ian Armstrong."

"We'll have to see what happens, but I'd be kidding you if I told you that we were on anything less than a very slippery slope."

George nodded.

"In the meantime, I'll make sure that nothing changes before Easter. I'll play the 'Moderator' card if I have to: no-one wants any sudden disruptions on the eve of *that* little visit. That's the most that I can promise at this point."

"Reverend Parker . . . Bob . . . can anything . . . save me . . . 'at this point'?

"Are you asking a theological question?"

"No."

"I thought not. All I can say is this, and I know that it's not much of an answer: I sense that the next little while is very important."

"He means in ze exercise of your diplomatic skills."

"So do I," George agreed with Parker.

"You meant somezing considerably different: vone of your little schemes or somezing."

"Good," said Parker. I'm glad that we agree on that."

"Oi!"

*   *   *

As the door closed behind him, George heard the phone ring and Parker's voice answer, "Hello?" But George could only think of one thing as he walked down the hallway: bed.

Rounding the top of the staircase to the ground floor a little faster than usual, he miscalculated the required arc and connected heavily with the banister which spun him to his left, sending much of his music to the floor and a large number of loose sheets cascading down the stairs as he teetered precariously on the edge of the top step.

The film ground into slow motion, the appalled face of George figuring prominently as he staggered at the top of the staircase, struggling against gravity with his failing sense of balance. His eyes and mouth opened wider as he yawed towards the yawning decline, even to the point of tipping over its very lip. He finally saved himself from the quick, gravity-assisted trip to the ground floor and a probable broken neck by intentionally giving up the fight for an instant and using it to strategically plant his foot on the second step from the top in order to halt his descent.

"Bravo," said Freud, expressing a sentiment that was echoed around the theater. "Just like a ballerina."

"Almost saw you arrive in Heaven at *that* point," said St. Peter.

"That would have been okay with me," George said flatly.

On screen, George sat down on the top step, and surveyed the wide distribution of his scattered music. He snorted when he noticed that he had actually managed to keep some of it in his hand.

"Not worth it," an older and wiser George muttered in the theater. "I almost got killed, and there I was, trying to save a few pieces of paper that wouldn't have gotten hurt anyway, a little wrinkled at worst. Pointless. That's 'obsessus' for you, I guess."

"Ja, zat's it exactly."

George began to gather up his music.

At Jesus' signal, the thought track resumed.

"*(Where's the descant . . . there . . . that goes with this . . . my . . . my hymn book! Where?)*" George looked about, puzzled. "*(Idiot! Left it in Parker's office.)*"

George trudged back to the good Reverend's door, and reached for the handle when he heard Parker's voice. He stopped, hand hovering over the doorknob, then slowly withdrew it, listening intently.

"He what? . . . Yes, yes . . . you're sure?" Reverend Parker asked. "She must be . . . yes . . . yes . . . very upset with him after that."

"*(Her? Who's 'her'? Who's 'him', for that matter?)*"

"I'll bet! . . . Yes . . . yes . . . that certainly sounds like Molly."

"*(Molly!)*"

"No, she certainly wouldn't take *that* lying down. Certainly not from her favorite organist."

"*(Wouldn't take **what** lying down?)*"

"That's it for her and the choir, eh? Uh-huh . . . kinda sad after what . . . thirty, thirty-five years?"

"*(Not for me!)*"

"And the music committee? Nothing to stop her from joining that now, of course."

"*(Oops! I forgot about that! Enough! I've heard enough!)*" George, immediately absorbing the implications of what he had heard, wasted no time setting off down the hall again, his hymn book forgotten.

"*(Doomed. Doomed! I don't want to **hear** any more.)*"

"Neither do I." George sighed.

"I think that in this case you really should," said Jesus.

Parker spoke, as George, now well out of earshot, sped down the hall. "She isn't, eh? . . . . *Not* joining the music committee . . . too embarrassed by the whole thing? Well, that's something at least . . . Yes, yes . . . that lets us have a little room to breathe, as it were . . . Yes, yes!" Parker laughed. "Indeed! Time for bigger 'breaths'!"

*   *   *

"*(I knew she'd be my downfall . . . from the first time she opened her mouth.)*" George rounded the top of the staircase for the second time, slowing considerably, and headed his office. "*(Molly, Molly! George's folly!)*"

George accelerated up the center aisle of the church, bounded up to the chancel, and through the "secret" panel to the relative safety of the private and the familiar, where he took, immediately and emphatically, to his couch. "*(Nemesis,)*" he thought, slapping his open palm to his forehead, "*(thy name is Molly!)*"

"Passing excellent," said Shakespeare, reaching for his quill.

"*(A plan, a plan: my kingdom for a plan!)*"

"Hey, that's mine!"

"Like *you* never borrowed."

"*(So. I have until Easter,)*" thought George, scratching his temple. "*(. . . last chance . . . last chance . . . so, what now? What now?)*"

"Did you have any ideas?" Bach asked.

"Lots," said George, "and all of them futile."

"Or vorse!"

"Worse," George agreed.

"*(Tired . . . so tired . . . what can I do? . . . No energy! . . . Maybe . . . maybe I should just go fishing and forget the whole stupid thing . . .)*"

"Used to work for me," said St. Peter.

"I liked making things with wood," said Jesus.

"Most zerapeutic," said Freud.

"*(If only I could . . .)*"

"You vill? Perhaps?"

"*(No, no, no!)*"

"Nein, nein, nein."

"*(Think!)*"

"Zat's how ze trouble starts in ze first place!"

"*(I have until Easter, and then it's probably all over . . . unless . . . unless . . .)*" George sat up. "*(Unless I can . . . Easter . . . Easter: yes, that's it! If I can completely outdo myself when the Moderator comes, make it truly unforgettable . . .)*"

"Zat you succeeded in. Zat und zen some!"

"*(Will that work? . . . will it? What other choice do I have? Let's see: Music? done, mostly. Singers? hired. Players? hired, but maybe a few more. Organ . . . ?)*" George laughed inwardly. "*(Do I dare? . . . I do have more pipes . . . but . . . where? **Where?** There is a bit more room in the attic . . . the . . . ohhhhh! . . . yes, but **that** would be something . . .)*"

"*(Desperate situations call for desperate measures, and this would certainly qualify on both counts.)*"

"*(The sound, the sound! It would be magnificent! The depth! Literally! Pipes in the basement, and with all that resonance!)*"

"*(But so much work! Is there time, is there time? Barely.)*" George sighed, long and deep. "*(Sleep . . . ?)*"

"*(And it would take some . . . tools . . .)*" George's thoughts were slowing down . . . drifting . . ."*(. . . a sledge hammer . . . for one . . .)*"

"*(. . . leave it . . . for now . . . sleep . . . on . . . it . . .)*"

Chapter, the Forty-Ninth:

... Desperate Measures

"George!" Tom, the Irish-Canadian verger of St. Christopher's United, open lumber jacket, lunch pail in his beefy left hand, called out. "Where you going with the sledge hammer?"

"To my office. I just picked this up at Allen's hardware for a neighbor—he can't get there before closing time weekdays because of his job."

"Pretty fast on your feet zere, George."

"Not really: I made it up in advance."

"Zinking ahead, zen."

"Oh . . . well, that's good of you," Tom said over his shoulder.

"On your way home?"

Tom turned, shuffling backwards. "As should you be, George, as should you: 'all work and no play,' you know."

"Thanks, I won't be long."

"See that you're not," he called out, turning finally to go.

"How suspicious was he, do you think?" Bach asked, as George headed deliberately to the newly designated basement pipe room.

George shrugged. "Why would he be?"

Bach laughed. "Well . . . it's not every day that you see the organist walking around the church with a sledge hammer, although I'm sure that you're not the first one to entertain the thought."

"Oh, he bought the cover story. Why wouldn't he? Besides, the truth was too strange to guess."

"Zat should have told you somezing right zere."

George surveyed his new basement pipe room, and hoisted his new sledge hammer. "I've been working on the railroad!" George sang softly, as he brought the great hammer down resoundingly on the concrete floor.

The repeated smashing of steel against concrete stabbed through the silence in the theater.

"More nails in my coffin, Lord?"

"I would say 'yes', but by then you would have a hard time finding a place left to drive one in, even with *that* hammer."

Having run through all he knew of *I've Been Working on the Railroad*, the echo of George's hammer, growing louder and louder as he put his back into it, was next accompanied by the singing of *The Ballad of John Henry*.

"George?" Bach asked, deeply shocked, "What *is* that dreadful song?"

"American folk music: The Ballad of John Henry."

"You weren't thinking of using anything like that in church, were you?"

"No, no, only in the basement."

"He lay down his hammer, and he died, Lord, Lord . . ."

Chapter, the Fiftieth:

Holy Week

"Well, George," said Jesus, "I think that, now, all the wheels have been set in motion."

"Is that a good thing?"

"That's up to you."

"I was afraid of that."

"Our Lenten tale with Easter soon shall bloom," said Shakespeare.

"Yes, this being Holy Week, but into what?" Jesus asked, looking squarely at George.

"I know, I know . . . that's up to me. Just . . . Lord?"

"Yes, George?"

"Could we . . . ?"

"Yes, George. It's hard to watch, I know; and from here to Easter Sunday, there is very little that is truly new, so yes, we can pick up the pace."

"Thank-you, Lord."

"You're welcome, George."

*   *   *

George sat hunched over his office desk, putting pencil to music manuscript paper, swiveling every once in a while with a slight squeak of his chair to the old upright piano beside him, and then back again to his page, playing or humming or singing, *Jesus Christ is Risen Today.*

"That's better than—what did you call it?—'American folk music'?" said Bach.

"Yes. 'John Henry'."

Bach pointed at the screen. "Sounds like you're hard at work on another descant."

George nodded.

George worked.

"Hmmm . . . interesting: a rising phrase to match the text: good word painting."

"Thanks."

"You're welcome." Bach supplied a running commentary: "Ahhhh . . . the 'alleluia' will . . . fall . . . yes, and the next phrase will rise as the first one did, this time a little higher, up to the high 'A', in fact—nosebleed territory for the sopranos."

"How did you know?"

"I know harmony, I know counterpoint, and I know *you*. Ah, there we are," said Bach, smiling, as George's vocalizations produced the predicted 'A'.

*　　*　　*

One of the seraphim fluttered up from the back row to whisper in Jesus' ear, turned with a smile to George, and then fluttered gracefully back again.

"They think you look a little like a cherub, George," said Jesus, pointing to the screen. "That's high praise from them, professional 'praisers' that they are."

Head down on his desk, George snored, apparently like a cherub.

"Dreaming, perhaps? Vhat about a little look see?"

"No!"

*　　*　　*

"They're waiting for you." Brian Tyler gently shook George's shoulder. "The choir . . . they're *waiting* for you."

"Huh?"

"It's Thursday, George. Thursday, as in 'choir night in Canada', and three days before Easter, the last rehearsal before the big day, and they're all in their pews. Come *on*."

"Coming," George answered groggily.

"What were you dreaming about *this* time?"

"Same one."

"Same one as what?"

"You don't want to know."

"*Ve* do," said Freud, indicating himself and the dead psychiatrists in the back of the theater, who nodded in unison.

"No."

"Just a hint?"

"Some . . . dumb dream I have sometimes. That's all."

"Ja? A recurring dream? Vhen did it start?"

"I don't know. When I was a kid, I guess."

"George! A recurring dream? Und a recurring dream from *childhood*, reappearing under stressful conditions later in life. Ze significance!"

"No!"

"*Nein?*"

"Nein!"

"Ja," Freud sighed, "*nein*."

Tyler also sighed. "You're starting to make a habit of this. Get some sleep, will you? At *night?*"

"Too many late nights?" Bach asked.

"Yes, and I still wasn't quite finished."

"Not surprising. *Did* you finish?"

"Yes. I finished it, and it finished me."

* * *

"George! I demand to be moved."

"But I thought you'd sat there forever, Mona, and you wanted to stay there."

"That was before. I want to move *now*."

"What she means is that there's no point in sitting there now that Molly isn't coming anymore, and she's in need of another alto to lean on," George explained

Much to everyone's surprise, on both sides of the screen, George, more from being too depressed to care rather than from any other consideration, answered Mona with one word: "Okay."

*   *   *

Rehearsal over, George took the bottom step, and turned to the music library, where choir members left their music folders. "I was hoping to see Kathy. In fact, I really wanted to see her."

Just inside the door, they came face to face. Before his mouth could fully open, she uttered a hushed "Hi", and side-stepped him, leaving him speechless, managing, finally, to mumble a mildly embarrassed "Hi" to her retreating back.

*   *   *

Halfway up the aisle to the chancel, George saw her. A few steps later, she saw him as she got up from the semi-darkness of one of the pews where she had, evidently, been at prayer. Caught in each other's gaze, there was a slight stiffening, and the barest hint of a slowing on both their parts.

For the first time, he felt a sense of sympathy for her.

As they neared, she turned her head, and said, with only enough brusqueness to maintain her equilibrium, "Good evening, George."

George answered, "Good evening, Molly."

*   *   *

"George!"

"Yes, Billy?"

"I can't do this . . . up!" William, the youngest member of the children's choir, was having trouble with his choir gown.

"You can't?"

"No! It's too . . . *much* for me!"

"I know just how you feel, Billy. I know just how you feel."

*   *   *

"*(Curly, Larry and Moe,)*" thought George, as Ben Smiley, Rob Taylor and David North entered through the forbidden "secret" panel for the *n*th time—George had lost count. He decided to keep playing, not wanting to interrupt what had actually been a decent start to the anthem on the sopranos' part, not for the likes of *those* idiots. Rather than quickly and wordlessly fish out their music and drift into the singing smoothly, they were on the edge of whispered hysterics as they shuffled sheets of music noisily, and only half-swallowed their laughter.

After half a page of this, with only Ben Smiley managing to find a correct note, their behavior had been sufficiently distracting that the girls lost their focus, and the challenging counterpoint that should have been developing with the alto entry fluttered down like autumn leaves around them.

The inevitable eruption arrived, delayed only momentarily by George's depression. "What are you clowns *doing* back there!"

The silence filled up quickly with teenage embarrassment and resentment, unvoiced, but palpable, regardless.

George turned his eyes apologetically to Jesus, looking for understanding. "My nerves . . . my nerves were rubbed *raw*."

"I know."

In the chancel, George continued, "It's not enough that you're late—oh no! You can't manage to find your own notes because you're too busy feeling that you're somehow tremendously amusing, and as if *that* weren't enough, you have to mess up what *we're* trying to do."

'   George shook. He stared at them long and hard, his lips twitching, plainly on the edge of further invective.

"Don't say it, George," said Bach.

The chancel being out of range of Bach's good advice by virtue of both time and space, George took a deep breath and opened his mouth.

Freud shook his head. "You'll be *sor—ry.*"

"I'm sure the girls are *not* impressed."

"Ouch," said Cecilia.

"I shouldn't have said that to them."

"You're right," said Jesus. "And *that*, by the way, was 'the last nail in your coffin.'"

Chapter, the Fifty-First:

Safe . . . but Just

"Why so late?"

"Oh, I have my reasons," said George, obviously enjoying himself despite his accumulated fatigue, creating an air of mystery around Jimmy's visit.

Jimmy, just as obviously, was in no mood for it. "George, it's Easter weekend. Every church wants its organ tuned. I've tuned three of them today, already. You insisted on having me arrive at nine o'clock at night for God knows what reason, and I have a family waiting for me at home."

"Sorry, Jimmy. I had no choice. You'll see why."

"Okay," Jimmy said wearily. "Let's get on with it."

Reaching the chancel, George went for the organ console, and Jimmy for the pipe room nearest to it—their usual routine for a tuning.

"George!" Jimmy exclaimed through the grille cloth. "What have you *done* in here?"

George headed for the pipe room. "What *haven't* I done?" he said, entering.

Together, they surveyed the ceiling.

"That's grille cloth!" said Jimmy. "On the ceiling! Tell me it's just . . . decoration or something."

"I can tell you anything you want me to tell you."

Jimmy craned this way and that, trying to see through the mesh until his eyes adjusted sufficiently to barely discern some sense of depth and shadow behind it.

"George," he repeated heavily, "what have you *done?*"

George shrugged. "Added a few pipes."

"A *few?*"

"Well, maybe a few more than a few."

Jimmy couldn't take his eyes off the ceiling. "You did hint at this last time, didn't you?"

George nodded.

"I never thought you'd actually go through with it!"

"Neither did I, but one thing led to another."

"I'll say it did! At least tell me that you didn't do anything structural; tell me that, at least."

"Well, not too much."

"What?"

"A few two by fours."

"A 'few'? How do we get up there?"

"This way."

*   *   *

George stood with Jimmy, ready to unlock the door to the church attic, off the stairs from the rear gallery, when he stopped. "Jimmy, do organ tuners take any sort of oath?"

"You mean like doctors or priests or lawyers? About secrecy or something?"

"Yes."

"Not that I remember."

"Well, I want you to take one now."

"What's on the other side of that door, George?"

"First, the oath."

"I like that," said Shakespeare.

"I don't know if I can do that, George. I don't know."

"Swear by his pipes," the Bard whispered, committing it to paper.

"Jimmy, this *has* to be a secret."

"I don't know. You're not the one who pays me, even. I don't know."

"Okay, okay, till Sunday afternoon, that's all I need. Just keep it to yourself until Sunday afternoon. It won't matter after that: everyone will know what I've done by then anyway."

Jimmy sighed, not once but twice. "Okay, George, if you say so."

"Swear?"

"Swear."

The door creaked open, and George threw the light switch, taking Jimmy's breath away.

"My God, George! It's like a second organ up here. Just look at it!" Jimmy didn't move for a long time. "Alright," he said finally. Let's have a look at it, then."

*   *   *

"Very impressive, George. I see that you've emphasized the higher partials."

"What else would you expect in the ceiling?"

"True." Jimmy thought it over for a moment. "Then . . . aren't the lower partials *under*-represented?"

"No."

"Then . . . where are *they*? Or should I be asking?"

"Only if you're prepared to reaffirm your oath."

"You can't mean . . ."

"I can."

Jimmy's eyes narrowed to slits as he struggled with the clues. "That grille cloth! That grille cloth . . . at the *back* of the pipe rooms . . . by the *floor* . . . but how? *How?*"

"This way."

*   *   *

George could not have been more mysterious, nor Jimmy more in awe, if they had been the first ones to enter King Tutankhamun's secret burial chamber.

Jimmy was left framed in the doorway of the basement pipe room, his eyes darting continually up, down, and sideways, nodding and shaking his head, absorbed in his own inner debate over the possibility of what he was seeing.

"So what do you think?" George asked.

"I think I need to sit down," said Jimmy, which he did, on the nearest available object: a wind reservoir. "It's certainly a piece of work. Say, this wind reservoir's pretty large for the number of pipes, isn't it?"

"I need to overdrive them a bit, given the route the sound has to go."

"Same in the attic?"

George nodded slowly.

"Where are you getting the power?"

"Rolls Royce jet engines," George deadpanned, then smiled. "The usual, but connected in series rather than in parallel where needed, which is just about everywhere except the original pipe rooms."

"What about the vibration?"

"Damped by anchoring to the structural supports."

"With overdriven wind chests? Any structural strain?"

"Not too much."

"That's where you have to be careful, then, George."

"Don't worry, I've done my calculations, so to speak."

"But have you eyeballed it with someone at the console?"

"That's what *you're* here for, after the tuning of course."

"How many pipes are we talking?"

"I lost count."

"I'd better write to my wife."

*   *   *

"Lord thundering Jesus!" Jimmy exclaimed, bursting up from the basement.

"That's kinda catchy," said Jesus.

George sat at the console.

Jimmy was giddy. "I've never seen anything like it! And it's a *hell* of a sound."

"*That* I'm not too fussy about."

"He only meant—"

"I know what he meant."

Muted giggles from the back of the Paradise—stony lack of reaction from the front.

"The sound, the sound! It's astounding. The music of the bloody *spheres*. There's, there's no *words*. The congregation won't know what hit them!"

"Oi!"

"But George!"

"Yes, Jimmy?"

"You've hit the max. You're getting some vibration in the beams up there in the attic: they're bearing more of the load since you took out those two by fours. And that strip of supporting concrete you've left at the feet of those columns in the basement pipe rooms couldn't be any narrower."

"It *is* safe, though," George insisted.

"Yes," Jimmy agreed, "but just. A few more pounds per square inch of wind pressure, a little more vibration, and . . . I don't know. I've never dealt with anything like this."

"Neither have I."

"There's a lot of weight resting there, George."

"I know."

"Whatever you do, don't increase the wind pressure any more, or I don't know *what* will happen."

"I won't."

"Even overweighting the tops of the wind reservoirs could be disastrous."

"Don't worry. No problem. The central wind reservoir is upstairs next to my office, and I keep a careful eye on it; the others are all under lock and key."

"Good," said Jimmy. "If you put too much weight on top . . ."

"I know, I know: if enough air is called for by sufficient notes and ranks being engaged, like big chords on full organ, for instance, and the weight is too great, not enough air will spill out the top, the pressure to the pipes will be too great, and the vibrations might be strong enough to threaten the integrity of certain parts of the structure—"

"Which is a fancy way of saying that things could fall on people's heads . . . *big* things."

Chapter, the Fifty-Second:

Ready or Not

George dropped to his knees in the warm darkness of the chapel.

"*(That's it; done: the last pipe set and tuned, the music written and rehearsed . . . I'm ready . . . as a musician, at least.)*

"*(I'm so tired . . . so, so tired. I'm disappointed in everything . . . I . . . I'm so disappointed . . . in . . . myself.)*"

George huddled in his pew, suddenly feeling the hint of a chill. He rose, stepped into the aisle, and walked to the front. Facing the altar, he fell again to his knees.

"*(Now it's Easter . . . in a few hours. With everything I've done, I may save my job. And the organ, the organ! That will blow them away! But so what? I thought that if I was the problem, then I could be the solution, but it certainly hasn't worked out that way.)*

"*(I lost Kathy . . .)*

"*(I wanted this Easter to be . . . I wanted my life to be . . . different. I don't know exactly how I wanted my life to be, but I did want my life to work; I wanted to heal myself and my relationships and . . . and . . . but how? I try to fight the depression . . . but I don't know how to anymore . . .)*

"*(Lord, please help me . . . and . . . and . . . Our Father, which art in Heaven, hallowed be thy name . . .)*"

Chapter, the Fifty-Third:

The Big Day

For most of the members of the congregation at St. Christopher's United Church, Holy week consisted solely of Easter Sunday. A few of them went to the Good Friday service, but it was such an embarrassingly low turnout that it was held in the chapel rather than in the church. Fewer still had even heard of Easter vigil, and would have chosen to spend their Saturday night otherwise, regardless. Maundy Thursday simply did not exist. For most of the congregation, Jesus, in effect, rose from the dead without ever having died.

Easter weekend was following the expected pattern in all respects, right down to the weather. Good Friday was dark and stormy; Holy Saturday dry, but windy and unsettled, brooding; Easter Sunday dawned gloriously sunny but for a low bank of gray cloud flecked with daffodil yellow from which the sun was emerging as George rounded the final corner to the church.

The steeple seemed to pierce the sky, as George approached the church and viewed it from the perspective of St. Christopher's big, front double doors.

Just inside, Rev. Dawson greeted him. "Beautiful Easter Sunday, isn't it, George?"

"It certainly is, Reverend Dawson. Are you the first one here?"

Dawson smiled. "Always am. You appear to be the second. Good for you! Lots to do, eh?"

"You can say that again."

"Sometimes I think we don't fully appreciate what the organist does."

"I think that often," said George with a weary smile.

Dawson nodded thoughtfully, first contemplating some sort of appropriate pastoral response, then deciding that another occasion, one when George's time was less spoken for, might be better suited to the purpose. "Carry on then."

George headed into the church, slowed as he passed the chapel doors, and hurried to his office to prepare for the most important day of his career, and of his life; indeed, his *lives*: this one *and* the next.

Chapter, the Fifty-Fourth:

Several Pairs of Feet on the Stairs.

George was gathering up music from his desk when he heard voices from the door to the pipe room opposite his office. "Come on!" someone whispered with all the intensely of a commando leader behind enemy lines, followed by the sound of several pairs of feet on the stairs. George stopped and went out, followed closely by Bernie, first looking down the empty stairs, then heading into the pipe room.

"I think we need some narration here, George."

"I thought I'd recognized David North's voice."

"Ze young fellow zat you embarrassed in front of ze girls, along viz his two friends?"

"That's the one. I thought at first that they were just cutting through the pipe room again, but then it dawned on me that they only did that coming to rehearsal, going *up* the stairs, never going *down* the stairs on a Sunday morning. Usually, even *I* wasn't there that early."

"So what vere zey up to?"

"They had removed the weights from the main wind reservoir, the one that fed all the others. Not only that, they had taken the weights with them—disappeared! I had to get them back."

"Vhy is zat, exactly?"

"The air reservoir," George explained, "is essentially a big box with a free-floating, weighted lid to regulate the wind pressure going to the pipes. If a few notes are being played through only a rank or two of pipes, for instance, little air pressure is called for, so most of the pressure spills out the top of the air reservoir, holding the weighted lid higher. If *many* pipes are sounding, *much* air pressure is called for, so the lid sinks, having little air pressure to hold it up."

"Ja, I see," said Freud, sounding, however, a little less than certain.

"Try this, then: weighting the lid on the wind reservoir regulates the air pressure; the greater the weight on the lid, the greater the air pressure to the pipes. If it's too little, the tone is weak; if it's too great—not a problem at *that* moment—the sound will be harsh, and the supporting structure might not like all the vibration from the increased airflow; it could even be dangerous after I'd removed some of the wood, and dug up the floor. That's what Jimmy had been worried about."

"Ja, gut."

"I had to get those weights back, and I couldn't. I looked everywhere and asked everybody. North and his two friends were nowhere to be found; no-one had seen them, either, but I knew it was them. In the end, I was left back in the pipe room with no weights and no clue what to do beyond finding a substitute of some sort, but what? It had to be the right weight. I tried several things, but it was no good: they were either too light, too heavy, or too awkward, until—"

"Woof!"

"Ja, George? You veighted ze vind reservoir viz your dog?!"

George nodded, smiling, obviously pleased with his ingenuity.

"Up, Bernie!"

"Woof?" Bernie obeyed, but without enthusiasm.

"Stay."

Sitting atop the main wind reservoir, head tilting this way and that, Bernie looked doubtful in the extreme.

Sitting at George's feet in the theater, Bernie, looking more than doubtful, covered his eyes with one of his enormous paws.

Chapter, the Fifty-Fifth:

Final Cadence

The first eight notes of the Easter hymn *Jesus Christ is Risen Today* floated softly, almost subliminally out of the quietest rank of pipes in the echo organ at the rear of the church, behind the congregation. Then, George shifted to the swell organ at the front of the church, repeated the opening motif and walked it through a variety of positions in the scale, playing it on a modestly expanding combinations of pipes. This formed a pastel counterpoint against which the full hymn tune emerged at half tempo in a masculine-sounding solo rank of pipes on the great organ: the unhurried rising of the sun out of the mists.

The organ prelude had begun.

"It's beautiful," said Jesus, with Bach and others agreeing as it grew in richness and power.

"I wanted to hint at the Resurrection: the moment, its arrival, not in some blinding flash but with the gradually quickening from within, first in wisps across the threshold of nothingness into being, then in gathering currents, and finally in torrents: the miracle of life returning out of death."

And Jesus marveled.

The improvisation grew in precisely the manner that George had described it, until the triumphant tune sounded in full organ, or at least full organ in the usual sense of the term: the full number of pipes that were housed on the ground floor; the rest, both above and below, being reserved for the appropriate moment later in the service.

A series of softer reflections from the organ followed, forming a slow, terraced, decrescendo arc, returning almost to the subliminality from which it had come. Seeing the choir and the rest of the chancel party spread out in readiness across the back of the church in the small mirror that always sat atop the organ console for precisely that purpose, George ended the prelude in a modestly ornamented plagal cadence and awaited the call to worship.

Wes Smallwood, chairman of the lay readers committee—for everything, there was a committee in the United Church—approached the lectern,. "Please turn to hymn number three hundred and fifty-seven. Let us approach the temple of the Lord, and render worship unto Him."

George played the last phrase of the processional hymn, left two beats rest, and began the verse, leading the choir, clergy and congregation in the hymn *Jesus Christ is Risen Today*.

As the choir processed up the main aisle of St. Christopher's United Church, subtle changes in the appearance of what was happening on screen became evident to the theater audience. The perspective shifted to the first two choristers, who were leading the processional party towards the chancel. Then the angle drifted lower so that the pews they were passing on either side appeared to grow higher, then further apart: two great walls of wood metamorphosing into water pluming high in the air above their heads, with the dry land beneath their feet.

"What's *that*?!" said George. "The parting of the Red Sea or something?"

"Looks like it, doesn't it?" Jesus agreed.

"What's next? Pharaoh's army pursuing the choir up the center aisle of St. Christopher's?" George turned and glared at the projection booth. "Who's *doing* that?"

Jesus smiled apologetically. "Cecil B. DeMille. His name was in the opening credits, you may recall. There is no-one better in Heaven for religious cinema. I told him that I wanted a docudrama. It would appear that he is emphasizing the 'drama' side of things over the 'docu'."

Jesus closed His eyes, and the fountains of the deep receded, allowing the reappearance of church carpeting and choir pews, as human proportion and perspective returned.

An older gentleman hurried down the aisle of the theater from the back and stood beside Jesus. "I *am* sorry, Lord. The Old Testament reading this Sunday is of the Israelites passing through the Red Sea, I remembered something that I had once done, and I got a little carried away."

"Yes, you did," said Jesus, but with a smile of understanding. "Now, more 'docu', less 'drama'. There's more than enough 'drama' in the 'docu' anyway. George has seen to that."

"Yes, Lord," said DeMille, who smiled quickly at George, and returned to the rear.

The church, meanwhile, had grown darker, the daylight fading while the electrical light remained constant. For any theater patron who had failed to notice the transformation, there were shots of the clouds gathering at various altitudes outside St. Christopher's United, including a bevy of great thunderheads directly above.

The choir and congregation settled into the second verse when there was a resounding crash of thunder, cracking and rolling off into the distance in its reverberation. The congregation became suddenly more erect, and their singing considerably louder than it had been moments before.

"I remember that!" said George.

"I'm sure you do," said St. Cecilia, smiling.

"*You* did that?"

"I helped," she beamed. "The thunder head was close by. It would have released its energy sooner or later."

"Never had I heard such singing at St. Christopher's United Church," said George.

Jesus smiled. "They probably thought that God Himself was knocking at the church doors."

"That would have been something," George said.

"Not necessary, though," said Jesus. "We were already inside."

"You *were?*"

"We're at every church service, George." Jesus laughed. "One day, perhaps, We should simply appear in the chancel, deus ex machina, so to speak,"—He nodded to Shakespeare—"and say, 'Good morning, everyone! Surprised? Why? Didn't you come to see Us? Well? Here We are!'"

"That *would* be something."

"Perhaps it's time that We did it. Straighten out a few misunderstandings while We're at it . . . it's tempting."

The choir and clergy had, by now, made their way to the chancel where the singing continued, the sopranos adding George' new descant to the last verse, soaring in rising phrases above the choir and organ, brass and tympani joining in, the first trumpet doubling their descant.

When the hymn's final chord had echoed away, Rev. Parker declared, "The Lord is risen."

"He is risen indeed," the congregation answered, reading their response from the service bulletin.

Completing what, in the United Church, amounted to a grand liturgical event, the choir sang, "Alleluia", and everyone sat down.

Rev. Parker continued. "Jesus said, 'I am the resurrection and the life; he that believes in me, though he die, yet shall he live, and whoever lives and believes in me shall never die.'"

"That is exactly what I said," Jesus agreed.

"Let us confess our sins to Almighty God . . ."

The congregation of St. Christopher's United gave heartfelt voice to their manifold sins and wickedness. After the formulas for all the most popular sins were read aloud from the green service book, Reverend Parker invited his parishioners to make a personal confession to God, presumably to make certain than none of the more creative sinning was omitted. The choir solemnized their confession by singing the litany, "Lord have Mercy. Christ have mercy. Lord have mercy."

"Now let us be comforted and be glad," Parker continued, "and hear the Good News: God so loved world that He gave his only Son, that whoever believes in him should not perish but have eternal life. Let us pray . . ."

"When are we going to hear your organ modifications?" said Bach.

"In the Handel."

"Why did you wait till then?"

"I considered using them as early as the prelude, but I thought that it might be too distracting for people to hear music coming from the ceiling at such an essentially meditative time. I preferred to wait for a big moment."

"You got zat!"

"I know, I know." George's left eyelid began to twitch.

Lessons were read, prayers were made, psalms were intoned, and hymns were sung. The Israelites escaped their Egyptian pursuers while Cecil B. DeMille sat on his hands, St. Paul admonished the brethren with the conviction that comes from personal revelation and the raw fervor of the converted, and Jesus Christ rose from the dead, all for the benefit of the Easter Congregation at St. Christopher's United Church.

Parker stood. "As you may know, we have a visitor with us, today: the Moderator of the United Church of Canada, Ms. Sarah Dey."

In the congregation, there was much turning of heads and craning of necks.

"Welcome," Parker added, nodding in her direction.

Sarah Dey, Moderator of the United Church of Canada, beamed her pleasure, nodding with unfeigned enthusiasm.

"Along with her widely acknowledged administrative and leadership abilities," Parker continued, "she is an inspired and insightful homilist, and so we are indeed privileged that, as part of her visit with us today, she has agreed to preach the sermon. Ms. Dey?"

Ms. Dey mounted the steps to the pulpit amid much thoughtful nodding and whispered acknowledgement of the event from all directions.

"Sarah?" said Freud. "I zought you said zat ze Moderator vas like a—vhat did you say?—United pope, ja? Zey have female popes?"

"And what would be wrong with that?" Cecilia asked.

"Nozing. I just vondered. Ve didn't have zem in my day."

"We still don't," George explained, "at least not the Catholics, but the United Church of Canada does. Not only that, but the Moderator can be a lay person like Ms. Dey. The requirement that he or she had to be a member of the clergy was dropped years ago."

"Good morning," Ms. Dey said brightly.

"Good morning," the congregation responded, a little less leadenly than was its custom.

"Thank you for your kind introduction, Rev. Parker. What he did not tell you is that some years ago, he loaned me a copy of the textbook on homiletics that he uses to teach that subject to candidates for the ministry at Queen's University, and so, in a very real sense, everything I know, I learned from him. I keep promising him that I will return the book."

This was generally considered to be amusing.

"I bring you greetings from United Church headquarters where your contributions to the Church, both financial and pastoral, are most gratefully received."

"Which is why we were privileged with her presence," George offered.

"True enough," said Jesus.

"It is my great pleasure to be with you this morning, and I am especially honored to have been asked to preach the Gospel this Easter Sunday. When I looked over the scriptures for today to choose my text, I was struck immediately and immensely by the role that women played in two of them."

"Here we go." George sighed.

"Shh," said Cecilia. "I want to hear this."

"It's an old joke," Ms. Dey began: "When God created man, She was only kidding." Scattered titters arose, mostly, if not entirely, female. "I wouldn't go *that* far, of course."

"That's good, at least," George muttered.

"Miriam, high priestess of the Israelites, sister to Moses and Aaron, danced and sang the victory of God over the Egyptians in the oldest known passage of the Bible. Why is she such a neglected figure now?"

"As if they'd stood a chance," George muttered.

"A little one-sided once Dad rolled up His sleeves," Jesus agreed, "but they were really asking for it."

"And 'The three Marys' were intimately bound up, in one way or another (depending on the particular Gospel writer), with the life, the death, and, in what we're most concerned with today, the resurrection of our Lord, Jesus Christ."

"Good friends, one and all," said Jesus.

"They went to wash His body," the Moderator continued, "and they were the first witnesses, after the angels, to the empty tomb and to the Risen Lord, Himself, the male disciples having scattered in fear and doubt. One wonders, given that the devotion of these women was so great and the fact that they were so favored by Jesus, why don't we hear more about them now?"

We're about to, thought George.

"You seem to be getting a little restless zere."

"I was. My career was on the line, and I had to listen to an hour of feminist Bible diatribe."

"Und vhat are you doing up zere now?"

"What no organist at St. Christopher's United had done in twenty years, I was told."

"Vhat's zat?"

"Walking out on the sermon."

"It bozered you zat much?"

"No."

"Vhat zen?"

"I got so nervous, I had to go to the bathroom."

*   *   *

George went into one of the washroom stalls.

Ben Smiley emerged from one of the others and fell immediately to washing his hands.

Humming emerged from George's stall, punctuated by the odd snatch of lyric.

Ben froze for a moment, then made for the door on tip-toe.

"My turn to narrate," said Jesus. "Ben Smiley was taken of the urge, so to speak, at about the same time you were. Now here, he has just recognized your voice, and guess what he is feeling?"

"Fear and loathing?"

"No. That would be his two friends, Taylor and North. Freed from their influence, he is experiencing something quite different: guilt. At first, he doesn't know what to do with it. What he finally settles on is this: he returns to the scene of the crime . . . see?"

Ben Smiley was heading for the pipe room, just as Jesus had said. And as he opened the door, Bernie, who had been less than thrilled about being perched atop the wind reservoir in the first place, hopped down and stood, tail wagging, tongue at the ready.

Smiley Jr. responded with the only useful word, among various other one-syllable possibilities, that occurred to him: "Sit."

Bernie sat, hoping by all rights for some form of reward. Instead, he was treated to the sight of Ben Smiley's back, as the guilty teen went to the far corner, began fishing the "missing" weights behind a temporary work table that George had been using, and replaced them, one by one, on top of the wind reservoir.

"Oh, my God!" said George. "So *that's* what happened!"

"It gets even more involved," said Jesus. "Ben Smiley, having finished replacing the weights, gives Bernie a quick pat, and then leaves quickly, fearing discovery. Notice, if you will, the door—slightly ajar. Now, Bernie, thus encouraged, heads for the door, and after a little clever paw work . . . there . . . gets it open, and looks around for some attention, which he finally receives . . . from . . . you."

"Oh, no!"

"Oh, yes!"

"Bernie! What are you doing out here? How did you get the door open?"

Much nuzzling and waggings of tail. Finally, some attention! "Get back in there. You'll ruin everything!"

"Now," Jesus resumed, "Bernie, dutifully but not joyfully, goes back into the pipe room and resumes his post with a little paw dragging and other forms of passive resistance, including some not altogether unexpected whining."

Said whining was heard in the theater, both from the sound system and from the original whiner, now ensconced tightly at George's feet, with no wish to see the morning's events unfold afresh. Watching the screen, Bernie saw, understood (after the fashion of dogs), and again covered his eyes, this time with both of his great paws.

"Of course, you were in too much of a hurry to notice that the weights had been replaced," Jesus observed.

George's voice sank to a whisper. "Yes . . . and then there was too much weight on the lid of the main wind reservoir . . . and so the wind pressure was too high . . . and the vibrations would put *such* a strain on the structure . . . *exactly* what Jimmy was afraid of."

*   *   *

"And you missed a fine sermon."

"I did?"

"Truly."

"But all that feminist—"

"Pain, George, pain, all that feminist pain, but she didn't get stuck there, which is what you were afraid of. She moved on, and she preached a fine sermon. Here, let's listen to the end of it, at least."

"Men and women are different," said Dey, "beyond the obvious physical differences. And I hope it will not be thought sexist of me to say so, but the concerns of men and women are also different. Their experiences and perceptions of life are different, and no amount of education, no amount of affirmative action, and certainly no amount of wishful thinking will ever change that. And do you know what I say to that? I say . . . 'Thank God.'"

"You're welcome," said Jesus, signaling for the film to pause, freeze-framed on Ms. Dey's thankful face. "She figured it out. She understands it, and you need to understand it, too."

"Understand what?" said George.

"When Man was created—'male and female created He them', remember?—woman was placed closer to the mystery of life, by virtue of her role in the giving of life, if nothing else—and there is much else. That is why I saw Mary and the others first. They *came* first, because they understand life and death in a way that men do not, and that affects everything they do throughout their whole lives, which is a goodly part of why you have such trouble understanding them."

"Kathy?"

"Yes, Kathy . . . and Molly, too."

"Molly, *too*?" George asked in rising panic.

"Yes, Molly too!" Jesus laughed. "You don't have to *kiss* her, George, just *understand* her. And listen to Sarah Dey! She knows more than you give her credit for. She's not some rabid feminist. She heard the message that I left mankind through Mary Magdalene and the others, and she is repeating it faithfully."

"What's that?"

"That men and women need to learn to listen to each other more, to learn *how* to listen. And now is a good time for you to start." Jesus signaled for the film to resume.

George listened to Ms. Dey.

"Mary and Peter needed each other," said Dey, "just as men and women everywhere do. It was Mary who was the first to experience the mystery and the wonder of the resurrection, and she communicated it to Peter, who started the wheels turning in the early Christian community. They each, with their own ways of understanding and doing, needed the other, and so do we, and the good news is that we are learning more and more to get to know each other better, and more importantly *how* to do that, and not just through husbands taking furtive peeks at their wives' copies of *Men are from Mars, Women are from Venus*."

There was scattered squirming (largely male) and snickering (largely female), reflecting the reality of what she had said.

"And so, this Easter Sunday," Ms. Dey concluded, "We celebrate not only the reality that Jesus rose from the dead, and the new and abundant life that He thereby gave us, but the manner in which He let us know of His gift to us, passed down in this truly 'Good Book' for almost two thousand years, for those who have 'ears to hear' and 'eyes to see', in what happened between Mary and Peter so long ago, that we might see that the unfolding of life's deepest mysteries requires both men and women together, sharing, each with their own unique perspectives, gifts, and connections to life. For this we give thanks to God. Let us pray . . ."

*   *   *

George slipped noiselessly back onto the organ bench.

"The offering will now be taken," said Parker.

George played a few quiet phrases to set the key and the mood, then signaled the choir to rise.

The "Amen" chorus from Handel's *Messiah* began with quiet energy. George's instrumental introduction on the organ was articulated smoothly and precisely, the choral entries were confident, and the music built in waves through the choral fugato, punctuated and augmented by brass and tympani, to its final stretti of overlapping phrases, and the last triumphant cadence, with more pipes and voices than had ever been heard at St. Christopher's United.

There was a moment of stunned silence in all quarters, even George's, after the final chord had finished echoing off the plaster walls of the chancel and throughout the building. George signaled for the choir to sit.

He began his improvisation. Here, it was his intention to finally "pull out all the stops". He began in the same manner as the prelude, upon a single rank of the echo organ at the rear of the church, but made it build more quickly, bringing in other ranks of pipes, before taking advantage of his new modifications, adding, for the first time, some of the pipes in the attic, starting with those furthest from the chancel, then others closer and closer, the congregation becoming aware, in various degrees of astonishment, of having the music ripple across the ceiling.

The resulting waves of gathering phrases washed up to the chancel, rising in glorious crescendo to form the accompaniment for the main theme, newly stated in the bass, growling its way up from the basement, causing members of choir, clergy and congregation to look up, down and sideways, seeking the multiple sources of the rapidly expanding riot of timbres.

The virtuosic choreography of George's hands and feet created fresh counterpoints of pitches and tone colors such as had never before been heard at St. Christopher's United Church.

"Astounding," said Bach.

"Okay for twelve semitones, I suppose," George mumbled unenthusiastically.

"For as long as it lasts," Jesus added darkly.

Rank upon rank, the organ multiplied itself amid much wonder and gripping of armrests, prayer books, and pew companions. One of the sidesmen who was taking up the collection simply stopped.

Rev Parker rose when he saw a few flakes of plaster flutter down and settle on the altar.

George became aware of a slight vibration in his bench, but told himself not to be faint of heart. He fought against a vague sense of anxiety, pushed down on the swell pedals, opening the shutters, and hit the foot switch that would bring the last few ranks of pipes into play, to produce full organ in the newest and fullest sense of the word for the final cadence of his inspired improvisation.

And then, a lot of things happened in a very short time . . .

With a determined wave of his head, George signaled for the choir to rise. The congregation responded, as they always did, by rising with them. George held the fullest C major chord of his life, while thanking God for the gift of improvisation. He left a two beat rest—during which, those with the most sensitive hearing heard a sad, muffled "woo-oof"—and brought in choir, congregation, brass, and tympani, with full organ:

Praise God from whom all blessings flow . . .

There was not a single soul in the building who was not keenly aware, in one way or another, that this was an experience that he or she had never had before. Reverend Parker, remembering a detail that he hoped he had attended to in the placement of various items on the altar, noticed a few more grains of plaster landing on the open service book before him. George noticed that the tone of the organ was a touch more strident than he had anticipated, as if the wind pressure were higher than it should be, as if Bernie was, in fact, a little heavier than the missing weights that he had replaced . . . maybe a *lot* heavier. And the vibration reaching him through the organ bench had markedly increased.

Praise Him all creatures here below . . .

And praise Him they did, many of them finding their voices as never before, a few in the chancel now sensing a vibration through the soles of their feet, one or two shifting their weight in an unconscious effort to rid themselves of it.

Praise Him above, ye heavenly host . . .

The falling of plaster continued, then increased, not just Rev. Parker, but various members of the chancel party (with the curious exception of George) experiencing some degree or other of fallout.

Praise Father, Son, and Holy Ghost . . .

In the space of a few beats, the rain of plaster increased further, first to chunks, then to slabs, and then the plaster was accompanied by beams of wood as the vibrations increased beyond the capacity of the structure to bear them, choking off the final statement of faith as the weight of the descending superstructure caused the floor to give way, the thin concrete borders in the basement pipe rooms to crack and fall into the pipe wells, and the columns to tumble, burying the final

A-meh—

Chapter, the Fifty-Sixth:

The Fellow in the Back

The Odeon Paradise was filled with leaden silence, except for the fellow in the back of the theater, the one whom Peter had been muttering about for some time now. In fact, the fellow in the back was being unceremoniously borne towards the exit, babbling and cackling, by four burly angels.

"Dead, dead, all dead! Hee-ee, hee-hee, heeee-hee-heeeee!"

"Who is *that*?" George did not appreciate *anyone* laughing at his death.

"Satan," Jesus answered matter-of-factly, as he signaled the projectionist to stop the movie.

"*Satan*?!"

Satan's exultation was approaching the delirious. "Ha! Hee! Hahhh, hee, hee, heeeeeeeeeee-hee, hee, hee, haaaaaaaaaaaaaaaah—die, die, die, die, dieeeeeeeeeee!"

"That's who was being discussed so calmly? *Satan*?"

"Yes," said Jesus, as matter-of-factly as before, raising his voice only enough to be heard through Satan's unholy racket. "Peter does not appreciate his presence, as you may have gathered."

St. Peter nodded grimly, his reasons for feeling as he did now abundantly clear.

"So why is he here, then? Why is Satan in Heaven . . . at *my* movie? And why is he laughing? And like . . . *that*."

"*That*" was a continuing wonder. If nothing else could be said of him, Satan certainly knew how to enjoy himself.

"I'm *dying* here! I'm *dying* here!" George erupted, pointing pointedly at the screen, causing only a modest abatement of the demon's merriment.

"Well," Jesus explained, "he *was* a full-time resident here, once upon a time: the brightest of all God's angels, in fact, until he got a little too full of himself—there's a lesson there, George! Now, we let him sneak in every once in a while, and it cheers him up a bit, temporarily at least, to think that he wins one from time to time."

"Wins one? *Wins* one? Me dying is him *winning* one?" Again, George indicated the screen. "*That's* winning one?"

"In his mind, yes. Try to see it from his point of view. It's all an illusion, of course, but it's the best he can hope for, given the way that *he* looks at things."

George's eyes looked as though they were poised to rotate in opposite directions. And he was not prepared to be understanding, not in the least. "Get hIm BacK HeRE NOW!" George demanded, rising from his seat, twisting to the rear, and gesticulating wildly in the general direction of the back exit, which Heavenly security (with Satan hoisted aloft) had almost reached.

Abruptly, the angels who bore the supine form of one vastly amused and highly animated arch-fiend came to a halt, as did everything else in the Odeon Paradise, even Satan's one-man, traveling celebration of mass death in the chancel, at least long enough for him to register a reaction to George's outburst, and to gather his thoughts sufficiently to express them. "Me-ee? Me? Someone wants to speak to . . . meeeeee?"

Satan looked up and twisted his head unnaturally in George's direction. "George!" He grinned. There was nothing quite like death to cheer up Satan, especially when it came coupled with an opportunity for any form of self-expression.

"Careful, George," was the unsolicited advice from many quarters, including the Lord Himself, Who added, "He's a handful, even for Me."

"I am *not* afraid," George replied, moving confidently into the aisle and facing the back of the theater resolutely.

"Then you're in sore need of a second think," said St. Peter.

Jesus touched Peter's sleeve, stilling him.

George advanced steadily toward the rear of the Odeon Paradise as Satan dismounted his perch atop the shoulders of Heavenly security and made his way forward to meet him against the backdrop of fallen timber and plaster that filled the screen.

Softly, it started: first one voice, then two, and then others: loud, louder, and louder still, the chant reverberating in the organist's ears, reaching Super Bowl proportions, pennants inscribed "George" appearing as easily as had the buckets of Paradise Popcorn so many reels earlier, waving all around him: "George! George!! George!!!"

The pounding evocation of his Christian name came to an abrupt but powerful and resonant end as George and Satan stopped a few paces apart, halfway up the center aisle of the Odeon Paradise.

"You're *Satan*?"

Satan looked vaguely like . . . George! . . . but different enough to avoid any undue confusion: taller, heavier, older—not a perfect imitation by any means.

"I am . . . for yoouuuuu," he answered, smiling ingratiatingly.

Satan's attempt at "relating", however, only served to annoy George further.

Peter was about to warn George once again to be careful, but Jesus stopped him and anyone else who was similarly inclined with a thought. Thus, silence provided the aural backdrop for George's moment of truth just as the tableau of death on the screen did its visual.

"When have you ever done anything for me?" he asked the father of lies.

"When? *When*?" The very idea rendered Satan breathlessly incredulous. "*I* led you to the attic; *I* led you to the basement pipe room: *I* taught you to think . . . *big*, and *I* can give you . . . morrrre, *much* more; *I* can give you . . . *anything.* How about an organ as big as a planet? That would give your little friend Frrreud here something to write about! And Herr Bach here a case of terminal organ envy! Ha-ha! How would you like *that*, George?" Satan grinned with the hope of winning the soul of the organist/choirmaster standing before him, right here in the bosom of Heaven, and right under the nose of Jesus!

"I already had an organ," George responded more slowly, sobered, his anger tempered now with sad and bitter remembrance, determined, but controlled, "and it killed me . . . me, Bernie . . . *Kathy* . . . and I don't know *how* many other innocent bystanders . . . people I loved . . . *people.*" George shook his head. "I don't want your organ, Satan. I'll stick to the twelve semitones. Bach was right about them: the rest is only decoration. And to think, I was killed by . . . by the wrapping paper! Now, you offer me a bigger box, with fancier paper, maybe even a few ribbons and bows. No thanks!"

Bach beamed. "Well done, George!"

"Ohhhhh," Satan purred. "I see. Bach is pleeaaasssed with you, is he? Well, of course he is. He just neutralized his chief competition! Why *wouldn't* he be pleased? And, at the same time, he stripped you of all your beloved pipes, and left you with his twelve little semitones . . . so many?" Satan whipped around, pointing an accusing finger. "How very generous of him. He didn't show you what he does with them, though, *did* he? *Did* he? Nooooo-oo, he didn't." Satan paused, his timing that of a prosecuting attorney, before continuing, now oozing warmth and utter selflessness, "I can show you how to write like Bach—*no*, better than Bach, selfish old Bach—pieces as good as his, every day . . . between the coffee and the cornflakes . . . *every* day! How would you like *that?*"

"Only Bach can write like Bach."

"That's what he *wants* you to believe." Satan sneered. "That's what he neeeeds you to believe. That's what he—"

"That's what *I* need to believe, too!"

"Whaaaaat?!"

"I want to write like . . . me. What would it profit me to gain the appearance of his gift and lose the substance of my own?"

"You can have both!" Satan shrieked, suddenly sprouting horns.

"I don't *want* both: I just want to be . . . me."

Satan began to pace, making odd gestures: scratching himself as if he were becoming allergic to George's answers. Then he stopped with a shudder. "Here is something that I know . . . knoooow that you want."

George blinked, and Kathy stood before him, smiling seductively at him, and wearing a very, very low cut dress, her cleavage angled provocatively towards him.

Peter could no longer restrain himself. "The Devil hath power to assume a pleasing shape, George."

"I know," George answered, over his shoulder. "*I* saw Faust. *And* I remember the ending." George looked sadly for a moment at the young woman before him. "You're not Kathy," he answered slowly. "I lost her up there," he said, pointing again, this time as if with his last strength, at the still scene of falling death on the screen. "You may be able to give me her pleasing shape, but you cannot give me *her*, and she's the one that I want; the one that I . . . love. You can't give me Kathy: only *she* can do that."

"Well done," said St. Cecilia.

Then, George remembered a bit of scripture that seemed to fit the situation perfectly, indeed, even as no other words could: "Get thee behind me, Satan!"

And Jesus marveled.

Satan's eyes bulged in rage, as he took a threatening step towards the mere man who had dared to command him.

George stood his ground.

Bernie growled into lumbering action, charging his way up the center aisle, ears flapping and jowls flopping, faster than anyone but Jesus would have thought possible.

"You have no power here, Satan!" Jesus declared. "Be gone!"

Satan snarled, but having a wary eye for the fast advancing canine, sped for the exit, Bernie in hot pursuit, barking wildly, finally stopped short at the door, to watch the Devil run like Hell, presumably in that same direction.

The theater audience broke into wild cheers, popcorn filling the air and pennants waving wildly, a welcome breeze arising courtesy of no less than the Holy Spirit Itself. "Well done, George!" was the most frequent comment being uttered in all the tongues of men and angels!

George made his way back to his seat, exhausted by his close encounter with evil, but surrounded, in the eyes of all those gathered, with no less an aura of glory than a matador in full triumph.

"Come, George," Jesus said to the weary organist. "Rest."

And Jesus led George back to his seat, where he sat down and stared numbly at the screen.

Chapter, the Fifty-Seventh:

A Bright Light at the End of the Tunnel

"Now," said George, with a limp gesture towards the screen, "where were we?"

"In the process of getting you from there to here," Jesus answered gravely. "If you're ready to complete the journey?"

George nodded heavily.

"Roll 'em," said Jesus.

The movie resumed with a slow motion shot, zooming and spiraling in from above, of George's face, open-mouthed in disbelief and a deep sense of betrayal at the great mass of falling death from his own creation.

A long camera shot from the back of the church showed the two huge support columns falling inwards, deflecting off each other and crossing awkwardly, the ceiling and then the roof caving in, and plaster dust rising in a cloud above the chancel before the eyes of the horrified congregation.

In the next shot, George, his soul having separated from his body, surveyed the situation from somewhere above the chancel, looking down on the column that lay across his body, and was then pulled upwards, first slowly, then faster, and then faster still, watching the church grow smaller, until he was caught up into the clouds.

Silence enveloped the theater. Many in the audience were nodding slowly, remembering the details of their own deaths.

The light blue and wispy white of the sky faded to dark gray as George fell through a tunnel for what felt like the longest time.

A low moan rose up in his throat, growing louder in volume and higher in pitch, exhibiting a pronounced musical quality that, under other circumstances, the young church musician might have appreciated.

"Once a musician, always a musician," Bach observed, to the complete agreement of the other musicians present.

George saw a bright light at the end of the tunnel, and as it drew nearer, the falling sensation was transformed into one of rising, rising on a powerful current of air in what struck George as being rather like the inside of a gigantic organ pipe. George's low moan became a surround-sound scream, the light rushed in upon him, and he was blown, cork-like, out of the end of the pipe, and shot upward.

"Look at him go!" one voice declared a few rows back.

"The height!" cried another.

"The distance!" a third enthused.

Shakespeare, absorbed in his art, whispered as he wrote, "He . . . who . . . lives . . . by the pipe . . . shall . . . die . . . by the pipe."

"Can't a guy die in peace?" George asked sadly.

A respectful silence resumed.

Every eye in the theater followed the arc of George's rise and fall through the air, their faces tracing his path up, then down, moving from left to right, stopping motionless and wide-eyed when George landed heavily in a heap, yelling.

A bearded man whom George now knew to be St. Peter looked over the nearby counter . . .

George's raw vocalizations slowly sorted themselves into vowels and consonants, then into syllables, finally coalescing into these, the first coherent words to come out of his mouth:

"JESUS CHRIST!!!"

Jesus arched His eyebrows at George, who grimaced apologetically on behalf of his former self.

"Taking the Lord's name in vain," St. Peter tutted from behind the counter, "is *not* the way to arrive in Heaven."

"Perhaps understandable under the circumstances," the fisherman now allowed, his appreciation of George having grown considerably since witnessing his close encounter with Satan.

"He certainly knows how to make an entrance," Shakespeare remarked.

"He does indeed," Bach agreed.

George took in his surroundings: a bearded man in white robes behind a marble counter . . . several others (some with *wings?*) retreating in the face of his unholy outburst . . . what appeared to be *gates* . . . ?

"Are those, by any chance, made of . . . p-pearl?"

"They are."

"The Pearly Gates?"

"That's right."

"You mean . . . *the* Pearly Gates? Of Heaven? I'm . . . *dead?*

"That you are."

Chapter, the Fifty-Eighth:

Dead

It was all too much for George: dying and then watching it happen all over again in wide screen Technicolor and surround sound. "I'm dead," he moaned from his seat in the theater, lowering his head, allowing it to tilt awkwardly to one side. "I'm *dead*."

"Zere, zere, George, it's not so bad," said Freud.

"Understandable, though," said Jesus. "How often does one die, after all?"

"A coward dies a thousand deaths; a brave man only one," Shakespeare offered.

"That's a comfort," George responded sarcastically.

"Zat vhich does not kill me makes me stronger."

"You said that before. And this *did* kill me."

"Ah, ja. Sorry about zat."

Peter offered, "O death, where is thy sting?"

"Where? *Where?* I'll tell you 'where'. Right in the—"

"Relax, George," said Jesus, "You're among friends."

"Or walking through the pages of Bartlett's quotations! I have a copy of it—*had* a copy of it—you know." George stared morosely at his feet. "Dead! I'm dead! *They're* dead! Kathy, Bernie . . . everyone in the chancel, *aren't* they, and *I* killed them! Killed them all! Jesus, Joseph, and Mary!"

"Yes?"

"Yes?"

"Yes?"

"Oh, God!" George moaned, cradling his head in his hands. "No, no!" he said suddenly, looking around, breathing heavily. "It's just an expression."

"Dad doesn't go to the movies, usually," said Jesus. "You won't be seeing him here."

Even through the numbness of George's shock at reliving his own death, the possibilities inherent in what Jesus had just said sank in. "Won't be seeing him . . . *here*? Somewhere else?"

"Yes."

"I'm going to see God?!"

"You already have, if you want to get technical about it: God the Son you see before you; God the Holy Spirit you have felt. But in the sense that *you* mean it, yes: now you're going to meet Dad, face to Face . . . and to have a good stiff drink!"

"We're going back to . . ."

"Yes, George. We're off to The Cross and Crown! And this time, everyone's invited!"

Chapter, the Fifty-Ninth:

Better Make It a Double

He had a long white beard, hair to match, and long, flowing, white robes. The Man behind the bar turned to George.

"What'll it be, George?"

"Oh, God!"

"Yes," He said matter-of-factly.

George swallowed hard. "Scotch?"

"Coming right up."

"Better make it a double." George looked over at Jesus in rising panic.

"It's alright, George." Jesus smiled reassuringly. "He makes really good drinks."

"Nothing up My sleeve," said God, grinning. He stretched forth His hand, and a double scotch appeared. There you go," He said, sliding George's drink across the counter.

"Dad, this is George; George, this is My Father: God."

"Welcome to My humble establishment. If there's anything you'd like, the Cross and Crown will do its best to provide it for you."

"I think I need to sit down."

"There's a booth right over there."

*   *   *

"Dad likes you," said Jesus.

"He likes everyone, doesn't He?"

"Not when they feel 'His terrible wrath'. That *is* something. You should see it!"

George began to look uncomfortable all over again.

"Relax, George. Here comes Dad, now."

The thought did not relax George in the slightest.

God approached with a tray in His hands, and put drinks on the table for George, Jesus, Saints Peter and Cecilia, Bach, Shakespeare and Freud, then sat Himself down among them.

"George?" asked God. "Why do you keep staring at My beard?"

George started to answer, then caught himself. "You don't know?"

God the Father and God the Son shared a smile.

"*You* tell him, Junior."

"Dad is making conversation. He is also a very good listener."

"Yes. Well . . . I went out with this girl once . . . I met her at a church I played for."

God nodded.

"After a couple of dates, she said she couldn't go out with me anymore because she was a born-again Christian and I wasn't."

"Yes," said God, stroking His beard. "Sometimes, they get a little sticky about that sort of thing."

"*She* certainly did. I said that it shouldn't matter if we believed slightly different things about . . . You know . . . You. We both believed in the same God, after all, even if the details differed a little."

God, a good listener, just as Jesus said He was, nodded thoughtfully as George continued.

"I used the metaphor that I thought God had a white beard, while she thought that He . . . You . . . had a gray beard—and what did it matter, anyway?"

God broke into a grin. "I have a *white* beard. Everyone knows that!"

Everyone, knowing that, laughed . . . except for George.

God tried again, "It was gray once upon a time, but I was younger then."

More laughter . . . George, again, excepted.

"You didn't like My little jokes?"

"No . . . I liked them."

"I know," said God. "They were so funny you forgot to laugh."

"It's not that . . . I guess I'm just a little nervous."

"No need. You're just having a friendly little drink with God."

George raised his glass and attempted a smile.

"That's the spirit!" God looked over George's shoulder, and said, "Actually, *that's* The Spirit over there. He likes the booth in the corner."

George turned to look, but was stopped by God's growing grin. George did laugh a little this time, then checked to make sure it was alright, which of course it was.

"That's better. Now, My Son here tells me that you've been feeling a little low lately. What seems to be the trouble: personal problems?"

George nodded. "Yes. I lost my girlfriend, my job is . . . *was* . . . on the line . . . and I *died*."

"That's quite a list. Sorry about the last one."

"Why? *You* didn't do it."

"No, but it was I who decided that people *would* die in the first place. It's a rough one, I'm sure—that's what my Son tells me. At least you've got it over with, eh? One per customer, isn't that right, Will? For 'the brave man', at least?"

"Forsooth."

"But I can see that something else is bothering you, George. Speak to Me of that."

"Nothing, really . . . I guess. I just thought of that . . . dream . . . I had . . . when I was a kid.

God's eyes narrowed. He nodded in obvious interest.

Shakespeare's eyes opened wider for the same reason.

Freud was on the verge of drooling like one of Pavlov's dogs.

"Vhat vas it?"

"It was . . ."

"Ja?"

"You remember . . ." George told Freud " . . . the recurring dream."

"Jaaaaa, ze recurring dream from childhood zat suddenly reappeared under ze stresses of life at St. Christopher's—jaaaaa, most significant."

"It's . . . a little embarrassing."

"You're among friends," said Jesus.

"Ja!"

George hesitated, pursed his lips, and finally shook his head.

"*Nein?*" And Freud's "nein" was almost a whine. For most of the movie, he had been waiting for such an opportunity, and now, just when he had finally given up hope, it had appeared, only to disappear again.

Jesus caught George's eye, and directed his attention to Freud with a nod of His head. George immediately saw the disappointment that was writ large upon him: real suffering, by Heavenly standards.

And, after a few moments of inner struggle: "Sigmund? I'm going to make you one very happy psychiatrist."

"Ja?!" Freud understood immediately. "Und can ve put it on der kleine—uh, zat little screen over zere?" He indicated the television in the corner.

"Oh . . . well, could I just . . . tell you about it?"

"Sure."

As George composed himself for the telling of his recurring childhood dream, the only sound was the rustling of paper from the notepads of a few dozen other dead but happy psychiatrists seated nearby.

"Okay. When I was a kid—I don't remember exactly when—I had a dream that . . . this is embarrassing . . . that I was . . ."

George took a deep breath, let it out slowly, and then blurted out, "that I was chased out of Heaven," upon which he lowered his chin, which had begun to quiver, and looked around, wounded, defensive.

"Hooh!"

"Somehow, I found myself in Heaven, and it looked very much like the suburbs of Toronto, where I grew up. Everything was just so: the grass was cut, the flowers were blooming, and the white picket fences were all freshly painted. I don't know what I did wrong—something small, I think—but it certainly got a lot of attention—something of the order of cutting through someone's backyard—and then some lady in curlers came out and chased me with a broom!"

"Und you ran?"

"You bet! You should have seen her!"

"Vhat did she look like?!"

"Kinda like . . . like Molly."

"Faaaascinating!"

"I'm not sure how it went from there, but one way or another, I was chased out of Heaven."

Freud slowly put down his pad, nodding in empathy. "Fantastic! Zat, George, vas ze genesis of your neurosis, right zere!"

"It was?"

"Ja. Zink about it: you vere a little boy, lost in Heaven, und for some iddley-fiddley little zing, zey *drove* you out. Ze injustice! Und listen to zis! You've been trying to get back in . . . ever . . . since."

George's wore his agreement like widow's weeds.

"Pretty eager about it, too," said St. Peter, the fisherman's face full of sudden understanding.

"Sorry about that."

St. Peter waved the apology away as being understood, accepted, and unnecessary.

"And with the pipes," said Bach, "remember?"

George remembered.

"And a humble servant of Holy Mother Church," said Jesus without even a trace of irony.

George appreciated that.

"Vell, George . . . you can relax now."

"I can?"

"Sure!"

"You got through the gates, didn't you?" St. Peter offered.

"Into My office . . ."

". . . the theater . . ."

". . . the bar."

George looked around the Cross and Crown, feeling a little encouraged.

"Und, George . . . understand zis also: you've been taking a broom to yourself . . . ever . . . since."

George nodded slowly, swallowing.

"No-one's been chased out of here, whether it be with a broom or a flaming sword," said Jesus, "not since the guy with the giggles and a bunch of his buddies, a long, long time ago, and he was really, really asking for it."

"Then why did it happen to *me*?"

"It didn't."

"It vas a dream, George."

"But why?"

"Ze details you can vork out for yourself later, but zis much I vill tell you: zings vere a little strict at home vhen you vere little; somevone vas a bit of a—vhat you say it?—'neat freak' or somezing, und you vere a sensitive soul—still are! Also, you vere growing up in ze shadow of ze church, vhat viz your dad being a church organist und you preparing to follow in his footsteps und all. Now, alvays, vone zing relates to anozer, und sometimes zey're all mixed up, ja? Und ze dreams of children are most potent, even shaping zeir lives, George, zeir entire lives."

"So, it's okay to put away my broom now?"

"Zat's right!"

"Forsooth!"

"Truly!"

And so on.

And when the clientele of the Cross and Crown had had a suitable opportunity to express itself, God addressed the gathering: "Drink up, folks. It's getting on near closing time, and no-one wants to miss the end of the movie. Tally-ho, what?"

George looked questioningly at Jesus.

"Dad heard somewhere that God must be an Englishman," Jesus explained, "and He's been saying that, on and off, ever since."

Chapter, the Sixtieth:

A Prayer for George

"Normally, I sit at His right hand," said Jesus, nodding in the direction of God's box seats, where He sat with Gabriel and several other archangels, "but I thought you and I might keep our seating arrangement for the last scene. Dad understood."

"Last scene? What's to see? My dead body?" George asked sadly.

"No. All the bodies have been removed. Watch."

A lone woman, dressed in black, a shawl about her head and shoulders, made her way up the center aisle of St. Christopher's United to the wreckage that was the chancel. There, she stopped, and reached over the yellow police tape to place a single red rose on the shattered organ console.

"Who is it?" asked George.

At Jesus' signal, the camera angle swung up and over the woman, then settled, even more slowly, in front of her deeply bowed head.

"I . . . I can't see."

Moments later, and in no hurry at all, she raised her head. It was . . .

"*Molly?* Putting a flower on the organ?"

"She *is* on the flower committee, *and* the altar guild," said Jesus.

"But why?"

"Why not?"

"She *hates* me!"

"She does not."

"Zat's your projection only, George."

"*Feels* real."

"George, get ready for this: she *likes* you."

"No!"

"Yes! Look!"

Molly's lips were moving silently, and tears coursed down her cheeks.

"What's she doing?!"

"She's praying."

"For what?"

"For your soul, George. You two may not have seen eye to eye, but she had a real soft spot for you. It didn't seem like it because she was every bit as caught up in what she perceived her mission in the church to be, as you were in yours, and as misfortune would have it, your goals were not always compatible."

"Ja, competing obsessions."

"Yes," said Jesus, "and if she hadn't liked you, she would have given you a *really* hard time."

George stared at the screen.

"George?"

George turned slowly, and looked dumbly at Jesus.

"You weren't expecting that, now, were you?"

George shook his head slowly, eyes wide, mouth open.

"No," Jesus said gently, "and, you're not quite as annoyed with her now as you were before, *are* you?" He asked, a grin beginning to appear.

George shook his head even more slowly than he had in answer to Jesus' previous question.

"And, if you don't mind me saying so," said the Lord, a smile like sunshine itself radiating from His holy face, "you look a little . . . mollified?"

Chapter, the Sixty-First:

A Few More Thoughts for George

"I never knew," George said quietly.

"Neither did she," said Jesus, "not until after she left the choir, anyway—not a surprise given the level of antagonism between you two. That's one of the reasons that I suggest turning the other cheek, especially in situations like that. It tends to lessen the hostilities. People are usually in fundamental agreement if they dig deep enough, and 'turning the other cheek' is sometimes the best available shovel."

"Yes, Lord."

"Another little piece of advice: do unto others as . . . well, you know the rest."

"Yes, Lord."

"Any other thoughts for George?" Jesus looked around the table.

"Ja. Don't vorry; be happy!"

George smiled in spite of himself.

"Remember," said Bach, "it's all about those twelve little semitones, not about hundreds or even thousands of pipes."

George nodded.

"Don't forget to write," said Cecilia.

"Why? Am I going somewhere?"

"*Music*, George, write music."

"Oh."

"Now, take off your shoes and socks, and roll up your pants," Jesus instructed.

"Huh?"

"Take off your shoes and socks, and roll up your pants," Jesus repeated, a little more slowly this time, "unless you want to get your pant legs wet."

"Are you sure?"

"Always. Now, take off your shoes and . . ."

" . . . and socks, and roll up my pants," George repeated and performed with Jesus' nodded encouragement.

"I did this with My disciples."

"He did," Peter confirmed.

"But, but," George sputtered as he removed his last sock, "if anything, it is I who should wash *Your* feet."

"That's what Peter said."

"I did," Peter also confirmed.

A bowl and a towel appeared, and Jesus washed George's feet. "Remember, George: he who would rule must first learn to serve. Now, the conductor must rule—that is certain—but he must also serve, especially when his is a ministry: a ministry of music, as yours is."

"Is? *Is?* I *am* going somewhere, aren't I?"

"That's right," said Jesus, toweling off George's feet, "all clean. Now, it's time for the other woman in your life."

"You mean . . ."

"Yes."

"Kathy?"

"Yes."

"*Kathy?* How can I face her after what I did to her . . . I-I *killed* her . . . her sister, too . . . *and* her parents. I *must* have. They were all in the chancel when . . . when—"

"How you face her is up to you, George, but face her you must . . . if you love her?"

George nodded weakly.

"She needs you, George," said Cecilia.

"Yes, she does," said Jesus, "and she's every bit as wounded as you are. Right now, you need each *other*."

"Take care of her . . . *this* time?" Cecilia added.

"Where is she?" George asked steadily.

"You'll find her easily enough," said Jesus, smiling. "She's waiting for you . . . she's waiting for you . . . she's waiting for you . . ."

Chapter, the Sixty-Second:

Maundy Thursday

" . . . they're waiting for you . . . they're waiting for you . . . they're—"

"*Huh?*"

Brian Tyler steadied George on his office chair. "The choir, George. They're *waiting* for you."

George looked around his office in incomprehension. "What am I doing *here?*"

Tyler hesitated. "Sleeping?"

"Oh . . ." George felt some instinctive need to cover his tracks, but he wasn't entirely certain what his tracks *were*. "I just wasn't sure what was happening."

"What's happening is that this is the last choir practice before Easter, the choir is waiting, and you're asleep."

"Asleep?"

"By the look of it, yes."

"Ohhhhh!" George couldn't quite hold it in. "Then . . . I'm alive!"

"Obviously! Although I *have* seen you look better. Now stop horsing around, George. You have a rehearsal, an *important* rehearsal."

Asleep? thought George. *Has it all been a dream? Bach, Freud . . . Jesus? A* dream?

"Then . . . then . . . I just had the strangest dream . . . I think."

"What were you dreaming about *this* time?"

"I've heard *that* before!"

"What's happening, George? Deja vu, or something?"

"'Or something', definitely 'or something'. And in such *detail.* It went on forever! I . . ." How much could he say?

"You can tell me about it later."

"Right . . . later."

He never did.

"Let's go."

"Okay . . ." George squinted, straightening up in his chair.

"Come on, George. As if you haven't got enough problems already. Let's go!"

"Sure."

"And stop staring off into space like you're trying to rewrite the theory of relativity."

George shook his head. "That's already been done."

"Come *on.*"

"Sure."

"You keep *saying* that, but you're not *moving.*"

"Sure . . . I mean . . . coming right away . . . You go on. I'll be right there."

"Are you sure?"

"Sure."

George grinned.

Tyler looked doubtful, but he left.

So that was it! It was all a dream . . . wasn't it? Another thought entered George's head, a fragment of an old Christmas story: "The spirits had all done their work in one night." But this was Easter . . . almost.

George looked at his desk, and saw his music folder, picked it up, and with an effort, picked himself up, then headed, with some vague sense of purpose, for the chancel.

George stood, framed in the doorway of the "secret" panel (the worst kept "secret" in Christendom), took in the choir as they, in turn, took him in, and headed to the organ console . . . smiling.

Once there, he placed his music on the stand, opened it, hesitated, and looked up at the choir who looked (first a few, then a few more, and finally all of them) at him, the chancel pregnant with expectation.

George slowly closed his music, stood, and walked to the center of the chancel, standing between the two halves of the choir.

"The Hallelujah Chorus." George folded his hands in front of him, looking down, composing himself with a conscious effort.

There was a rustling of scores.

"No," said George. "No music, not for me, not for you."

The choir looked up, puzzled.

"No music. Memory. Concentrate. Here are your notes." With the appropriate hand gestures, indicating bass, tenor, alto, and soprano parts, he sang their entry notes, ending in falsetto on the soprano entry.

"One, two three, four . . ."

"Hallelujah! Hallelu—"

George waved them to a halt. "Think of what the word . . . *means.*"

A few choir members looked at each other, but most of them simply stared at George as he focused their attention on what they were singing.

And he was smiling!

"Again."

George waved them to a halt a second time, but further into the piece than the first. "Better," he said. A compliment! "Now, the mechanics, think, 'articulation and accent' . . ." George got specific . . . still smiling!

This time, they got through the first section.

"Good. Now, the first fugue subject . . . you remember it, I'm sure."

Slowly, the choir adapted to this new approach as they proceeded, section by section. Many of them were amazed to see that they remembered the music by heart, although it was not really not that much of a surprise, considering how long the church had been putting on its annual Messiah.

"The last fugato passage: it's a little uncertain in spots . . . we need to do something about that."

"Extreme staccato?" Mona Cooper's voice was laced with sarcasm.

George stopped. He also stopped smiling, but his smile was replaced by something else also not usually seen on his face during rehearsal: relaxation. Tyler wondered if George was truly awake, then decided that he was, that there was some other explanation—what, he did not know.

"No . . . absolute . . . adaaaaagio," he drawled, provoking a few smiles. "Slow motion. Get your music out."

Then, George did something to Mona that he had never done before, something that neither of them would have predicted: he *smiled* at her . . . at *her*.

In her shock, she blurted out, "You're the boss!" which echoed halfway between an admission and an accusation.

George stopped. "Am I?" He reflected on the thought, as if it had never occurred to him before. It had a ring of strangeness to it. Something was wrong, he could *feel* it . . . what *was* it? Something about the dynamic of his leadership, even though he had worked so hard to achieve and sustain it, no longer suited him.

He who would rule must first learn to serve, Jesus had said. George had to do something . . . something *now*.

Suddenly, he knew what it was.

He left . . .

George returned with a large bowl of water and a towel. These he placed in the center of the chancel along with his piano bench. "It's Maundy Thursday, The Lord's Supper. Jesus washed the disciples' feet. He said . . . He said that he who would lead must first learn to serve."

"He *did*?!" Mona asked—she was a regular at Bible study.

George caught himself. "Well . . . perhaps not in precisely those words . . . I don't know," he smiled good-naturedly. "I just know that this is something that I should do." He looked intently at Mona.

"Oh, no, you don't! Not with *my* feet!"

George smiled sadly, and she felt a twinge of guilt, but it could not match her rising sense of panic. For the second time in one rehearsal, she blurted something out. "Do Smiley's!"

There was a sharp, collective intake of breath. George's looked at Bill Smiley, who, having no idea why he was being volunteered for the honor, stared back at George. Someone muttered something to Smiley that ended with " . . . humor him."

"Okay," said Smiley, perhaps in response to the pressure of many eyes, or perhaps because he heard the word "humor", but for whatever reason, he said, "why not?" and walked to the center of the chancel, removed his shoes and socks, and brandished his feet.

George smiled, refusing to allow the assault on his nose to find any expression on his face, took up Smiley's feet, and washed them, thoroughly, to the widening eyes of everyone there, as gently as if they were those of his own child. "Bill," George whispered as he dried them, "we're going to have to do something about those feet."

"What's that?" Bill whispered back.

George shrugged, knowing that this was too public a moment for details. "Maybe wash them on a regular basis."

"You?" Smiley asked, dimly aware that there was something was going on beyond good foot hygiene.

"Door's always open," George concluded, with a flourish of his towel.

"Thanks, George."

"You're welcome, Bill." Political correctness was made to serve man, thought George, not the other way around.

There was silence in the choir pews as Smiley returned to his seat.

George looked up, and everyone understood that he was not finished.

Janet Stewart, who, being a practical nurse, was not squeamish about such things, was the first soprano to come forward. "I don't know what's happened, George," she whispered as she sat down, "but I think I approve."

"It's a long story."

"I'll bet it is."

Again, George looked at Mona, simply because, of those present, it was her that he was most in need of learning how to serve. Molly, if she were there, would have taken precedence, but, seeing as she was not . . . . It was a greater challenge in its own way than Smiley's feet were in theirs, but it was the right thing, he knew.

George nodded encouragement, and in a state of bewilderment and disbelief, she went to him. "George, are you having a nervous breakdown?" she whispered hoarsely.

George smiled, and shook his head.

"What Bible, exactly, have you been reading?"

"A special edition for organists who have become too full of themselves."

Mona began to enjoy the movements of George's hands in spite of herself. "Where did you learn to do *that?*"

George shrugged modestly. "From Someone Who was *very* good at it."

Mona nodded.

"Mona?"

"Yes?"

"Call Molly. Ask her to come."

Mona looked alarmed on Molly's behalf.

"Ask her to trust me," he added.

Irene Dalrymple, easily the oldest soprano in the chancel was next.

"George?"

"Yes, Irene?"

"I'm wearing pantyhose," she confided in low tones. "Would you settle for my hands?"

"Your hands would be just fine."

When Mona returned, Rev. Parker was with her. George, by this time, had cleansed several sopranos, two altos, one bass, and, of course, Smiley, but the number of those willing to come forward was dwindling.

Rev. Parker remained outside the chancel, that being his sense of the moment. George and he looked at each other briefly and wordlessly. Parker saw something in the organist's eyes that he had never seen there, perhaps anywhere, before. He knew without thinking it through that, as a man of God, he had to trust it, which he indicated with a nod, first to George, and then to some in the choir who seemed to be looking to him for pastoral guidance.

The number of choristers heading to the center of the chancel grew until there was a modest but respectable line, and it began to look as though everyone would eventually join it.

Darlene Parker, with a mother's intuition, whispered, "Be good to my daughter," to which George nodded solemnly, touched by her mother's trust, his own love of her daughter, and the memory of things regretted.

When Kathy's turn came, George looked up at her, up at her beautiful *blue* eyes, wordlessly seeking her permission, which she, in turn, wordlessly gave, each realizing that the time for them to talk had not yet come.

Molly, who lived a scant two blocks away, walked slowly up the aisle and into the chancel with the aura of one who was doing the hardest thing that she had ever had to do. She sensed something of the same sort about George, and it compelled her.

They faced each other silently, as the last choir member replaced his footwear, and went back to his pew.

Finally, they both knew what to say.

"You, I have wronged," George began.

Molly knew precisely how to answer, including the appropriate, almost liturgical, syntax. "And I, you."

George returned to his music stand, silent for a long time, and finally spoke. "There's nothing like a clean choir."

"Turn now to the 'Amen Chorus'."

"You know how to pick them, George!"

"Thanks."

George and Molly appeared, in their own special way, to be bonding.

"That contrapuntal passage is a little stubborn, isn't it?" George stroked his chin, thoughtfully, resisting what, only the week before, would have been the obvious.

"It's okay, George," said Mona. "We *want* to do it extreme staccato."

*   *   *

The last choir member, Brian Tyler, left, nodding solemnly, too moved to speak. George was . . . different. Everyone had seen it, even if they didn't know what to make of it.

*   *   *

The rehearsal had been fantastic, George thought. He had gotten more work out of his choir while asking—overtly, at least—for less. Now there was an irony that even Shakespeare would have appreciated. *Shakespeare?*

And why had he gotten more? Because he had *given* more. It was obvious! It was *so* obvious . . . now. You catch more flies with honey than with . . . what was it?

Didn't matter.

* * *

He hadn't gone home. Too much to do. Too much thinking to do. Sleep would have been impossible, anyway. And who, exactly, was doing the thinking? Him? Or had his thoughts taken on some demi-life of their own? Or was it the characters who were populating them? George didn't feel like he had much control over it.

And the organ? What of that? He had worked an undeniable wonder, and it would sound stunning at Easter. There was a forest of pipes in the attic and an indescribable arrangement in the basement. When the time came, it would take people's breath away, but would it also take the lives of who knows how many people in the chancel? Now there was a past that was screaming to be changed . . .

He had to work out exactly what he should do for Easter. He had lived through it once already—or had he? And then seen it on the screen of the Odeon Paradise? And if it had actually happened, could he change the past? He'd better!

If tonight were any indication, and it actually was the past that he was trying to change, the answer was yes. It would certainly look different—no walls of water—without Cecil B. DeMille. *Cecil B. DeMille?*

* * *

Three in the morning. Sitting in his office. George knew that sleep would not come. How could it? There was too much to absorb, too much to understand.

He had to play the Good Friday service in the chapel in six and a half hours. A little sleep would help. If only he had a good stiff drink. When had he had his last one? At The Cross and Crown? A double, wasn't it? With God. *God?*

All he knew for certain was that he had been changed. How? Had "the spirits" done it "all in one night" as they had for Scrooge? Just different spirits? Was it a dream? A bit of undigested food? Something . . . real?

It *must* have been a dream, but it felt so real! 'Felt so real,' indeed!" he snorted. "But it did. It did!"

Wearied by the mental effort, George eased himself over to his couch. Bernie had long been asleep on the rug at his feet. *Good boy. Did you dream it too?*

*   *   *

"Not bad, George, not bad at all, but you need to be a little more careful what you say."

"Lord?"

"If you're going to quote Me, be sure that it's from the Bible."

"You mean with Mona? 'He who would lead must first learn to serve.' That one?"

"Yes. That was a paraphrase. What I actually said was 'Whosoever will be great among you, let him be your minister; And whosoever will be chief among you, let him be your servant.' They tend to pick nits in Bible study, you know? Like that girl who thought that Dad had a gray beard, remember?"

"I remember."

"And don't talk to anyone about what happened in Heaven, except maybe to Bernie."

"Yes, Lord."

"We don't want you to get locked up, now, *do* we George?"

Chapter, the Sixty-Third:

Good Friday

"Good morning, Rev. Dawson."

"Good morning, George! Come in!"

"You're here early."

"Not for *me*. What's your excuse?"

They both smiled.

"I don't think that I've had the pleasure of having you dropping by my office before. What's the occasion?"

Parker wouldn't have been so direct, wouldn't have wanted to risk scaring a person off by shining too bright a light on their purpose like that, but Dawson had a way of "getting on with things" . . . curious in a man who seemed to enjoy going on so.

"I was in early."

"You were in *late*," Dawson corrected him, good-naturedly.

"Can't fool you."

"You want another spot in the prayers?"

"No, I just saw your door . . . Rev. Dawson?"

"Harry. It's about time, wouldn't you say?"

"Harry. Why do you think the Good Friday service is so poorly attended?"

Dawson flexed his eyebrows—the equivalent of a carpenter cracking his knuckles before picking up his hammer. "Many reasons, I suppose. Mostly, I think, because people come to church to feel good, and Good Friday is, for them at least, misnamed. They can't relate to the darker, stormier side of Christianity. I suppose they prefer the stars to the nails. Natural enough."

"Yes: the crown to the cross. Of course."

"Exactly."

Curious, thought George. *He's brief enough here. He could have gone on and on.*

"What is it, George?"

"Nothing, really. I was just comparing your . . . delivery, I guess I could call it, just then and . . . in the prayers."

Dawson laughed. "Yes, I do go on, don't I?"

"Oh, no, I didn't mean—"

"Oh, yes. The older members of the congregation seem to like it, though, and I do spend most of my time with them. They remember, too, when this was my church; now I'm 'minister emeritus' or something like that, 'in residence' yet—what a thing!—and some of them miss my sermons. I don't know why. I guess you get used to things being a certain way."

George smiled. "I guess so." It was a brief smile.

"What is it now, George?"

"Oh, nothing."

Dawson nodded. "After I got married, I learned that the word 'nothing' could have many shades of meaning."

"Nothing—" George caught himself. "Just feeling a little guilty, that's all."

"Why's that? My . . . 'delivery'?"

"Okay." George took a deep breath. "Because I used to be a little, well, critical of your . . . 'delivery', and you were nice enough to take my prayer request."

Dawson took it in stride. "Don't worry, George: I've heard it all. Even collected a few nicknames on account of it." He plainly enjoyed a good laugh at his own expense. "You wouldn't have one for my collection, would you?"

George couldn't help himself. "Yes . . . Reverend . . . Neverend."

'Reverend Neverend' grinned. "That's what my *wife* calls me!"

* * *

George looked out the window of his office, fifteen minutes before he had to begin the prelude for the Good Friday chapel service. Rain streaked the leaded glass windows, and there was a feeling that the sun had gone out for good. "Pathetic fallacy," his high school English teacher would have called it. Shakespeare would have appreciated that . . . *Shakespeare?*

"Good" Friday, indeed. And would the next day be unsettled, and Easter Sunday glorious? Had anyone thought to do a study on the meteorology of Holy Week? What if . . .

No time now.

* * *

"Well, I don't think anyone would mistake this for Christmas Eve," Rev. Parker began, the hint of a smile appearing. "And why is that, exactly? Partly, of course, because people prefer birth to death."

True, thought George. *Who ever said, "My, what a beautiful corpse!"*

"And it's a rare person who goes out of his way to contemplate his own death. Someone once said that it's like looking directly at the sun: something makes us turn away. It simply hurts too much. But, equally painful, surely, in the long run at least, is to banish all thought of death, hiding it away in some dark corner of our psyches to fester into the stuff of nameless anxiety and nightmare. Good Friday is Christianity's answer to that problem. It asks us to have a good look at death, at least for a moment."

George drifted into his own thoughts, to look at his own "death" amid the terrible rubble of his own creation. Not to mention the innocent people who had "died" along with him. That was *not* going to happen again.

"But for us, as Christians, this Good Friday," said Parker, "death has a deeper meaning: that salvation is bought with the coin of suffering; that we must die, whether it be in the death of the body, or in any one of the 'little deaths' throughout the course of our lives that Thoreau wrote about; or perhaps even to some of our own desires, if we are to join in the fullness of life: that eternal life is bought through nails and thorns.

"And so—"

"And so" means he's almost finished, thought George, preparing himself to play the offertory organ music: no choir at this service.

"—we begin our Easter journey this Good Friday. And it is indeed 'Good' that we do so, for at the end of this 'fever of life', we will take that journey 'from which no traveler returns', and this will be our road map, the path that Jesus blazed for us, as we all experience our own passion, our own death, and our own resurrection. Thanks be to God."

*   *   *

"Good morning, George." Rev. Parker looked up from his desk.

"Good morning . . . Bob."

"Come in, come in."

George came in part way, but did not sit, and something about his body language told Parker not to ask him to. "That's the first time you've called me by my Christian name . . . at least, willingly." Parker smiled warmly.

"This has been a week of firsts," said George.

"I'll bet. For the choir, too."

It was George's turn to smile.

"I've been thinking. I'd like to find a way to donate some pipes to another church, maybe a small church that has to make do with one of those horrid little electronic organs . . . something like that."

Parker sensed the immensity of what he was hearing. "Yes," he answered slowly, nodding. "I'm sure we could figure out something. Some of the newer churches are lacking in that regard. Of course, they might not know what to do with them."

"Maybe I can show them." George smiled.

"I'm sure you can. You don't have any further use for them?"

"Well, maybe one or two ranks. It's kinda like potato chips, you know?"

"I could see that."

"Well, I guess that's it." George shifted his weight from one foot to the other as if to leave, and Parker sensed that George's journey, whatever its precise nature, must remain a private affair, despite the very public display of its fruits at choir practice.

"Very well, George. Looking forward to your music Sunday."

"Looking forward to your sermon, especially after today's."

"Thank-you, George. I take that as high praise from someone as accomplished as you are with what *you* do, but this Sunday's sermon will be from the Moderator."

"Oh, yes, that's right."

"You know, George, sometimes I think that the church gets so caught up in the mechanics of its organized forms of outreach that we forget that 'the Lord moves in mysterious ways, his wonders to perform': 'the wild side of the Spirit' I once heard it called."

Oh, I don't know, thought George. *He preferred the booth in the corner—didn't seem all that wild to me.* "I think I'll leave the theology to you, Bob. All I know is twelve little semitones."

"And you certainly seem to know what to do with them."

After George had left, Parker looked steadily at the door . . . "Somehow, George, I can't help feeling that you know a lot more than that, a *lot* more than that."

*   *   *

Three in the afternoon, Good Friday. There were as many living souls in St. Christopher's United Church as there had been at three in the morning: one organist, and one organist's dog. The organist was in the attic, busy, very busy. The dog was in the organist's office, bored, very bored.

George surveyed his creation. "Can you say, 'Frankenstein'?" he muttered.

Now *there* was a past (*and* a future) that was screaming to be changed, and *here* was where it had to be changed, and there was only one way to change it, only one way that was foolproof.

He could lock the door to the pipe room. That would stop the chain of events that lead, ultimately, to the falling death in the chancel. But locks could be jimmied, and there were other considerations. What would the congregation make of the sounds of pipes in the ceiling? And the basement? Would this enrich their sense of worship? Or distract them from it? What had he been thinking?

Only one way that was foolproof.

One nail less in his coffin.

*   *   *

"See, George? About ze obsessus?"

"Yes. I don't need it any more. Enough is enough."

"Nein, George. You don't get rid of it so easily, but it's an excellent start. Sehr gut!"

"But the music? Will *it* be as good?"

"Ahhhh, ja! Maybe better even, vizout all zat energy being eaten up by your neurosis.

"I'll do my best."

"I know zat you vill."

"Hello, George."

"Herr Bach!"

"No, no, George; call me Johann: we're colleagues, after all."

"I guess . . . but I'll never equal *your* achievement."

"That new descant isn't bad."

"Thanks."

"We use the same twelve semitones, remember?"

"I will."

"I know that you will."

"George."

"Yes, Lord?"

"How was your day?"

"Not bad. And Yours?"

"Good . . . in the sense that Good Friday is 'good'. Death is death, even for Me: it smarts."

"Yes, it does."

"Of course, it's only the first step; the situation does improve: 'no pain, no gain', you know?"

"Yes, Lord. Thanks for the encouragement."

"You're welcome. Oh, and George?"

"Yes, Lord."

"Remember: let's keep all this between you, Me, and Bernie."

"You can count on me, Lord; Bernie, too."

"I know that I can. Now, get some sleep."

Chapter, the Sixty-Fourth:

Ready as I'll Ever Be

"Well, Bernie. I guess you're it."

"W*oof*?"

"Yeah, I know: it's a *big* responsibility, but you're the only living creature I can share this with . . ."

*   *   *

George shut down the organ, and swiveled off the bench to survey the chancel, the altar, the choir pews, the openings to the pipe rooms, and finally, the ceiling.

"Thank *God* I found out about that!"

*   *   *

"Well, Bernie," he said, rising restlessly from his living room couch. "I'm going to see a movie."

*   *   *

An actor playing Jesus was washing the feet of several other actors. George had seen this version of the Easter story many times, and it was back at the local repertory theater for its annual run. It used to look so much more real. But then, how could an actor, any actor, compare with . . .

The popcorn also invited unfavorable comparison—now *that* was popcorn!

The appearance of the three Marys at the tomb engaged his interest in a way that they never had before. What did men know about such things, anyway? Birth and death? Peter and the others needed these women, and yet they seemed not to know it, certainly not these . . . actors.

He thought of Kathy, of how much he needed her, and how much more he loved her.

"I'm sorry," he whispered. "I'm so sorry."

*   *   *

And George slept a dreamless sleep . . . for the most part.

"George?"
"Yes, Lord."
"Are you ready for the big day?"
"Ready as I'll ever be."
"That's the spirit."
"Lord?"
"Yes, George?"
"Will I do okay?"
"Yes, George, you will, and then some."

Dawn slipped into George's bedroom. First Bernie cocked one eye open, and then, as the rising sun steeped his master's face in life quickening rays, so did he.

Thursday, George had dreamed a dream . . . or was it? He still couldn't be sure. Friday, Saturday, and now Easter Sunday . . . their events flooded in on him, animating him. A sudden energy thrust him into a sitting position.

Looking out on the widow, the spire of St. Christopher's United Church framed in the distance, one thought filled his mind: *And on the third day, he rose.*

Chapter, the Sixty-Fifth:

Easter

"This is it," thought George. "Easter Sunday. The big day. The Moderator's coming. What will she preach about? The three Marys?" He looked up at the cross that crowned St. Christopher's United as he rounded the final corner to the church. "At least no-one will die."

He stopped short on the sidewalk at the foot of the path up to the church, seeing it in a new light. "Somehow it doesn't matter as much as I thought it would. I could give this up . . . what a thought!" Entering by the front door, he headed up the main aisle to his office behind the organ console. The ladies of the flower guild had been busy: there were Easter lilies everywhere, even on the organ console, right where Molly had placed that single red rose . . . Molly? Jesus would know . . . *Jesus?*

George rounded the console, and headed for his office. He put on his robes immediately: he wanted to remind himself of why he was there: to exercise the ministry of music, for however long it was still his, to the glory of God—Whom he had now met, personally, if only in a dream . . . was it only a dream?—and not for the glory of George!

From the distant past, he remembered a name he had sometimes been saddled with in elementary school, the name of some obscure wrestler, of all people, that one of his friends' parents remembered from *his* youth: Glorious George? No . . . no, it was *Gorgeous* George. What would Freud have made of that? George laughed at the thought. Freud would have laughed too, and then started scribbling about it in that little notebook of his . . . *Freud?*

*   *   *

George was gathering up music from his desk when he heard the rattle of the padlock he had installed on the door to the pipe room opposite his office . . .

It held.

"Come on!" someone whispered, his disappointment palpable, followed by the sound of several pairs of feet on the stairs.

Not that it would have made much of a difference if George had let them have their fun: he had done more than lock the door, but it was simpler this way. Bernie, if he possessed the vocabulary, would have agreed.

*   *   *

Time to begin the prelude. Choir rehearsal had gone well. They had been with him! And somehow, George knew he would survive the challenge on the music committee . . . but should he?

And what about Kathy? What would he do? Could he do? Should he do?

Responsibility!

No time for that, now: too many *other* responsibilities.

One at a time . . .

The prelude went exactly as he remembered it in the dream—was it a dream?—ending with the same series of reflections from the organ as he had before, forming the same slow decrescendo arc of falling phrases, until, seeing the choir and the rest of the chancel party spread in readiness across the back of the church in his rearview mirror, he played the final cadence, and awaited the call to worship.

George noticed it getting darker—clouds gathering?—and then, in the second line of the second verse, just where he remembered it, there was a fusillade of thunder that unleashed the full flower of congregational singing. He had even anticipated it by adding a few more ranks of pipes to support the increased vocal volume. Was George changing the past? Was God Himself knocking at the door? No Red Sea this time: all "docu", no "drama" (not in *that* sense at least), but what if the Trinity were to appear? Jesus *had* called it "tempting".

The new descant, all rising phrases, written that way to represent Christ rising from the dead.

Bach had liked it . . . *Bach?*

*   *   *

Parker was in fine Easter voice. "Jesus said, 'I am the resurrection and the life; he that believes in me, though he die, yet shall he live, and whoever lives and believes in me shall never die.'"

"Works for me," thought George.

Prayers, confession, hymns passed in a blur; the liturgy of the word: readings from the Old and New Testaments; the sermon . . .

The Sermon.

Ms. Sarah Dey mounted the steps to the pulpit, just as she had before, amid much thoughtful nodding and whispered acknowledgement from all quarters.

To begin her sermon, she talked about the role of the three Marys that first Easter morning, just as she had in his dream. But behind the feminist complaint, he heard the feminine pain, and instead of the feminist diatribe that he had once braced himself for, he heard a feminine plea based on the necessary roles of both sexes, just as she had in his dream. He listened more carefully than he ever would have before. She helped him understand, just as she had in his dream.

Clearly, his had been no ordinary dream.

What had Jesus told him? "Men and women need to learn to listen to each other more; they need to learn *how* to listen."

He looked at Kathy, letting his eyes rest on her as long as he dared. *I'm sorry,* he thought. *I'm so sorry.*

"The men and women of the early church needed each other," Ms. Dey continued, "and so do we, and the good news is that we are learning more and more to get to know each other better, and more importantly, we are learning *how* to do that, and not just through husbands taking furtive peeks at their wives' copies of *Men are from Mars, Women are from Venus.*"

George realized that he had some reading to do.

"Just as Mary Magdalene and Peter discovered, the unfolding of life's deepest mysteries requires both men and women, together, to share, each with their own unique perspectives, gifts, and connection to life. For this, we give thanks to God. Let us pray . . ."

                              *   *   *

The Hallelujah chorus went even better than he had hoped it would. He would have to use that rehearsal technique again . . .

George absolutely lost himself in the Amen Chorus. That loss of ego yet finding of a truer self in the service of the music had always been his favorite thing about being a church musician. What had Freud called it? Ze sublimation of ze what? *Freud?*

With the organ improvisation begun, he remembered the falling of plaster, beams, and columns, but it couldn't happen now: George had seen to that. He had spent Good Friday and Holy Saturday disconnecting much of his previous work and returning the motors that supplied the air pressure for the pipes to their previous configurations—no need for all that power now.

The organ was still fuller and richer than anything that had previously been heard at St. Christopher's United, but it was all on the ground floor now, and it wouldn't kill anyone; still, when he came to the Doxology, he left a token rank of pipes out of the registration, just for sake of superstition.

"Twelve semitones are enough," thought George as he signaled the choir to rise and join with congregation, brass, tympani, and organ:

"Praise God from whom all blessings flow.
Praise Him all creatures here below.
Praise Him above, ye heavenly host.
Praise Father, Son, and Holy Ghost.
Amen."

"Alive . . . I'm still alive."

The rest of the service was anticlimactic, and he was barely aware of it, except for a special thanks to him, the choir, and the extra musicians that he had hired for "the beautiful Easter music"—Rev. Parker was determined to save George, it seemed—and the inclusion of his name in the prayers of intercession, sandwiched among those of various other church employees. *That* had never happened before!

The last hymn, the choral amen, the benediction, and the postlude all drifted past. George had given St. Christopher's United the Easter service music of its dreams—Evan Bawdry would be happy with him, or at least with the collection plate—and no-one had died, not one.

*   *   *

Back in his office, George removed his robe, and he knew what he had to do—now.

*   *   *

George made his way down the stairs outside his office and across the large room in the basement in time to see Kathy, her mother, and sister leaving the women's choir room. He slowed and stopped a short distance from her, allowing her to avoid him if she wanted to, but something about his calm, sad smile made her stop. Her mother and sister scanned the situation and made their own way to the stairs and up.

"Happy Easter, Kathy."

"Happy Easter, George."

"Can I talk to you for just a minute? I have something I . . . something that I need to say . . . maybe outside?"

"Okay."

They crossed the floor, went up the stairs, and out the side door into what was now a beautiful Easter afternoon.

"Kathy . . ." George began. He looked briefly at the sidewalk, and then back at her, into her beautiful blue eyes—how could he have ever forgotten *them*. "There is so much that I didn't know . . . so much, now, that I *have* learned . . . too late, I guess . . . but I have to . . ." George struggled against his gathering tears, determined not to influence her with either pity or persuasion.

She looked at him, both calming and tensing at the same time.

"I let you down; I was selfish; I thought mostly . . . of myself . . . and now I've seen . . . more than I can tell you. I don't know how to say it . . . I . . . I love you, Kathy. I think I always have—I know that I always have—but I didn't know . . . what love . . . *was,* exactly. I didn't know a lot of things."

The look on Kathy's face could not be described. The combination of love and fear, relief and disbelief, made her unreadable, not that George was trying to: he had made the conscious decision to unplug his "radar".

"And now that I *have* learned—I wish that I could tell you so much more—I don't know what to do." George shook his head. "I suppose that I'm being almost incoherent."

"No, George. No, you're not."

George nodded, grateful. "I do know that I must resign—"

"No!"

He looked up, surprised.

Kathy explained. "Things were bad, really bad with the choir, but you're winning them back; you've won them back, really: they don't understand, but they can see, *everyone* can see, that something has happened. You don't have to leave. I'm sure of it!"

"I know that. I won't get fired—*that* danger has passed—and the choir, most of them, anyway, will stay on, I think, but I'm not just a musician, not even just a *church* musician. The organist/choirmaster must be—I don't mean to give himself airs—must be a minister of music, in a way, and my—*God*, this sounds so pompous—my . . . 'ministry' . . . has been terribly divisive. I've caused a lot of pain here. A few pretty notes won't make up for that."

Kathy opened her mouth to speak, but George shook his head, feeling that he did not deserve the kind words that he sensed she was about to say, or the understanding that he sensed he was about to receive, and he needed to finish what he had to say before his emotions overwhelmed him.

"So I *will* resign, and . . . I won't ask anything of you, but I will tell you what I . . . wish . . . I had done for you . . . when you asked me to . . . once."

"You don't have to."

"I need to. I wish . . . I wish more than anything, that I had been . . . your friend, as you had asked me to . . . 'Friends lasts', as you said. 'Friends' is good; it's so . . . *friendly*, and it's what you wanted . . . needed . . . whatever . . . and I loved you enough, certainly, to *be* your friend, but I was so . . . lonely . . . and I acted out of my need rather than out of my love. I was so stupid, stupid . . . I'm sorry, Kathy . . ." he whispered " . . . I'm *so* sorry."

"That's okay," she said.

"Thanks, Kathy, but I did what I did . . . there's no escaping that. I just wish . . . I just wish that I could do it over . . . it's too late . . . I suppose . . . now? To be . . . your friend?"

Kathy shifted uncomfortably. She had not expected this. She wasn't prepared: it was too sudden, too emotionally immense, even to take in, let alone deal with now; but she *had* to deal with it now . . .

So Kathy did what most people would do: first she panicked, then she grasped at straws, and the straw that she grasped was her memory of what George once said to her, in the closest thing that she had ever had to a similar situation, reversed though it was.

Looking down, and using the same words that he had used, she said, "I have lots of friends."

"I understand," said George, staring across the street.

*   *   *

George looked around his office . . . one last look: so many memories! The shelves lined with music, the music stand—it had been his father's; he would, of course, take that with him—the pipes! Still so many stray pipes!

The letter of resignation was in his hands. He let it drop lightly down on the desk in front of him. "Not important now," he thought.

George looked at the phone. How he wished he could call Kathy, as he once had, the time he so begrudgingly accepted her offer of friendship—if only . . . Her number was etched in his memory—would he ever forget it?—but he could not use it, not any more.

The irony of it all!

The phone rang.

If thoughts were wishes!

"Yes . . . yes . . . you do? . . . you're sure? . . . Yes, I would . . . I'd love to . . . for sure. . . . Yes . . . yes . . . yes . . . my friend."

Chapter, the Sixty-Sixth:

No Ordinary Dream

Meanwhile, back in Heaven, there arose a great rejoicing as Jesus, Freud, Saints Peter and Cecilia, Bach, and all the others watched George replace the phone in its cradle on one side of the split screen, and Kathy do likewise on the other. Gabriel sounded his trumpet, popcorn filled the air, and there was nary a dry eye among cherubim and seraphim alike.

So it was in George's dream, late Easter Sunday night. George smiled as he lay asleep in his bed, as he stood beside his Savior in the Odeon Paradise, and as he appeared on the silver screen, having just spoken to his dearest friend.

Surely, this was no ordinary dream, George later thought.

Jesus turned to face the theater audience, one hand on George's shoulder, as George and Kathy's smiling faces filled the screen behind them, in the final scene of *Pipes: the Story of George*. And Jesus said, "Once again, in your sight and in your hearing, the lost *has* been found, the longing satisfied, the soul's deepest sadness given over to rejoicing . . ."

Cheering, laughter, more airborne popcorn.

" . . . finally," Jesus added, smiling. "And now, we have something to do, and somewhere to go."

"What shall we do, Lord?"

"Whither shall we go?"

"Yes, tell us, Lord!"

"We return to the Cross and Crown . . . annnnnd . . . the drinks are on Me!"

"Hurray!"

"Yahoo!"

"Tally-ho!"

* * *

God Himself set up the glasses, and the sweet nectars of Heaven flowed from spigots of gold.

"Who will propose a toast," Jesus asked.

Freud composed himself for the happy task, straightening his stance, squaring his shoulders, and raising his glass. "Loch Hiem! George, may all your dreams be full of joy, und all your couches be for sitting or sleeping!"

"Loch Hiem!!" the patrons of The Cross and Crown echoed, accompanied by the raising and clinking of glasses.

St. Cecilia was next. "To George! May your marriage be full of harmony, your children all musicians, and your soul alive with song!"

"To George!!"

More raising and much clinking.

"To George, and to all of us!" Shakespeare declared. "'We are such stuff as dreams are made on.' May all our dreams be filled with joy and bliss!"

"To George, and all of us!!"

And every glass was raised and clinked.

"May I say something?" George asked with a humbled spirit.

And Jesus, smiling, nodded His approval.

George first looked at the floor, and then looked up with a new firmness of purpose. "I have learned so much . . ."

To which there was general and heartfelt assent.

" . . . from You . . ."

At which Jesus looked well pleased.

" . . . and you . . ."

Bach beamed.

" . . . and you."

And Freud took out his hankie.

"In fact, all of you . . . gave me my . . . *life* back."

"Zat you gave your*self* back, silly."

"With a little help."

"Hmmm, ja, I suppose."

"I don't know how I can ever repay you."

"Keep writing those descants," Bach suggested.

"Be good to Kathy," St. Cecilia added.

"Live well," said Jesus.

"I will try."

"Yes, you will," said God Senior. "And there is something else you have it in mind to do."

"Don't look surprised, George," said Jesus. "He knows everything—I told you that."

"I . . . I would also propose a toast, if I may."

"You may indeed."

"I feel a little like . . . Ebenezer Scrooge on Christmas morning, and there's one line from that story that I can't get out of my mind, corny as it may be . . ."

"Corny is good up here," said Jesus.

"I'm glad because this certainly qualifies: I'd like it to be my toast: God bless us, every one!"

"God bless us every one!!"

And, rising to the occasion, God said, "I bless you, every one!" causing all gathered together there to further rejoice. And then God smiled a Godly smile, and, with a twinkle in His eye, raised both His glass and His voice in great exultation: "Hip, hip?"

"Hooray!"

"Hip, hip??"

"Hooray!!"

"Hip, hip???"

"Hooray!!!"

And after the hipping had ended, and the hooraying had sufficiently subsided, a voice arose out of the general rejoicing. "May we sing a song of praise," someone asked of God.

"You may, indeed," He answered.

And everyone knew which song would be most pleasing unto God:

"For He's a jolly good Fellow . . ."

Jesus motioned for George to accompany him to the door, saying, "It's time We got you a cab, George."

"Yes, Lord."

And all those gathered in The Cross and Crown waved, raised their glasses, and called out their warmest farewells and fondest of wishes for George's future as he left.

Reaching the door, Jesus put a warm hand on George's shoulder for the second time that evening, saying, "Go in peace, George, with God's speed and all the hopes of Heaven behind you until that day, many years from now, when you and I shall meet again, face to Face."

And George, in the midst of his great joy, was possessed of a sudden sadness. "That long, Lord?"

"Yes, George. Unless you start tinkering with that organ again."

"I won't. I don't have even have an organ now, or at least I won't after my resignation takes effect."

"'Holy Mother Church' has many daughters, George, and I'm sure that one of them would be the richer for an organist/choirmaster of your depth and accomplishment; so is Herr Bach."

"Will You . . . will You ever . . . visit me . . . in my dreams, at least . . . even if it's just once in a while?"

Jesus smiled. "I will. *We* will. Good night, George."

And George smiled also. "Good night, Lord."

*   *   *

And as George slept a dreamless sleep, one of the heavenly revelers asked this of Jesus: "What shall we do now, Lord?"

"Yes, Lord," another asked, "tell us, to what great work shall we turn our hands?"

Indeed, "Tell us, Lord," was the general request of the patrons of The Cross and Crown.

And the Lord answered. "What work? 'What *work*' you ask? Well . . . there is another movie goer arriving shortly," He said, looking at His watch, "but, in the meantime . . . let's dance!"

THE END